THE PETTICOAT SKY

CHARLESTON BRIDES ~ BOOK 3

ELVA COBB MARTIN

WILD HEART
BOOKS

ISBN-13: 978-1-942265-45-0

The hand of Providence has been so conspicuous in the course of the war that he must be worse than an infidel that lacks faith.

~ George Washington, August 20, 1778

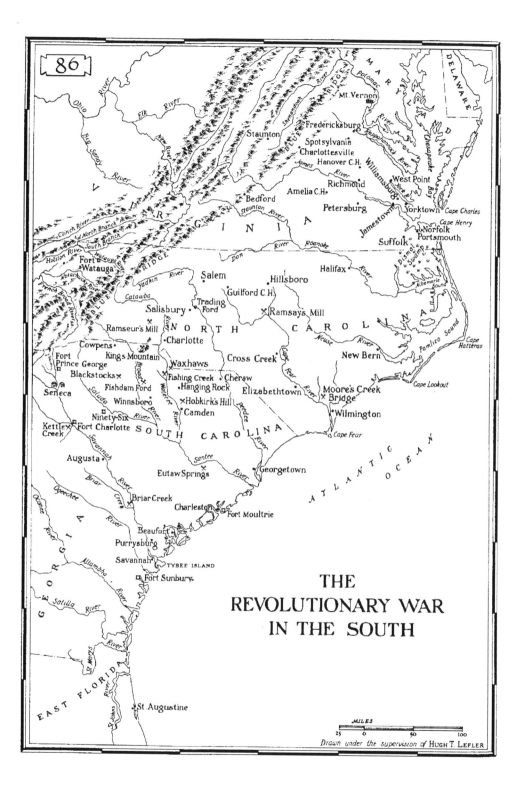

THE
REVOLUTIONARY WAR
IN THE SOUTH

Drawn under the supervision of HUGH T. LEFLER

CHAPTER 1

CHARLES TOWN
OCTOBER 31, 1779

A traitor is everyone who does not agree with me.
~ King George III, Great Britain

The wind whipped through Anna Grace Laurens's hair as she galloped her mare back toward their Charles Town plantation through the hardwood forest she loved. In the fresh morning air, the war her brother fought with the South Carolina militia against the British faded in its heaviness. Woodsy scents of pine, sweet cedar, and birch laced with the damp earthy smell of decomposing leaves wrapped their rich scent around her.

But even as they flew along the familiar trail, something jangled against her nerves like the forewarning rumble of a storm coming.

A burly black form burst through the brush in front of her, and Jolie reared. Anna clung to her saddle and stifled the scream rising in her throat.

Big Jim. Her heart slowed its pace as she recognized their most faithful, loyal servant. His dark skin glistened with sweat and the whites of his eyes blazed in the forest shadows.

Prince, her father's large brown mixed hound, raced from beside the man and pranced around Anna's horse. Jolie shook her thick silver mane, snorted, and kicked out at the barking animal.

Anna Grace managed to keep her seat and pointed the tip of her whip toward the pet. "Sit, boy. Quiet."

The dog moved to the side of the path and sat, but emitted a low whining sound.

She patted the damp neck of her beloved horse and turned to Big Jim standing near, trying to catch his breath. "What has happened?"

Now that she turned a good look toward him, his torn, bloody clothing revealed wounds on his thick arms and chest. Her heart picked up speed as questions pressed in her throat.

He jerked off a faded, dirty field hat and gulped. "Miss Anna, I'se got bad news. Turr'ble mens in green coats, evil mens, they come just after you left this morning, and they's set fire to the big house." He swiped sweat from his steaming forehead and swallowed again. "They done burned the rice barns, yo cattle stalls, and took all the slaves and best stock."

Fury lined his dark brow. "They slaughtered yo papa's animals they didn't want. I heered the men say Tarl'ton ordered it done to all rebels."

With every word the man spoke, her chest clutched tighter. Not their plantation. Their livelihood. She stared at the sky above Laurens Hill. A stream of smoke rose into the air beyond the border of trees. Her stomach clenched and her body trembled. With her next breath, the odor of burning wood, rice straw, and charred beef stung her nose. "I must get back to help...." She clamped her heels on the mare's sides.

Big Jim stepped forward and grabbed Jolie's bridle. "No, Miss Anna. I begs you. Don't go back. Turn this horse around and flee for yo life. I'se got a cave and done put my Mary Lee in it and they'll never find us, but you—you need to run away as fast as you can."

"But I must return. Help my parents." Her shrill whisper sliced through the peace of the moss-hung oaks.

He held firm to the horse's bit, even when Jolie nudged hard at his chest. He hung his head, and a tear made a shiny track down his cheek. "Miss Anna, I ain't tole you the worse. Yo mama and papa been shot and killed. The men were yelling about your brother Henry being a rebel and this is what rebels' families git. I tell you there's nothing to go back to, but them green-coat soldiers. They'll hurt you, Miss Anna. They'll hurt you bad."

It couldn't be. His hoarse words blasted through her, and she fought the blackness trying to claim her, to drag her from the saddle. "My parents are what?" Not Mama and Papa. They were still sitting at the breakfast table like they'd been when she left for her ride. Papa reading the paper, and Mama perusing the latest letter from Aunt Reba. She clutched the pommel and the thick silver mane flowing over it. How could they be...?

Jolie stamped her hoof and nudged Big Jim again, pulling her back to the present.

"Yesm, I saw it all. I'd never left them if I could've helped 'em." His thick lips tightened and his eyes blazed. "But I took care of the two who did it." He swiped another tear. "When the soldiers leave, I'll go back, bury yo mama and papa and do what I can for the place." His hoarse voice broke on the last words.

Sounds of horses, curses, and laughter emerged in the distance through the trees.

Big Jim stiffened and slammed his hat back onto his thick black hair. "They's coming. Will you flee, Miss? I kin lose them in the swamp. You follow the river to the town and safety. You got people there who can help you."

With tears gushing down her cheeks, Anna reined Jolie around and urged the mare into her fastest gallop toward the Cooper waterway. The hound loped along beside her. Now she knew why he was no longer with her father. Prince would've never left her papa if he still lived. She gulped back choking sobs.

When she glanced behind, Big Jim disappeared into the tangle of undergrowth from which he'd emerged. The man had left his safe cave to come and warn her. *Keep him protected, Lord.* She swiped the tears coursing down her cheeks. Her abundant hair popped from its pins and spread out behind her like a fan.

The fresh morning and the sun growing brighter overhead no longer filled her heart with well-being. Nothing could push back the darkness that hovered around her. It was as if she, the exhausted horse beneath her, and the drooling dog bounding alongside them, split a path through a shadow land of terror.

O God, help me. Help us all.

The hoof beats behind her grew closer, and a drunken holler echoed through the trees. "Lookie, lookie what's running ahead of me, men. And with that red flame of hair. She'll belong to the one who catches her." Then other shouts and laughter burst forth.

~

Captain John Vargas stood on the quarterdeck of his sloop, the *Sand Dollar*, with his eyeglass trained on the distant shore of the Cooper River. His mother and father, Georgia and Samuel, joined him.

"Look, son, I see smoke rising beyond the trees on the far bank. Could it be a house burning?" His mother's voice trembled.

"It's in the vicinity of Laurens Hill Plantation. Tories or that Butcher Tarleton must've been at work early this morning." He sucked in his breath at the sight of a horse and rider galloping toward the river with a horde of green-coated men in close pursuit. "Someone is fleeing on horseback."

Georgia reached for the eyeglass. "Oh, John, it's a woman. I see her red hair flying out behind her. Do something, son." His mother gasped when the horse and rider jumped from the steep bank into the river.

The pursuers pulled up to the edge, then two men dismounted and started casting off their green coats.

"Oh, yes. We'll give those monsters something to remember." John, with his father close behind him, flew down the quarterdeck steps and toward the nearest cannon, yelling for his first lieutenant and their experienced gunner to come.

First Lieutenant William Burns rushed to John's side and helped the gunner push the cannon into the gun port. "We'll put some stingers in their hide, that we will, good captain, the Lord willing. And I do think He'll be happy to save that lass." His Scottish burr and words encouraged John, as they always did.

John drew out his eyeglass and gauged the distance. "Up toward the cliff. Let's send a round into that green horde."

The gunner aimed the weapon and loaded the shot.

The cannon boomed through the quiet morning, and the ball landed in the midst of the pursuers. Horses reared and screamed. The two Tories on the ground looked across the waterway at them, grabbed their coats, and leapt into their saddles. As Burns and the gunner sent another shot, the group turned and galloped away.

"Blast some more after them for good measure. Just don't hit the river." John shouted orders back to the men as he and his father ripped the rowboat free and lowered it into the water. They slid down the rope on the side of the ship, dropped in, and grabbed the oars.

Rowing as fast as he could, with his father working in perfect rhythm with him, John scanned the clear waters around the horse struggling to swim to the lower shore downstream. He could discern the animal's lifted silver face and movement, but no human head bobbed nearby. Where was the rider? Had the flowing river swept her downstream?

He and Samuel stopped rowing at the approximate place the horse and rider had jumped into the waterway. John stood, jerked the gun and sword from his baldric, then cast the leather strap and his shirt to the floor of the craft. He looked around the area for a swimmer. "Where could she be?"

Then he saw something white and dark red floating, weaving on the river's surface, waves covering, then revealing a small pale face framed by long auburn hair. He dove into the cold water and drew the woman toward the boat. She was lightweight, even with her thick, soaking skirt and tresses.

"Lift her with care, son." His father leaned out and reached for the feminine form with its wet hair draped over a porcelain face, then brought her aboard.

John climbed into the small vessel. "Is she dead?"

His father frowned, looking into the soft face still as the grave. "I don't think I see her breathing."

"Give her to me." John lifted the cold, soaking form and draped her over his shoulder. He gave two sound thuds across her small shoulders, like he'd seen William Burns do to a half-drowned sailor who fell overboard.

The girl coughed, and water gushed out her mouth and nose and down John's back. Joy surged through him.

Sitting on the bench with her laying on his lap, he watched as she took regular breaths. Color came into her lovely face, and her eyelids with their dark lashes fluttered, but didn't open. "Why is she not waking up?"

"Look at that bruise on her forehead, son. Maybe she hit her head on the saddle when the horse jumped into the river." He smiled. "But if she's breathing, I think she'll be all right. Your mother and Mammy June will make sure of that."

John laid her gently on the floor of the craft. He folded and placed his shirt under her head.

A sudden bark alerted him to another creature needing rescue. A hefty dog scratched at the side of the boat as if to climb aboard. John reached for the thick leather collar around its neck and helped the animal scramble in. The wet red hound shook, showering them with his cool droplets, then laid down beside the girl with his head across her middle. Large, soulful brown eyes moved from John to his father as they rowed back to the *Sand Dollar*.

~

*A*nna Grace awakened in a soft bed. She looked up into the smiling face of an older, angelic, blond-haired woman sitting nearby. Had she died and gone to heaven? Yet the room seemed to rock as if on a ship, and she reveled in the warmth of a blanket covering her. The memory of being drenched and cold faded.

Glancing behind the angel, she saw a tall black servant, a red kerchief covering most of her thick curly hair threaded with gray. "There now. There's our young lady. She's returned to the land o'the living, and we sure is glad."

The living? Tears filled Anna's eyes and flooded down her cheeks. "*Pour ma mere, mon papa.*"

The two women looked at each other. The blond one patted her shoulder.

Something wet brushed her hand and then licked it. *Prince.* She touched the familiar head thrust from the other side of the bed, and the dog barked and wagged his tail. He sat on his haunches and pushed his nose close to her.

"Hello, boy. I'm so glad you made it, too. You're about all I have left." Just thinking of her family brought a fresh gush of tears. Dear Henry. What would he feel when he returned home from his militia duty? She would never tell him the raiders came because of his enlisting with Francis Marion's men. She swiped at the wetness on her cheek. At least she still had a brother, or hoped she had.

The servant poured a cup of tea on a side table and offered it. Anna Grace sat up and took the drink. Her head ached. She reached up and touched a bruise on her forehead.

The blond woman smiled at her. "You may have bumped your forehead on the saddle when you jumped into the river, dear one."

The terrible plunge came back, and she shivered, almost spilling the contents of her cup. Her two visitors stared at her with concern. She took a deep breath, steadied her cup, and examined the cabin. Its accessories evidenced a woman's touch, from the fluffy bedspread to the rocking chair covered in soft cushions. A silky curtain hung at the corners of the bed, and a thick rug blanketed the floor. She sipped her tea and fingered the ruffle of the yellow gown she wore. Someone else's clothing. "Where am I?"

The woman spoke. "You're on our son John's ship, the *Sand Dollar.* He saw you jump into the river and sent some cannon shots to disperse your pursuers. Then he and his father rescued you and your dog. I'm his mother, Georgia Ann Vargas, and this is Mammy June."

"I am Anna Grace Laurens." Tears threatened again and her throat tried to close. She sat her cup back on the side table. "A man named Tarleton and other Tories burned our plantation and...murdered my parents." She couldn't suppress a sob.

A harsh expelling of breath in the entrance drew her gaze. A tall, striking man stood in the doorway, his white shirt stretched over thick shoulders and blue pants stuffed into high black boots. His dark curly hair swept back in a queue framed a strong, bearded face tanned to a golden bronze. He wore a sword and brace of pistols in a red leather baldric.

"Here is John, our son, captain of this ship." The blond woman stood and turned to him. "She has regained consciousness, dear. Her name is Anna Grace Laurens."

He strode forward, his weapons bumping and clanging. His tall, powerful form dwarfed the cabin space. Prince lifted his nose from the bedspread and growled.

The man glanced at the dog but didn't hesitate until he stood beside the bed. Scents of sea and leather emanated from him. Blazing green eyes under thick brows searched her countenance.

Anna patted Prince's head. "No, boy, he's our friend. He saved our lives." She lifted her face to the captain's. "And we are most grateful, sir."

When their gazes met, heat climbed up Anna Grace's neck and spread to her cheeks. She pulled the coverlet closer to her chin and looked away.

"I overheard you tell what happened, and I want you to know how sorry I am, Miss Laurens." His eyes glowed with warm sympathy, then flashed like sunlight on steel.

He turned to his mother. "Now you understand why I've insisted you and father leave Windemere and go to the island. No patriot is safe with the green coats and Tories raiding the countryside."

His mother shrugged and sighed. "Yes, Captain John, I think you are right. What happened today confirms it. We'll be much safer at Salt Marsh until this horror is over."

Anna lifted her face toward the handsome man again. "Sir, can you tell me about my mount? Did you see anything of my poor Jolie when you rescued us?"

He smiled, showing even white teeth. "Good news on that point. She swam to the lower shore downstream and climbed out. You need not worry about her. She looked like a fine horse, and anyone who finds her would want to take good care of her—even those who raided your plantation." He leaned closer. "I'm sure they're long gone now, and I hope you can rest easy, Miss Laurens. You're safe here." He turned and left, leaving the room feeling empty.

She lay back on the pillow and blinked away moisture. Rest easy? Would she ever again? Whispers and the retreating footsteps of his mother and the servant were the last thing she heard before falling into a fitful sleep.

~

*L*ater that evening, when the sunset shot pink and purple rays through the port hole, Anna Grace awoke and sat up against her pillows. A knock sounded at the door, and then it opened. The tantalizing smell of food filled the cabin. Mammy June placed a tray with a bowl of steaming soup and a wedge of bread before her. Until that moment, she hadn't realized how hungry she was.

The servant also placed a lantern on the small table beside the bed. "Ma'am, kin I git anything else for you?"

"No, thank you very much." She smiled at the woman as she turned and left.

The thick, warm liquid and fresh bread invigorated Anna. Prince, too, when he received her leftovers. As her strength returned, her sorrow morphed into anger like she'd never known. Revenge burned across her mind and brought a bitter taste into her mouth. She placed the empty bowl and spoon back on the tray and clenched her teeth.

Justice. Why not implement it any way she could? She could shoot and use a sword as well as most men. Her father and brother had made sure of that. But how could she, even with her weapons expertise, have hope of avenging her parents' murder and their destroyed plantation?

If Henry were in Charles Town, he'd help her. But there was no telling where, and for how long, he would be riding with Colonel Marion's men, exacting as much damage as possible against the British.

She sighed. And so was her childhood ally and almost-fiancé Burton Rand. He and her brother joined Marion's militia together. For a moment his familiar, dear face filled her mind. He would not like what she was thinking.

I need to do my part, too.

"And I will find a way," she spoke into the falling darkness. Prince lifted his head from the floor at the sound of her voice, and she patted him. With that decision made, she blew out the lantern and lay back on her pillow. The gentle rocking of the vessel as it moved down the Cooper River eased her into a fitful sleep.

CHAPTER 2

Strength and honor are her clothing, and she shall rejoice in time to come.
(Proverbs 31:25)

ohn stood on the quarterdeck the next morning and gazed across the Cooper River. The auburn-haired beauty named Anna Grace flowed into his mind. He'd never seen eyes quite her color. Not brown, but bronze, or topaz, with golden flecks that matched the blond tints in her mass of hair. He inhaled a deep breath and, with effort, pushed the tempting picture away.

A different face, almost as lovely, replaced it. But this countenance mocked him. Ruth Garfield's last words chilled his heart again like they had a year earlier when she had uttered them without a trace of regret. *I must marry the duke, John. My family is insisting. It's a lifestyle I deserve and want.* Then his childhood sweetheart had flounced away from him at the soiree, and he'd left the party to lick his wounds. Never would he allow another woman to ensnare his affections as she had.

He looked around the *Sand Dollar.* His forever love. He liked every inch of the 200-ton coastal schooner with her four masts and a crew of eight to handle her. Perfect for his work among the Charles Town islands and quick trips to the Caribbean for trade. If the British ever discovered his secret help to the patriots and caught him, he'd rot in the deepest dungeon until they hanged him.

He smiled. They couldn't catch him. In the taverns, the British soldiers spoke of the Devil of Charles Town who continued to escape their capture.

"Son, what are you grinning about?" His mother walked up on the quarterdeck. "Could it have anything to do with our attractive passenger?"

John turned his gaze seaward and inhaled a deep breath of the fresh, damp air, now tinged with salt. They were within a day's sail of the Charles Town Harbor where the Cooper River flowed into the Atlantic. Best to let his mother think he smiled because of their lovely guest. She knew nothing of his clandestine trips to the Caribbean for supplies to help the patriot cause. And he *had* thought about their guest. "You're right. She is fair to look upon with that sweetheart face and mane of hair." Not to mention her eyes that seemed to see into his soul.

His mother moved to stand beside him at the railing. "Are you thinking about asking Anna Grace to accompany us to Salt Marsh?"

"Would you and Father mind? She said she's an orphan."

"No, we would love to have her if she'd be happy to stay with us. I'll invite her at our evening meal. I believe she'll be able to come to your captain's table."

Before long, they all sat at his oak officer table and enjoyed a thick stew and corn bread. John watched Anna Grace, lovely in her borrowed blue silk dress, when his mother invited her to visit Salt Marsh with them.

"We have a comfortable house on one of the secluded sea islands, and we'd love to have you, dear, until it's safe to return to Charles Town." She patted Anna's hand lying on the table.

The girl tucked a curly strand of auburn hair behind an ear and blessed his mother with a wonderful smile, showing even white teeth and a dimple in her chin. "Thank you so much for the invitation, but I must decline. I'm not without family whom I can go to. You see, I have an uncle who owns Laurens Mercantile in Charles Town near Gadsden Wharf. Rufus Laurens is his name. Also, I have a brother, Henry, who is in the militia with Colonel Marion. He'll come back to the city when he can. So could you please put me ashore at Uncle Rufus' place?" She shifted topaz eyes to John.

His mother turned her gaze on him, too. "Can you, son? Do you know where the place is?"

He knew the location of Laurens Mercantile. He and Rufus carried on secret trade for the benefit of the patriots when John made trips to the West Indies. What kind of pickle would it be for a girl like their guest to get mixed up in that business? He searched her eyes. "I could, but I don't recommend it, Miss Laurens."

"Please, call me Anna Grace." The invitation in her voice sent warmth up his spine.

He shook it off. "I'm taking my parents to a safe hideaway because of the dangers daily increasing for all who desire independence from the king. I urge you not to go into Charles Town, even if the patriots now hold it. The British are angry as wet hens for being run out and will try to retake the city. I believe they'll use every kind of force they can."

She thrust out a pretty lip. "I'm not afraid. My uncle is in good standing with the patriots and the Tories, and I should be safe in his care. He tries to stay neutral for his mercantile business."

John's face stiffened, and he leaned forward. "I tell you, young lady, you will be at major risk. The latest news is that General Clinton is planning a combined sea and land expedition to surround Charles Town, cut off all supply lines, and bombard the city until all patriots surrender. They plan to retake the colony. Eventually, they're coming back in force."

His mother gasped. "John, are you sure?"

His father nodded. "He's right, ladies. I heard the same news."

Anna's face paled but she sat up straighter. "Please, I'm confident I'll be fine. Uncle Rufus is a well-known merchant, and he has a good affiliation, even with the British, if they should...return to power. I trust he can take care of me."

Trying not to grit his teeth, John shook his head and stood. "If you insist, Miss Laurens, we'll honor your wishes in the morning." He strode out of the cabin.

What an obstinate young woman. Beautiful, but stubborn.

~

That night Anna gave up the idea of sleep. The thought of arriving in Charles Town on the morrow both excited and frightened her. Would she be sorry she didn't go with the captain's family to a safer place? How could the British retake the city with it full of patriots? She slipped back into her dress, drew a wrap around her shoulders, commanded Prince to stay, and left her cabin. Perhaps a breath of fresh air would settle her.

She tiptoed down the corridor and up the steps to the deck, her skirts rustling despite her effort to be quiet. The moon, like a ghostly galleon, sailed in and out of the clouds above. Sounds of snoring sailors in their nooks, interspersed with the lapping of water on the sides of the ship, floated on the night air. She found a shadowed spot at the forecastle, away from the sleeping hammocks.

Taking a deep breath of the fresh salty scent, she peered across the ship. The night guards walked their rounds, but didn't look her way. She leaned on the railing and glanced at the white foam churning below as the schooner moved upon the sea. A gentle wind lifted her hair from her shoulders, and she shivered in its coolness. They had to be close to the Atlantic and the Charles Town harbor.

"You should not be on deck alone at night, Miss Laurens."

Startled, she twisted around to meet the unsmiling face of the captain. His white shirt sleeves whipped in the breeze and his bicorn sat at an angle on his curly dark hair. She pulled her wrap closer. "I wanted a fresh breath of air, thank you. My cabin is a little stuffy."

He moved to lean on the railing beside her, and she became aware of the strength and warmth that emanated from him. His scent of leather and spice tickled her nose, and his closeness tightened her breathing. She moved a step away.

He smiled. "Or have you had second thoughts about going into Charles Town?" His low, condescending voice tripped something inside her.

She glared at him. "No, I have a duty to fulfill and I plan to do it."

"A duty?"

She gripped the railing and took a deep breath. "Yes, I will find some way to avenge my parents' death against the British." An exciting new thought flashed into her mind and, before she could discern the wisdom of sharing the idea, out it came. "Maybe I'll spy for the patriots." As she spoke it, resolve flowed through her.

He snorted and shook his head, and then he leaned down, his face within inches of hers. "Anna Grace Laurens, that is the most foolish idea I've heard from a young woman like you. You don't understand what you're talking about. Both the British and the patriots sentence suspected spies to hanging as fast as they catch them, and many have already lost their lives. It's not a game to enter into without forethought." His eyes blazed into hers.

She inched back. "Truly?"

"Yes. The English are angry as hornets about the colonial rebellion, and they're going after our patriot spies with a fury. They want to stamp out this uprising fast. When they catch suspected victims, they sentence them to hang on the flimsiest of evidence and...burn patriot plantations. Does that ring a bell in your head?" His hard voice chilled her.

She turned away. To her vexation, moisture formed behind her eyelids. She clenched them shut. How dare he remind her of her loss? Why did she even tell this infuriating man her idea? Of course it was dangerous work, but she wanted to help the patriot cause. She must do *something*.

He placed his hands on her shoulders and turned her to face him. She swiped away a tear. "I'd give a lot to know you were safe with my parents at Salt Marsh, Anna Grace." His softened voice, his touch, and manly scent so close sent tremors through her.

She looked up into his countenance, no longer tight and harsh, but concerned. About her. His uneven breathing feathered her cheek, and her heart thudded. He exuded some kind of dynamic vitality that drew her, but she must resist.

She pulled back. "Why should you care about what happens to me, Captain?"

His glance settled on her lips. "I don't know, but I do." Then he released her.

She took a deep breath, then crossed her arms and stretched taller. "Well, I am going into Charles Town, and I won't change my mind. Sorry if that disturbs you, sir."

He frowned, and then his captain's authority settled back on him like a cloak. He whipped off his hat and gave her a curt bow. "Fine, Miss Laurens. Please return to your cabin and stay there until we arrive in the harbor at dawn." His low voice exuded annoyance.

She grabbed the edge of her gown and swished away, conscious of his frown following her until she made her way down the deck steps.

~

John stared at the outline of the Charles Town harbor glowing like an Australian opal in the pink and golden rays of the sunrise. He stood with his helmsman as the man guided the *Sand Dollar,* flying Christopher Gadsden's patriot snake flag, into the northern part of Gadsden Wharf. He eased the vessel in among almost two hundred ships from various ports over the Atlantic.

He didn't want to attract attention. How many times had he slipped into this dock with contraband goods—cargo not bought from British sellers in the West Indies and not carrying heavy English taxes? He had done it right under the noses of the inspectors since before the war began. His fast sloop always outran their border patrol frigates. Under cover of darkness, he did all his secret trading. Daylight required much more care. He had instructed his parents not to come aboard deck until they were well away from Charles Town, just in case.

Two of his crew, at his instruction, lowered the gangplank to the busy dock. Shouts and curses from crews and hucksters and bleating animals filled the air. Smells of unwashed bodies, undried leather pelts, and more pleasant scents of bread and bacon cooking somewhere down the wharf floated across the morning air.

Anna appeared from the hatch steps dressed in her own clothing, including her boots she'd been wearing when he rescued her from the river. Her dog strode beside her on a lead. Roses bloomed in her cheeks and her eyes sparkled as she walked to him on the quarter deck. The cool sea breeze played havoc with her auburn curls pinned back from her face. He forced his gaze away from the lovely vision.

"We've arrived." She looked across the dock and wrinkled her nose. "Whew, we didn't encounter such odors on our plantation." Then she lifted her glance to him. "Do you know where my uncle's mercantile is?"

He expelled a long breath. "I do."

"You do?" Her bronze eyes flashed.

"Yes. I will escort you. Are you ready to leave or have you changed your mind?" Her heart-shaped face turned up to him with all its loveliness. A smattering of freckles crossed her turned-up nose. Did she have any idea what a beauty she was? What he wouldn't give for her to change her plan and go to safety at Salt Marsh with his parents.

She frowned and stamped her boot. "No, I have not." Then she added with a softer tone. "And please thank your mother for all the help she's been. Tell her I didn't take any of the clothing she offered, because I'll have everything I need in Charles Town."

"Where will you live? Not over the mercantile, I hope." He couldn't keep the sarcasm from his voice.

She laughed, though annoyance flashed in her eyes. "Of course not. My aunt and uncle have a home on the corner of East Bay, and our family townhouse is three blocks from theirs."

He took a deep breath and drained all mockery from his tone. "But could you stay at your house...a young woman alone?"

"What is it to you, whatever I do, sir?"

"I'm just thinking of your safety, Anna Grace Laurens. We are living in troublesome times."

"Well, for your information, my mother's sister has lived in our home since she became a widow some years ago. Aunt Reba keeps the house in excellent shape and has the servants and supplies she needs to do it. Does that satisfy your curiosity about where I will live?"

He expelled a harsh breath and led her down the gangplank, with Prince padding at her side, sniffing at the new harbor smells. She pulled a thick wrap closer against the cool November morning air.

They walked around the wharf until they found the sign above wide, double doors, *Laurens Mercantile.*

Anna Grace knocked at the closed entrance until a window opened in a room above. A bearded man in a night shirt leaned out and grunted, "We ain't open yet, lady. It's another hour."

"I am Mr. Laurens's niece, please come down and let me in. We must send a message to him."

He grumbled, but shut the casement, and after a few minutes, heavy, limping footsteps descended the stairs. One of the double doors opened and he glared at them. At least, he'd changed into his trousers.

Anna Grace smiled and addressed him. "I believe your name is Jack, is it not, sir. You and your wife have indenture papers with Uncle Rufus and help at the mercantile?"

John had endured the servant's animosity whenever he came to the business. Jack suffered a carriage accident two years earlier that injured his leg, but Laurens decided it wouldn't hinder his work as a clerk and let him continue his indenture contract. But the fellow's attitude had soured.

Jack nodded. "My wife'll be down in a bit, if you need her. She's got to feed the boy."

"That's fine. But would your boy take a message for me after his breakfast? I am Anna Laurens and this is Captain Vargas who was kind enough to convey me to Charles Town."

He nodded but didn't look at John. "I know the captain." He moved from the doorway and headed toward the fireplace.

John acknowledged the man's cool greeting with a nod and hoped he'd say nothing else about his work with Rufus. The less the niece knew of his work for the colony and Washington's continental army supply, the better.

Anna proceeded him in and John closed the door on the chill dock air. Jack stoked the fire, added logs, and went about lighting lanterns in the dim interior with a hot stem of wood he took from the flames. A blended aroma of ripe cheese, whale oil, pickles, produce, leather, and tobacco filled the air, as well as the burning smell of pine in the fireplace.

A long counter included candy jars, a coffee mill, scales for weighing items, wrapping paper, and string. The light revealed side walls with shelves displaying fabrics, sewing goods, shoes, hats, and stockings. Bins of farm products spilled across the middle of the area —potatoes, sacks of flour, rice, beans, salt, pepper, leather items, feed, and farm implements. One entire section displayed barrels of rum and bottles of wine housed in sectioned wooden crates.

Anna turned to the man when he finished lighting lanterns. "Would you be so kind as to give me paper and pen to write a note to my uncle?"

"Yes, ma'am. Right away." He gave it to her and turned to trudge back up the stairs. Soon, a boy of about thirteen descended, took her note, and hurried out the door.

His father also returned. "I have work in the storeroom. Please have a seat here until Mr. Rufus arrives." He disappeared behind a door in back.

Anna sank into a rocking chair near the fireplace. Prince dropped on the floor beside her and laid his head on his paws. John sat on a chair nearby, making a crackling noise as his weight settled on the corn-shuck seat. She looked at him and smiled. "Captain, you are welcome to leave. I'm sure my uncle will be here as soon as he can."

John removed his bicorn and leaned forward. "I said I'd escort you to your uncle's, and that's what I intend to do. I'll depart when I see him take responsibility for you."

~

*A*nna shook her head in annoyance and sighed. The man was impossible. "What do you do for a livelihood, may I ask?"

John smiled. "Gentlemen do little for a living, I understand."

"Are you a gentleman?"

"Probably not the kind you're used to."

"Are you in some type of business with your ship?"

"You might say I'm in the supply trade. I try to find and deliver whatever the patriots need."

She stared at him. What could he mean? Did he help provision Washington's army? She'd heard of the secret wagon trains that left Charles Town on the Kings Highway and headed toward Philadelphia and places General Washington might be. The work carried significant risk for anyone involved because the British were just as eager to stop all supplies going to the Continental army as the patriots were determined to get supplies there.

"Isn't that perilous work?"

"Not as risky as spying."

She lowered her head. Was her idea crazy and more dangerous than she knew?

He stood and walked to a shelf holding a few books. He pulled out a thick, black Bible. "My mother once told me Proverbs, Chapter 31, holds good signs for women. Let's see if there's one for you. Tell me your birthday."

She looked at him, puzzled. "My date of birth?" And a sign for her as a spy? What could he mean?

"I understand there's a verse for every woman in Proverbs 31 according to the day of the month they are born." He opened the Bible and flipped through the pages. "Are you going to give me yours?"

"My birthday is the twenty-fifth of January, 1762."

He grinned. "I can see that you're young and didn't need the year."

He ran his finger down the page. "Here it is, verse 25." He leaned toward the lantern and read. "'Strength and honor are her clothing, and she shall rejoice in time to come.'" His green eyes flashed. "That's your verse."

They both jumped at the sound of a carriage approaching on the wharf outside, coming fast by the sound of the horse's hooves pounding the dock and the jangling of its harness.

"That must be Uncle Rufus. He always drives his bay at a gallop."

The conveyance stopped at the open door and Prince bolted to his feet, barking.

"No, boy, no." Anna's firm voice calmed the dog, and he laid back down before the fireplace, but his dark eyes never left the front entrance.

A robust figure with a cigar clamped between his teeth entered with brisk, authoritative strides into the mercantile.

Anna Grace stood and ran into her uncle's outstretched arms. She burst into tears and pressed her face into his strong shoulder so like her father's. He patted her, and she lifted her head and took a deep breath.

"You smell good, just like…daddy."

"There, there, my dear. He moved the cigar from his mouth and shook its ashes behind him toward the fireplace. We smoke the same type of these Havanas. Glad you like the scent. Wish my Merle did." He kissed her forehead. "Young lady, I was so happy to get your message."

She pulled herself together and stepped back from his embrace.

He glanced up. "Why, hello, John. Thank you for your part in this. We—we thought we'd lost the entire family after we heard of the appalling raid." He turned back to Anna and handed her his handkerchief. "My dear, we praise God you escaped, but how *did* you escape?"

She wiped her face and blew her nose. "I was out for my morning ride when it took place. On my way back in, Big Jim ran out of the swamp to warn me not to go home. He told me…what had happened." Another tear spilled down her cheek.

"My girl, you don't have to talk about it for now, if you'd rather not." He cleared his throat, swiped at his eyes, and glanced at John a few yards away. "But I am curious how the captain here became involved."

John strode forward. "I can tell you that part of the story. My family and I were sailing down the Cooper River and saw her fleeing on horseback with Tory green coats pursuing her. She and the horse jumped into the water, and we frightened the men off with a few cannon shots, then rescued her."

Anna touched her uncle's arm. "Oh, Uncle Rufus, I so want to know what happened to my beautiful Jolie."

John spoke up. "I told her I saw the animal swim downstream and climb out, and that I believed anyone who finds her would be happy to take care of a fine horse like that."

"That's true, Anna. I don't think you need to worry too much about Jolie. Horses are scarce nowadays with the army taking so many, and I will do some checking. She may even find her way home. And, Captain, we are ever so grateful for your rescuing my niece and bringing her here."

John stood and shook the man's extended hand, then swiped up his bicorn from a chair and walked to the door.

Anna cleared her throat. "Yes, thank you for everything, John. Will —will we see you again sometime?"

He turned and winked at Rufus and then smiled at her and slapped his hat on his head. "Maybe."

~

*J*ohn strode out the door and down the dock to the *Sand Dollar* bobbing in the tide. Of course, he'd return to the mercantile. He and Rufus accomplished important business for the patriot cause. He couldn't deny how the thought of seeing Anna again already made him eager. But what effect would Rufus's niece arriving have on their dangerous, clandestine work?

CHAPTER 3

*I know not what course others may take; but as for me, give me liberty or
give me death."*
~ *Patrick Henry, 1776*

*A*nna's heart sank when her uncle insisted they drop by his
townhouse to greet his wife on the way home. Riding in his
carriage with Prince at her feet, she braced herself for the encounter
with Aunt Merle, a fervent Tory. How could a man and spouse be so
different? He a patriot, she loyal to the king?

Anna slid her glance to him, sitting beside her, the epitome of
goodwill and kindness. Dressed in his favorite deerskin breeches,
black shoes with shining brass buttons, and a simple brown waistcoat,
he didn't appear to be the rich merchant he was. Except for his fine
silk cravat and gold chained watch—additions Merle added to his
attire—he could be a plain working man of Charles Town.

She cast her thoughts aside as the charm of the city enveloped her
with each clip clop of her uncle's high-stepping horse through the
cobbled streets. How she loved their elegant settlement, which she'd
heard to be the richest in the thirteen colonies since rice became the
principal export crop. They passed grand, three-storied, palatial

homes. Ornamental, hand-carved, wrought-iron gates enclosed the imposing entrances and surrounded well-cared-for gardens in their fall plumage. Red, orange, and blue annuals peeped through the intricate metal bars. Hanging roses in various colors crept over the tops of walls. Shiny leaf camellias, fragrant gardenias, and blooming crepe myrtles lined carriage drives. Anna smiled as all the names came back to her. From a child, her mother had taught her to appreciate the fascinating flora that grew so well in their southern area.

The driver turned into the open gate at her uncle's impressive three-story dwelling and shouted, "Whoa." The magnificent bay stallion stopped and tossed his fine head, causing his harness to jingle.

Her aunt swept down the steps of the grand house to greet them. Servants in impeccable green livery stood at attention behind her. Dressed in a well-appointed gray silk dress with yards of fabric in its bouncing skirt, she appeared every bit the rich Charles Town merchant's wife she was. A fine gauze cap adorned her high coiffed white wig.

Anna commanded Prince to stay in the buggy and, assisted by her uncle's hand, alighted. She allowed her aunt to draw her into a light hug. Recognizing the Tory green rosette on the side of Merle's headpiece, she stiffened. The woman would never miss an opportunity to show her loyalty to King George. And she always smelled of lavender. Anna's mother had told her that ladies added that herb to the wig powder not just for fragrance, but also to kill head lice.

Anna restrained a smile at the thought her aunt may have that problem in her elegant hairdo.

Merle released her, and then her soft, white hands fluttered over her dress and wig as if hugging Anna may have upset their perfect lines. "Well, my dear, we are so happy you survived the attack on your plantation." The woman sniffed, straightened her back, and looked down her long nose. "As sorry as I am about what happened to your parents, my dear, I must tell you it is nothing more than those who rebel against our king can expect."

Anna gasped, and blinked as moisture gathered in her eyes.

Her uncle shook his head and steered her away toward the

carriage. "I'm going to escort Anna to their townhome. We only stopped for her to greet you."

When on the street to her own townhouse a few blocks away, he patted her clenched hands. "Don't let her throw you, dear. You know how your aunt is. But I'd have never heard the end of it, if I hadn't brought you by." He grinned. "Think of it like this, your coming to see her will prevent her dropping by your house later today or tomorrow. She's done her duty and made known her loyalty to the king loud and clear in her usual painful manner."

Yes, it was a relief to know she wouldn't need to dread a visit from Aunt Merle any time soon. She looked at her uncle's firm countenance through damp lashes. Unlike his Tory wife, he had discarded his white wig when the war for independence began. "How do you...live with such different loyalties?"

He chuckled. "With much care and caution, dear."

"What about your sons? How do they feel?"

"Warren is a patriot, I'm thankful to say. In fact, he's off with the militia and Marion. I hate to admit it, but James stands as firm as his mother for King George."

"I'm so sorry. Your life must be like walking between two barrels of gunpowder with a smoking brand in your hand."

He took a deep breath. "It's not quite that bad. I've learned to keep my patriot ideas and work separate from my home life." A sad smile played at the corners of his mouth. "And as long as I meet Merle's extravagant needs, she can, at times, be pleasant."

His glance rested on Anna for several moments. "I don't want to upset you, but I plan to ride out to your father's plantation in a few days to check on things. He put me as executor of his estate some years back, and I added him as mine. Brothers trusting each other. You don't need to go with me. I'm just letting you know."

Anna's heart lurched. "Please, I want to see the plantation again. Will you take me with you?"

He sighed and began to shake his head. "It'll probably be a heartbreaking sight. The word I got was that the main house and rice barns and stables burned to the ground, and the animals not taken were killed without mercy." He looked at her with sympathy creasing his lined face. "I understand one servant who escaped has buried...Charles and your mother. We thank God for that, but surely you don't want to go back until we get the place cleaned up some. I think it unwise. Are you sure about this?"

Anna wiped a tear that slid down her cheek. "I'm quite certain. I know Big Jim and his wife Mary Lee escaped. He told me he would...bury Mama and Papa after the Tories left." She gulped back more tears, touched her uncle's arm, and looked into his face. "I need to go for their sake." She swallowed hard. "And there's one more thing. I want to know if my Jolie found her way home after we jumped into the river."

Uncle Rufus sighed. "Your mare, huh? I know how much you set store by that Arabian you raised. If you insist, I'll let you come with me." Then a grin creased his face. "I've never been able to deny you anything, have I young lady, since you came into the world with that fluff of red hair and those topaz eyes? You were the prettiest baby, and the only girl in our two families. Did we spoil you?" His strong, familiar voice restored a measure of harmony in Anna's mind.

She gave him a trembling smile. "Well, I hope not, if spoiled means I'm no longer any good."

He chuckled and shook his head.

They arrived at Anna's front gate. Her mother's sister, Reba Collins, sat on the porch and appeared to be working on a hat in her lap. She owned the best millinery in Charles Town. When she looked up at the carriage driving up to their steps, Anna waved.

The woman's mouth fell open, and she stood, dropped the cap aside, and shouted for her man to unbar the entrance.

Rufus's driver shouted, "Whoa," and the horse stopped and stretched his neck.

Her aunt flew down the steps and nearly pulled Anna from the conveyance as she hugged her tight. Prince leaped down to the ground and sniffed around the walkway, wagging his tail.

"My dear, dear Anna." Tears rolled down her aunt's porcelain cheeks. "We thought they murdered your whole family when we heard the terrible news of the raid. Thank God they spared you." She glanced at the dog. "And is this Prince, your father's hunting hound? He's grown."

Moisture stung her eyes, but Anna lifted her head and nodded. When she gained control, she moved back from the warm embrace.

Aunt Reba pulled a lace handkerchief from her sleeve and dabbed at her eyes and nose. "Now, young lady, as soon as you get settled, I want to hear how you escaped and made it to Charles Town." She glanced at Uncle Rufus still in the carriage. "Thank you, sir, for bringing her home. Our debt to you grows much larger."

"We're family, Reba. You don't owe us anything." He turned to Anna. "Feel free to visit the store any time, you hear me? I'll put you to work, young lady." He grinned and motioned to his driver.

Anna wiped her face and blew him a kiss. Then she reached down for the leash trailing behind Prince.

Her uncle's servant clicked his tongue, and the bay proceeded toward the back courtyard and turned the buggy around as he'd done in the past. They left the drive and headed up the street at a fast clip.

Anna, with her aunt's arm around her waist, entered the house, and Prince came with them. She greeted her family's favorite servants, Sadie Mae and her husband, Moses. The woman worked as cook and lead servant over the housemaids and a kitchen worker. Moses supervised the stable and garden work, with two young male servants to do his bidding. A big grin creased his leathery, wrinkled face. She had seldom seen the man when he wasn't smiling.

Prince sidled up to the man and nudged his leg. The servant patted his head. "Big boy, ye 'member old Moses, do ye?" The dog wagged his tail and barked. The man always took care of the dog and had a place for him in the stable when her family came to live at the townhouse for the long, hot summers.

Anna wiped another tear. How she missed her people. There would be no going back to the rice estate to live. She stood straighter and lifted her chin.

But one day, with God's help, Henry and I will rebuild Laurens Plantation.

Aunt Reba clicked her tongue. "Come, now, Anna. Let's get you upstairs to rest. Do you want a warm bath, or do you prefer to relax until the midday meal? We can talk later."

"I'll rest for a while. Homecoming has been full of...memories and emotions."

"Of course, it has. It will become easier, my dear, with the good care I'll make sure you receive."

Anna followed Reba up the stairs and to her bedroom at the back of the house. The first sight of her well-appointed chamber with its scent of rosewater used in cleaning brought a baptism of peace and comfort in the familiar. She gave a long sigh.

Her aunt patted her shoulder and then left, closing the door behind her.

Anna lay down on the thick pink bedspread and stretched her taut limbs. As her eyelids closed, the striking face of Captain John Vargas with his amazing green eyes flashed across her memory, and her heartbeat increased. Had he sailed away from Charles Town? Would she ever see him again?

She banished that thought and brought Burton Ross's earnest, handsome visage to mind. They weren't officially engaged, but everyone knew they'd been promised to each other since children, by both sets of parents. The war had hindered a real engagement announcement and party.

Where was Burton now? Would he and her brother help keep each other safe fighting in the militia with Francis Marion? She would need to pray hard. Something her mother once said about praying flowed over her mind. *God's people and the enemy make the same mistake. They underestimate the power of prayer.*

～

*J*ohn stood on the quarterdeck of the *Sand Dollar*, reveling in the fresh sea breeze coming off the islands south of Charles Town. His father and mother still lingered over breakfast below deck, enjoying the rare English tea he had procured for them from his last West Indies trip.

William Burns, his First Lieutenant, joined him. The man was not yet middle aged, but already bald and proud of the fact, often going without a tricorn. He was tall, strong, and sinewy in all his limbs and hailed from Scotland. He loved to wear black clothing and high boots. His thick corded neck and dark beard, along with his shiny scalp, gave him a fearsome look, which never failed to impress enemies or the *Sand Dollar's* crew when he issued orders.

John had found him in a tavern in Jamaica three years earlier, when a throng of drunken pirates in the place seemed intent on destroying the man because his Scottish accent and booming voice irritated them. John walked in, surmised the situation, and helped Burns level most of the brawlers. They became friends, and William joined the *Sand Dollar's* crew at John's invitation. He always proved an asset in any battle on the high seas, and he knew good sailing practices and how to handle men. The man was also loyal and was a Christian and follower of the reformation leader Knox's teachings, which he sometimes quoted.

William leaned on the railing beside John, with his unlit clay pipe clamped between his teeth, and stared out across the capping waves. He removed it to speak. "You got plans for after you deliver your parents to that island, have you?" His Scottish burr with its rolled r's, unique vowel sounds, and word flow always sounded pleasant to the ear.

"Yes, but not for announcement to the crew yet."

"We going back to the Indies for more cargo, are we?"

"In a week or two."

"If the Lord be willing, I like to say." The man grinned and moved away.

John's parents appeared at the deck entrance and walked up the steps to him. His mother wore a shawl against the cool breeze.

His father reached for his hand and squeezed it. "Your mother and I enjoyed the tea you gave us. Thank you. Is there more to take to the island?"

"Yes, and you're welcome." He smiled at them.

"I dare not ask how you came by the tea, son." His mother patted his arm. "Please don't take unnecessary risks. You're the only son, *the only child*, we have, John." A shadow crossed her soft brow.

He'd had a little sister, but she died of yellow fever at age two.

His mother, even at middle age and her blond hair streaked with gray, was still beautiful. He gave her a quick hug. "Dear Mama, you keep praying and I'll continue being careful. Is it a deal?"

She smiled at him, took his father's arm, and gazed out to sea as the trim sloop maneuvered among the chain of islands along the coast. "This is a lovely trip, passing the beaches in their robe of autumn haze. We've never come in the fall." She turned back to John. "How much longer before we arrive at Salt Marsh?"

"Good news. We should land before dark."

His father took a deep breath. "I wish we could've talked Pastor Ethan and Marisol into coming with us. At their age, it worries me for them to stay near Charles Town. Will you keep check on them? Try to evacuate them before...the worse comes?"

"Yes. I knew as a pastor, grandfather would be hesitant to leave his flock, but maybe I can talk him into coming to Salt Marsh a little later."

∼

The following morning, as dawn streaked the sky in brilliant shades of pink, yellow, and blue, John docked the *Sand Dollar* in the deep water some distance from the Salt Marsh landing. Then he and his small crew helped his mother, father, and Mammy June unload their household goods and clothing from the ship to the smaller longboat for the trip to the dock. On the shore, shaded by tupelo trees in their stunning orange-red fall leaves, a young boy waved and then began ringing the large bell hanging from a crossbar between upright poles.

Servants spilled down the steps of the Georgian dwelling almost hidden many yards beyond the pier and surrounded by moss-hung oaks. They grabbed carts leaning against the rose harbor hedge and came running and laughing to help bring the stacked articles in the boat to the residence.

Later, standing in the great hall, Georgia took a deep breath and turned to her son. "John, it seems strange to be coming here in late fall instead of summer, but the holidays in this house ought to be fun."

Where would he be in six weeks when the Christmas holiday arrived? And where would the patriots be if the British surrounded Charles Town and cut off all supply lines?

"Hey, man." He turned to greet his father's mulatto friend and comrade-in-adventures, Jamie Boy, as he came up on the porch. John struck at the large outreached hand and they both laughed. A younger man with thick muscled arms and neck moved up the steps. His bright eyes stared at John, then down at the floor.

Jamie Boy folded his arms. "Want you to meet our boy, mine and Belle's. This is our Thomas. Your father told me you might can use a hand on the *Sand Dollar.*"

"This is your son? You can't mean it. Last time I saw him, he was little more than a grasshopper." John reached out a hand, and Thomas clasped it. Impressed with the young man's firm grip, he also noted his height and powerful build.

"You interested in sailing, Thomas?" He looked into the dark, excited eyes and saw the healthy, glossy skin of his face with its light shadow of brown fuzz on his jaw.

"Yessir. Ever since my dad told me the first story about his sailing with them Barbary pirates with your father."

"Oh, I see he's been planting seeds, has he?" He nudged Jamie's shoulder, and the man nodded, flashing a wide smile. Then he shooed his son away, and the young man disappeared around the edge of the house.

"The main thing is, me and his ma want to get him off our backs for a spell. Can you remember being fifteen and a half and nothing suited you around home anymore, in particular when you started getting a little hair popping out on your chin?"

John laughed, then he turned sober. "You've got to know my crew and I meet many dangers on the sea. Are you serious about wanting him to sail with me? I'd love to have him, but would hate for anything to happen to him."

Jamie took a deep breath. "That's just it. Belle and me, we're concerned he may slip off and try to join Marion's troops or a crazy independent rebel group. You know some slaves have done that. We feel sailing with you can't be no more risky, and you'd look after him best you could."

John pressed his lips together. "Yes, of course, I would, but..."

Jamie folded his arms and rocked back on his heels. "He can shoot a squirrel's eye out in the top of a tree, and you seen how strapping he is now. He's strong and could be some real help in a crisis. And he knows how to take orders, too. And he's smart. Belle's made sure of that. Taught him everything she can about learning, and God, and her herbal remedies."

John's father moved into their circle from the hall. "I heard what you two have been discussing. What do you think, son? Your mother and I would feel better knowing you had another sure ally in your crew, and you saw how big and tough the boy is now." He smiled.

John nodded. "All right, have him ready to sail with the *Sand Dollar* at first light, day after tomorrow."

Jamie whooped and slapped his leg, then hurried down the porch steps.

~

Two days later, John sailed back into Charles Town and took on cargo—rice, timber, and indigo—for trade in the West Indies. In those rich islands lived hundreds of merchants—Dutchmen, Frenchmen, Portuguese, and even some Englishmen—willing to sell anything to anybody, and without the hated English taxes.

He planned to pick up needed guns, swords, tools, salt, sugar, and fabrics, and looking glasses for those wealthy enough to ignore the war. Part of his cargo would go to Charles Town residents. But the significant portion of it, the weapons and salt in particular, would pass to a group of patriots who risked their lives driving wagons north on the Kings Highway to find Washington's army.

His work bringing needed goods into Charles Town from the Indies and those delivering the cargo to the rebel troops was dangerous business. The British navy kept a lookout for ships sailing north from the islands. Their militia waylaid every wagon train traveling north on the Kings Highway they were lucky enough to catch, confiscated the cargo, and executed all participants.

With his ship loaded in the trade goods, John stood with Rufus on the dock early the next morning, ready to catch the tide going out.

Rufus extended his hand. "I will pray for your safe return, and your hold full of supplies the patriots need. May God give you wisdom and protection to avoid the British warships combing the waters to suspend our supply lines. I've been told they're out in force now, and any ship not flying the English flag, the order is to sink it on sight, no quarter given."

John's lips tightened, but he shook the man's hand and ran up the gangplank. He'd escaped the many British frigates that tried to intercept his blockade running trade, and he laughed at the nickname they'd given him, "The Devil of Charles Town." But the devil didn't give him the wisdom and power to escape capture. Father God and his parents and grandparents' powerful prayers for him helped him avoid trouble.

As he gave the order to pull anchor and unfurl the sails, a chill of forewarning crept up his spine more intense than for other dangerous voyages. What did it mean?

CHAPTER 4

We must all hang together, or assuredly we shall all hang separately.
~ Benjamin Franklin at the signing of the Declaration of Independence

$\mathscr{A}$nna awoke and eyed the blue cornflowers on the wallpaper of her bedroom. What a merry time she and her mother had spent picking out the pattern two years earlier. She blinked back tears and sat up. Light flooded the room, so she must have slept late.

She arose, pulled on her robe and slippers, determined to make a good start in her new life. Would her uncle send word today about visiting the plantation? For a week, she'd heard nothing. She walked to her dresser and brushed her thick hair back from her face.

A soft knock sounded at her door.

She laid the brush down and turned. "Come in, please."

Jessie, the upstairs maid, came in and curtsied. "Mistress Collins, she say Mr. Rufus done sent a message to you and she's waiting in the breakfast room with it."

Anna threw off her robe. "Thank you. Will you help me get ready?" She pulled a dark dress from her wardrobe and her boots, instead of soft slippers, for walking around the plantation. Holding them up for a moment, she sighed. The terrible morning when the enemy soldiers came, she'd worn them while riding Jolie. Where could her dear horse be? Did anyone find her? Were they taking good care of her?

When Anna rushed into the yellow breakfast room, Aunt Reba was seated at the big table and smiled at her. But her smile dimmed as she spoke. "Are you sure you're up to going out to Laurens Hill, dear? It's going to be a sad sight for anyone's eyes. We let you sleep as long as possible. Rufus will come by in an hour." She took a sip of tea.

"Oh, yes. I wish to go with him. Will you accompany us?"

Her aunt set her cup back on the saucer and sighed. "Yes, that is my plan, young lady. But first, I need to see you eat a good breakfast."

Anna picked up her plate and moved to the buffet. She partook small portions of scrambled eggs, bacon, and a chunk of warm bread, and then sat at the polished table.

Her aunt arose and did the same, and then slipped into her chair at the head. She reached her hand for Anna's and said grace.

Before Anna took a bite, she glanced at her aunt. "But what about your millinery shop today? Have you someone to handle it while you're gone?"

"Dear, I've decided to close the business until this current crisis is over. I can complete what orders I have now here at home." She wiped her lips with a snowy, lace-edged napkin. "Besides, several of my best customers left for England after the patriots took Charles Town. So it's as good a time as ever to close shop. And Rufus says we need to make shirts for the rebels. He's going to send fabric."

Anna nodded as she placed a spoonful of food into her mouth. Thinking about the trip to the plantation, it was all she could do to swallow a few bites and wash them down with the herbal tea from the silver teapot. Her aunt, a patriot, would not serve English tea at her table.

Within the hour, she, Reba, and Rufus sat in his coach on the way to Laurens Plantation. Was she prepared for what she might see?

Her aunt had insisted she wear a warm shawl like the one she donned herself. In the chill November air, Anna pulled the welcome wrap close.

Two miles from the entrance to the estate, a rank odor assailed her nose. As the coach drew closer, the smell grew heavier. Coming to the edge of the planted fields, the horrible scent thickened to a stench that grabbed at her breath. Anna glanced at her uncle. His lips turned inward in a hard, tight line. Her aunt pulled a handkerchief from her sleeve and held it to her nose.

The horses pulling their conveyance snorted, stopped, and pawed the ground with their ears flattened. Their driver spoke to the animals and rapped the reins across their trembling backs until they progressed up the drive with jerks and stops.

A sheer black fright swept through Anna. What could the disgusting odor be that had even spooked the horses? She wrung her hands and the back of her neck ached as they advanced through the entrance to the plantation. The towering oaks that once stood guarding the mansion were a mass of burnt tree trunks, like tall black sentries.

Anna gasped, and so did her aunt, as what once was Anna's home came into full view. A weight pressed on her chest as she took in the shocking sight.

Her uncle rapped on the coach door and the driver shouted, "Whoa." The matched bays stopped, tossed their heads, jangling the harness, and blew air through their noses.

Anna gazed at chimneys, gaunt and darkened by fire, standing against the skyline amid piles of ashes and rubble. Charred pieces of walls, drapes, and half-burnt furniture lay as they had fallen in the blaze that destroyed her beautiful home. Her old hobby horse, scorched by the flames, along with trunks of clothing and old chairs that had been in the attic—or what remained of them—lay scattered about the area that had once been the first floor. Part of the framework of the winding staircase still stood, blackened and hanging in space. A sob escaped her lips, and Reba patted her clenched hands.

Then Anna saw the source of the putrid stench. Bodies of dead animals—pigs, sheep, cattle, and the older plow horses filled the area behind the house. Their carcasses, with legs stretched up in the air, lay bloated and decomposing in the sunlight. Some looked as if someone had slaughtered them fast for food, the meatier parts cut off, and the rest left to rot. Others appeared to have been killed for no reason with bullets or bayonets.

Anna opened the door and dropped out of the coach to her knees, sobbing. As waves of grief washed through her, bile rose up in her belly. She vomited her meager breakfast into the dried, burnt grass that had once been their green lawn.

The horses reared in fright, and Uncle Rufus cursed and jumped down to help the wide-eyed driver keep them from bolting. Aunt Reba disembarked from the carriage. She stooped to hold Anna's head and pulled a handkerchief from her sleeve to wipe her hot face.

Finally, the retching stopped, and Anna sat back on the ground battling a dark cloud that tried to blot out the sun overhead, the terrible smell, and the horrid sights.

A figure emerged up the side hill of the plantation. "Miss Anna, Miss Anna, you never should've come back here yet. But I'se got some good news for you." Big Jim came loping toward them. Mary Lee, his stalwart wife, ran close behind.

She stared up at him. "Good news, Big Jim? Is there any good anywhere in this god-forsaken estate?"

His dark face lit. "Yes'm. There is. Your horse, that Jolie, she come back home the next day after you left, and I'se got her down yonder in the only stable still standing. The place is too scary for her to run loose."

Uncle Rufus, who stood holding the bridles of the horses, nodded to the driver to take over and strode to help Anna to her feet. He held onto her and spoke gently. "I tried to warn you what this might look like."

She looked up into his worried face. "You could've never warned me enough. But I had to come."

Big Jim moved to take charge of the nervous bays. "I'se going to tie the horses to the one hitching post we still got, Miss Anna. Then me and Mary Lee will be coming right behind you to the stable. I got to see this reunion."

She wiped her nose and trudged with wobbly steps toward the

stable, helped by Uncle Rufus and followed by Aunt Reba, shaking her head and wiping her eyes.

A few chickens scratched in what used to be the chicken coop, the only creatures moving, except for the buzzards circling above the dead animals in the fields.

Jolie neighed a welcome as they entered the small barn. Anna fell across the mare's silver neck and sobbed. The horse nickered deep in her throat and nudged her. When she lifted her face, Anna tried to smile at her aunt and uncle. "I can thank God for bringing Jolie home safe, can't I? Seeing her makes me glad I came."

Aunt Reba nodded. "Yes, yes, you can thank the Lord, my dear. Healing starts with our thanksgiving." She turned aside to the servant. "Big Jim, Anna's parents...did you..?"

"Yes'm, I'se buried them side by side in the family plot up yonder on the hilltop."

She turned back to Anna. "Do you want to go see, or do it later?"

"I'll come now." She gave Jolie one last pat, took a deep breath, and followed the others to the family cemetery up the hillside beyond the destroyed house. Thank God its grove of oaks still stood, unscorched from the flames below. A few colorful leaves clung to the limbs and waved in the November breeze as they approached.

The wrought-iron fence around the graveyard stood intact. That was something else she could be thankful for. Her uncle opened the gate with their family name, Laurens, carved in its intricate metal. A few birds overhead tittered at having their solitude broken.

Aunt Reba reached out to clasp Anna's hand.

The smell of newly turned earth gave some relief from the stench behind them. Anna's boot heels sank into the grass and dried leaves as she walked past the markers of her grandparents to the fresh graves and handsome headstone her parents had erected some years earlier. A few wildflowers lay wilted on both the mounds. *Dear Mama and Papa.*

A dry sob escaped her throat. She had no more tears left.

"Miss Anna, me and my Mary, we could only find them wildflowers. All the rose bushes and yo garden flowers, they been burned." Big Jim's low voice exuded apology and respect.

"Yes, of course, Big Jim. Thank you both for what you've done. You did fine." Anna released her aunt's hand and reached out to touch the names carved in the cold, rough cement with their birthdays, but not their final dates. That was something she would ask Uncle Rufus to take care of. That thought—something to do, the beginning of a list— eased her pain. And they would have a real service here with their dear Pastor Clyde Allenby and his wife Ruby.

She lifted her head and looked up into the trees, hanging onto their last fall leaves. Then she turned to Rufus. "Uncle, do you think we might stop by the Presbyterian church we attended on our way back to Charles Town?"

"By all means. Let me talk to your servant here a few minutes while you and Reba walk back to the coach."

Anna Grace, with her aunt behind her, alighted and sat in the conveyance until Rufus finished talking to Big Jim. The servant strode down the hill to the small barn, entered, and soon emerged, leading Jolie with a halter and rope toward them. His wife came behind with a bucket of water. Anna stood and clasped her hands. "Oh, Uncle, can we take my Jolie back with us?"

Rufus strode toward the coach. "I don't see why not. You've got a stable at the townhouse, and I've no doubt you and Moses can take good care of her." He grinned and untied the reins from the hitching post, then climbed into the carriage.

Mary Lee offered the bucket of water to the bays, and they drank it empty.

Big Jim tied Jolie behind the coach, her silver head in reach of Anna Grace's hand when she leaned out the window. The horse nick- ered when she touched its soft muzzle.

"Thank you, uncle." Anna waved at the two servants as the carriage pulled away and started up the drive.

Uncle Rufus let out a labored breath. "I'll send a cleanup crew here by the end of the week, and more supplies for Big Jim and his wife. He thinks more of the slaves will come back from the woods and swamp once they know the raiders are gone for good and there's a place for them at the plantation. I'll order new housing for them to be built before winter sets in with earnest."

"That's wonderful. How can I ever thank you for all you're doing?"

He chuckled. "Well, you can keep your chin up, young lady, and help me out at the store a little when I'm at your estate overseeing things." His face turned serious. "I don't like to leave Jack in charge by himself too long without checking on him. There's too much temptation to pilfer or to give one's friends special prices."

"I'll be glad to support you anyway you need. Just show me what to do. But does your son...?"

Rufus sighed. "James is not a lot of help. He's too busy with his Tory friends. Spends most of his time at one of the taverns or in the back room of the hotel playing cards." Her uncle gave her a pointed look and whispered to her when Aunt Reba's head was turned. "Actually, I could use someone I can really trust—to keep a secret, for example."

Trust to protect a secret? Was he involved in something clandestine? She looked at his open expression and warm eyes. Not Uncle Rufus. He would not know how to act with duplicity. His kind face would give him away every time.

Two hours later, they passed the small stone Summerhill Presbyterian church with its wooden spire pointed up into the sky, and Rufus rapped on the roof for the driver to turn into the pastor's driveway beyond the sanctuary.

The minister and his wife sat on the porch in rocking chairs and stood when the carriage turned down their drive.

The middle-aged cleric, dressed in his black waistcoat and white collar, hurried down the steps with a smile. "Hello, Mr. Laurens, I believe it is." He glanced at the two women. "Oh, and Anna Grace. How happy we are to see you, isn't that so, Mama?" He turned back to his wife who was walking toward the carriage. She wore a simple orange dress without hoops and had her gray hair pinned in a low bun behind her head.

The woman pressed her hand against her mouth, then dropped it to exclaim, "Oh, yes. Anna Grace, how delighted we are to see you. We thought...we heard..."

Anna sighed. "I survived because I was gone on one of my early morning rides."

"Thank God." Both man and wife exclaimed in unison.

The woman seemed to collect herself. "Won't you folks climb down and come in for refreshment? I bet you've been down to see...the plantation, or what's left of it." Mrs. Allenby's words wandered off, and sympathy lined her soft face.

Anna took a deep breath. "Yes, and tea would be wonderful."

An hour later, they rode back to Charles Town, refreshed and having made arrangements for a memorial service the following Sunday for Anna's parents.

Aunt Reba's head lolled backward on the carriage seat, eyes closed, and soon her breathing became slow and shallow.

Rufus leaned toward Anna Grace, his face serious and voice low. "Don't forget what I said about helping me. I'll talk to you more next week. Come to the mercantile after lunch Monday. Will you?"

She smiled and whispered back. "Of course I will."

~

*M*onday morning, Anna dressed in her red riding skirt and warm gray cloak. Her friend, Abigail hadn't been at church the day before, so she'd determined to check on her. As she entered the barn, Jolie neighed a welcome.

Moses came from his work in another stall and had the horse saddled and ready in a few minutes. He patted the silver neck as Anna mounted. "Now be careful and happy today, you hear?"

Jolie tossed her head and stamped a hoof.

"We will be. I told Aunt Reba I'd be back well before dark."

Anna rode the horse at her smooth running-walk down Alexander Street toward Charlotte Avenue, where Abigail Hamilton Welch lived with her parents while her husband served in the Continental army with General Washington. How she would love a good talk with her dear friend. It had been much too long since they'd been able to chat. Their last opportunity had been at Abigail's small wedding a few months before the raid on Anna's plantation. So much had happened. Anna blinked back wetness and refused to let grief grip her heart.

The horse stepped lively and carried her tail high through the morning shadows and beams of sunlight. Taking a deep breath of the crisp, salty air, and appreciating the lovely, familiar streets of Charles Town, Anna acknowledged a blanket of peace cascading over her. This first harmony she had experienced since the terrible raid on her home was more than welcome.

Four patriot soldiers marching on the opposite side of the cobbled street, dressed in their blue waistcoats, red vests, and carrying muskets on their shoulders whistled at her. She smiled and gave them a playful salute.

Even in November and December, Charles Town exuded a special charm. The palmetto trees, with their evergreen bushy tops, looked rich beside tall oaks with their few colorful leaves clinging to dark intricate branches, all lifting their arms to heaven. Glancing over the walled gardens, easy to do as she passed on horseback, she drank in the red, pink, and white camellias starting to bloom, their colors vivid against glossy, dark green foliage. They would be in riotous blossom in January, as would the budding magnolias. In sheltered areas, she still saw wisps of pink, feathery sweet grass that had been in their full display in past weeks.

She passed maids sweeping porches and one man pushing a cart of sweet potatoes. Somewhere, a baker baked with cinnamon. Maybe apple pies?

Mrs. Hamilton would be aghast that Anna rode horseback—and not even side saddle—from her townhouse to theirs. She could just hear her now, *and without a chaperone*, the woman would remonstrate.

As she came to the Hamilton's hitching post, a servant ran out to take Jolie's reins. She walked up the steps to enter the three-storied Georgian house.

Abigail pushed open the front door and walked toward her smiling, her dark lavender gown swishing against the wooden boards.

"Anna, dear friend, I am so glad to see you. I saw you riding up the street from my window." She leaned to give a gentle hug.

Anna started at the paleness of Abigail's face. "I looked for you at church yesterday. Are you ill?"

Her friend smiled. "Not really."

An aggravated voice from within called out. "Abigail, who is it? Bring them into the parlor right now. You know my hip isn't good, and I can't run out to the porch like you just did. That was not at all like a lady, I must add."

Anna Grace smiled at Abigail and called out as the two of them swished into the house. "Mrs. Hamilton, it's me, Anna Grace." They entered the parlor where the overweight woman sat on a thick-cushioned chair with embroidery in her lap.

"Well, come here, my dear, and let me look at you." Her voice trembled, and then tears flooded her eyes. "I just can't stop thinking about the terrible thing that happened to your family. I don't know what we're going to do if the British try to take Charles Town back."

Anna knelt down beside Mrs. Hamilton, and moisture filled her own eyes. The woman patted her head. The rose scent she wore reminded Anna of her mother.

The elderly lady pulled a handkerchief from her sleeve and dabbed at her face.

Anna rose and moved to sit on the sofa beside Abigail.

Her mother looked back at the door. "And where is Reba? Surely you didn't come all the way to our house alone, Anna." Her voice took on an offended air.

Anna exchanged a glance with Abigail. "Aunt Reba was busy making a new hat. And the patriots have the city now, so I didn't worry."

The woman sniffed, shook her head, and took up her embroidery.

Abigail stood, pushing a wisp of hair back into her bun. "Come, Anna, we've lots to talk about."

She followed her friend upstairs to her bedroom. She plopped onto the middle of Abigail's high bed with its fluffy green taffeta spread and propped on her elbows. But her friend sat in the bedside chair. From this angle, a narrow gray streak showed in her thick, dark hair. Abigail was five years older, but they had been friends almost forever, since their fathers had built townhouses a few blocks away from each other.

Abigail leaned forward, her brown eyes kind. "Now, tell me all, Anna Grace. Especially about that handsome pirate I heard rescued you from the river." She leaned back. "Then I'll tell you my news."

Anna patted the satiny bedspread. "Oh, that. Well, his name is Captain John Vargas, and I think he's a privateer, more than a pirate."

"And?"

"He has a ship named the *Sand Dollar*, and he trades in the islands."

Abigail sighed. "Is that all you have to report?"

"He and his mother asked me to go to their island home that he insisted would be much safer than Charles Town. But, of course, I wanted to come here with Uncle Rufus, Aunt Reba, and you. Now what about your news?"

Abigail stood and walked to the window, her face pale and stiff as porcelain.

Anna sat up and frowned. "Yours is bad news, and you let me prattle on about nothing important."

Her friend turned to her. "It's good news and bad news. I'm trying to decide which to tell you first." Her voice shook.

Anna arose and went to her. She laid her hand on Abigail's arm, and her stomach knotted at the pain in her eyes. What had happened?

"Yesterday, I received a letter. Philip, my dear husband, succumbed to his wounds, and passed two weeks ago somewhere near Philadelphia." Abigail pulled a handkerchief from her pocket and dabbed at her eyes. "He's buried there with other Continentals who died in that battle."

A wave of pain pressed on Anna. "I am so sorry. I had no idea. Have you told your parents?"

"No. Father stays away days at a time, and mother...well, you know how she has fits of nerves, and this is so soon after my brother's death. You're the first one I've told. So many are losing loved ones." She turned sad eyes on Anna. "I hated to tell you when you've just lost both parents."

Anna shook her head. "This is what friends are for. We share each other's sorrows."

Abigail looked out the window. "We only had one week together before he left to join Washington's army. That's why my good news is...almost a miracle."

Anna took Abigail's hand. "What is your wonderful news, dear friend?"

Her friend's eyes brightened. "I think I'm with child."

Anna gasped and sank down in the nearest chair. "You had all this news and you've kept it to yourself. Glad I dropped by." She stared at Abigail. "How do you feel about...becoming a mother? That's not the way to ask it. I mean, with all that's happened..."

Abigail's face shone with a new light, and she patted her still slender middle. "God has lightened my grief over Philip, and I'm sure it's because of this little one I need to protect. I know He'll provide. I cannot give in to fear or grief." A tender smile flitted across her lips.

"You've got it right, my friend. And you know I'm here to help any way I can—and I'm sure Aunt Reba would say the same."

"Thank you. That means a lot."

"Are you having much morning sickness?"

"I did for two weeks, but now it's about gone. Mother is so concerned about her health and Father's gambling that she hasn't noticed my situation." Abigail sat beside Anna on the loveseat. "And that's just as well for now. I'd hate for her to be worrying over me."

Anna took a deep breath, searching for a new topic. "Well, if you're feeling up to a frivolous idea, let's talk about going to the Gadsden New Year's Eve soiree. Just everybody who is anybody in Charles Town will be there. I'm sure your family is invited. Aunt Reba and I have received an invitation, probably because of Uncle Rufus. But he'll be away on business that evening, and Aunt Reba isn't interested in going."

"We have received an invitation from Lieutenant Governor Gadsden, but I'm not sure I care to go. I feel all right physically, but Father will be out of town. And both Tories and patriots will be there. Feelings can run high."

Anna nodded. "You're probably right, but I still want to attend. I know Aunt Merle will come with her green cockade for everyone to hate. I'd like to see what color Della Ravenel wears. Do you know if she favors the patriots or the Tories?" Anna had not seen the young woman since the previous summer's last soiree, but who could forget the blond, blue-eyed beauty her brother had called *the most prissy belle of Charles Town* before he rode off again with the militia.

Abigail looked down at her folded hands. "Della is a beautiful girl. So sad her mother died three years ago. She's not had the training she would have received from a good parent."

Anna raised an eyebrow. Della didn't have a glowing reputation among the Charles Town elite, but Abigail could see or say no evil against anyone. Not so her mother. Mrs. Hamilton was known as the matron propriety keeper of Charles Town, who always spoke her mind about any infractions, no matter who the person might be.

"Well, if your mother comes, I bet Della will have her best manners on display. So do come, both of you."

Abigail smiled. "Mama does seem to carry that mantle of decorum with her. And if anyone doesn't notice, she makes sure they do before an hour passes."

They both laughed. The handsome face of a ship's captain flashed into Anna's mind. What would Mrs. Hamilton have to say if he attended the soiree? Probably nothing good.

~

Sailing back from the Indies, John's thoughts were not on the risks, or the excellent cargo he carried on board to Charles Town. The lovely face of Anna Grace Laurens kept floating across his mind as he stood on his quarter deck enjoying the sea breeze ruffling his hair and shirt sleeves. How was she doing? *What* was she doing? Was she keeping out of trouble? Did she have any idea the danger she and her aunt were in while staying in the city? Why wouldn't she consider going to a safer place, like *Salt Marsh?*

These thoughts would plague him for a while, then he'd cast them aside, reminding himself he must not get involved with her. Why set himself up for more heartbreak with the proud, stubborn Anna Grace? One disappointing love relationship was enough for him. He'd learned his lesson.

But her inviting amber eyes haunted him during the long days of sailing a placid ocean.

"A sail! A sail, Captain. Coming fast from the northeast." Thomas, Jamie's boy who had assimilated fine into John's crew, yelled from the eagle's nest, interrupting his thoughts.

John whipped his eyeglass from his sash and thrust it out in that direction. A chill zipped up his neck. A British frigate sailed straight toward them. They must have come from their home port in Jamaica, from which such vessels patrolled the Caribbean to prevent ships reaching the colonies with untaxed goods. And that two-deck man of war would have seventy-four guns to his sloop's meager twenty-four. Could the *Sand Dollar* outrun it?

The frigate came on fast, sailing closer. He could try to elude the pursuing vessel, which might be difficult with his full hold. His privateer ship flew the Gadsden American flag with its coiled snake and warning to the English, "Don't Tread on Me." If he exchanged it for the British jack, it might give them favor and the frigate wouldn't fire on them.

But what if they were ordered to drop anchor and allow the king's soldiers to inspect the *Sand Dollar* for untaxed cargo? They would find freight he had not paid tax on that he'd secured from the islands. Worse, they would recognize cargo he'd taken from a British merchantman the day before. The surplus English dog lock muskets being sent to the islands since the Brown Bess had replaced them in the king's army now lay stacked in his hold. Weapons the colonists would rejoice to get.

If the British boarded, the *Sand Dollar* would be confiscated by the enemy. And he and all his crew would face the hangman's noose.

CHAPTER 5

Don't fire until you see the whites of their eyes! Then fire low!
~ Israel Putnam, The Battle Of Bunker Hill

John's lieutenant, William Burns, came to his side at the initial sight and hail from their eagle's nest of the approaching vessel. "I don't relish being hanged and our ship sunk. What will we do, throw up the British flag, play it calm and hope they won't board us? Or should we try to outrun them, sir? I'm praying for your best decision."

John slammed the eyeglass closed. "Outrun them. But we must lighten the ship. Order the crew to toss half the sugar bags overboard."

William leaned over the quarterdeck railing and shouted to the men below. "Fill the main topsails, lads. We're going to throw out some cargo and hope to outrun them. Turn northeast until we lose them."

In an organized movement, a few hands hurried to the braces while others scurried aloft to set more sail.

Under the direction and Scottish burr of Burns, six crewmen hauled heavy bags of sugar up from the hold and cast them into the sea. "Move fast, me lads. Show what stuff ye're made of."

In a matter of minutes, the *Sand Dollar* thrashed northeast. Carrying every inch of sail the brisk trade wind would allow, she lay steeply over, plunging through whitecaps in her new direction. Waves burst on her weathered bow and sent sheets of spray flying. The taut rigging shrieked in the air currents, a remarkable transition from the quiet of earlier moments.

A cannon blast sounded across the waves and water swooshed up like a volcano, not far from their stern. Backwash splashed up on the quarter deck but missed John by several yards. He laughed. The *Sand Dollar* had swooped away just in time.

Burns bounded up on the quarter deck grinning. "A man with God is always in the majority, sir. We give Him thanks for delivering us."

He smiled at the man's quotation from his mentor, John Knox.

Once the frigate no longer bounced on the horizon, he gave the order to change direction northwest toward Charles Town. He prayed the brisk wind would hold to help them make up the time they'd lost sailing east on the choppy Atlantic to escape their pursuer.

✑

They arrived at the Gadsden harbor in the falling darkness a day late in mid-December. John posted three guards who would receive extra pay, one of whom was Thomas, Jamie's son. He paid off the rest of the crew, the men making no secret about their desired destination—a favorite tavern.

He and his lieutenant doffed warm blue waistcoats against the cold air rising off the water and, together, lowered a small boat to row to the dock of Laurens Mercantile. Would Rufus be there to rendezvous about the cargo a day late? As they rowed around the other ships and came in sight of the merchant's pier, the customary lantern glowed a welcome on the wall surrounding the backdoor entrance.

Rufus, his smiling face outlined in the light, leaned toward them as they glided in close to the dock and tied up. "Real glad to see you. Wondered if you'd run into serious trouble. Thank God you're here safe."

As the three of them walked into the back room of the mercantile, warm air brushed John's face. His breath skidded in his throat.

Anna Grace Laurens sat in one of the corn shuck chairs around the small table, with its candle lighting the storeroom. She wore a blue cloak and earrings that twinkled. The flickering light played over her thick, loose, shoulder-length hair and drew out its golden highlights. He'd forgotten how beautiful she was.

He cleared his throat. "Wha—t is Miss Laurens doing here, Rufus?" He turned to the man, frowning. His unhappy voice echoed in the room's stillness.

The merchant pulled out chairs for them and plopped into one beside Anna. He grinned. "My niece is now my assistant in our joint work, Captain. I've explained all to her."

Dread crept up John's spine, and he let out a long, audible breath. "Everything?"

Anna Grace turned bright imploring eyes on him. "It's perfect, John. I will love being able to help the patriots overcome the British any way I can for what they did to my family."

Rufus nodded at his niece. "She's quick, and I believe she can keep whatever secrets we have, John. And I need her here in the store when I have to be away a day or two a week. She'll tell me all that goes on." He patted her hands knotted in her lap. "Anna is someone I can trust."

John's brows drew together in tense lines. "But Rufus, this could be dangerous for her. You know how the Tories stop by here looking for anything to put their finger on to report to the British authorities. And who is going to protect her, if you're not here and someone, a redcoat, or even a patriot, takes a look at her and...gets ideas? Somehow, I don't think your man upstairs will lift a finger, not with that bad leg and his family to keep from harm."

Anna stiffened, and her amber eyes flashed. "I will have Prince here with me, sir. And I assure you he won't hesitate to defend me if the occasion arises. Also, I know how to use a musket and a sword." She bent to move aside her skirts and pulled something from her boot. "And I carry this with me now everywhere I go." She gripped a shining silver dagger in her hands.

William Burns emitted a low whistle and then spoke in a gentle voice. "Methinks the lassie is prepared best as she kin be. But it may better, Captain, if you stationed one of your men here with her. Maybe that bright young Thomas? He's itching for something more to do."

John leaned back in his chair. "That's a great idea, William." He turned to Rufus. "I have a fine young mulatto man, strong and willing to help the patriot cause any way he can, son of a friend of mine. I'll release him to serve Anna Grace. He should do fine. After sailing to the islands and back with him, I'd trust him with my most precious possession. What do you say?"

The merchant nodded. "If you trust him, so can I. Send him on over in the morning, and we'll get him acquainted with Anna Grace and the mercantile.

John regarded Anna. "Will you take him as a bodyguard of sorts? Not come here or go anywhere else without him?"

Anna slipped the knife back into her boot. "If it'll make Uncle and you happy."

They all stood, and John handed Rufus his cargo manifest. "We had to dump half the sugar to outrun a frigate."

The man nodded and glanced over the document. "Looks good, my man. Tomorrow night we'll be ready to unload your shipment."

Rufus walked into the mercantile and the sound of drawers and cabinets being tested and locked, floated through the door.

William Burns strode outside to the dock.

Anna moved toward John and gazed up into his face. "Are you disappointed I'm now part of this team?"

He looked away. Those lovely tawny eyes could do things to a man's mind, heart, and to his resolve.

"Does it matter if I am?"

"I'd like to think you won't dislike having some contact with me. I'm glad you bring in supplies for the patriots." She tipped her chin and smiled up at him.

He placed his hands on her shoulders, which was a mistake. "It's not the contact, Anna Grace Laurens, it's the risks we're involved in and what I feel sure the British are planning against Charles Town, and soon." How could he tell her he preferred to face the dangers alone and imagine her safe, warm, and happy in her house with her aunt? Better yet, with his parents at Salt Marsh.

His eyes dropped to her soft, full lips, and his thoughts became jumbled. Her shoulders trembled under his hands and a soft gasp escaped her.

He bent and brushed her lips with his own. Desire, like fire, spread over his body.

Anna pushed him away with both hands and kicked his shin with her hard boot.

The flame in his flesh dissolved into genuine pain in his limb. What had he been thinking to kiss her? He stepped aside from her. "Good night, Anna." Pushing out the door to the dock, determined not to favor the leg, he gulped the cold, salty air to straighten out his thinking.

He ducked his head when William looked at him, and then untied their boat. They rowed to the *Sand Dollar* in silence. Once, he rubbed the sore spot on his shin. Maybe Anna Grace Laurens *could* take care of herself, somewhat at least.

~

That night Anna slipped into her soft bed and lay back on her pillow, staring at the moonlight shining through her townhouse window. She touched her lips, still burning from the kiss of John Vargas.

All the time she'd known Burton Rand, he'd only kissed her twice, once at her sixteenth birthday, and later when he confirmed their pledge to marry. But neither of those kisses had prepared her for John's gentle touch on her lips. What did it mean? And who did he think he was, *or she was,* to allow such a thing? She smiled and almost laughed aloud at his expression when she kicked him. Had he ever had a response like hers to his amorous advances? But it was what he deserved.

Something nibbled at the edge of her memory, some words he had spoken earlier that evening. When they came back into her mind, she sat up.

He'd said he would trust Thomas *with his most precious possession.*

Those were his words. What or *who* did he mean by them? What precious possession would a half-pirate like John Cooper Vargas have? Of course, he called himself a privateer. But she had a good idea he became a pirate when circumstances offered it as a better opportunity.

His hands on her shoulders and the way he looked at her tonight had made her tremble. And the kiss...well she'd not think about it. She couldn't deny his handsome tanned face, strength, and magnetic charm attracted her. She punched her pillow. Blinking, she tried to replace John's strong profile and square jaw with Burton Rand's gentle countenance that she'd trusted since childhood. Why did her beau's face seem hazy after only six months absence?

She forced her mind to quietness and prayed for Burton and her brother's safety. The two friends rode, slept, and fought side by side somewhere in the Carolina backwoods and swamps with Francis Marion and the militia.

After she prayed, she slept.

Hours later, a terrible boom and flashing light through her window awakened her. She sat up and listened as the old clock in the hall struck three. After lighting a candle from a smoldering log in the hearth, she grabbed her robe and hurried up to the top floor of the house. She stepped out on the widow's walk and stared through the darkness down toward the harbor.

A fire near Gadsden Wharf licked up into the sky. She shivered in the early morning air and drew her wrap closer. A sudden wind brought the smell of burning wood and rice to her nose and muffled shouts of men to her ears.

Had a British ship slipped into the harbor and fired a cannon shot? She trembled. Uncle Rufus's mercantile was at one end of the pier...*and the Sand Dollar docked not far away.*

CHAPTER 6

The rebels did more in one night than my whole army could have done in one month.
~ British General Howe at Dorchester Heights, March 5, 1776

$\mathcal{A}$t dawn, Anna threw on a warm day dress, stockings, and boots, then a hooded cloak, and tiptoed out of the house. She made her way down the cobbled streets to the harbor in the dim early light. The brisk December air invigorated, but chilled her, and she pulled her thick wrap and hood closer.

The scent of sweet-smelling bread drifted on the breeze. Somewhere a bakery baked fresh loaves. Her stomach rumbled. She'd left before their servants served breakfast. She had to know what damage the cannon had done. As she reached the Gadsden dock, she scanned the ships, merchant offices, and warehouses as far as she could view. She released a tense breath. Laurens Mercantile stood uninjured in the morning mist. But what about the *Sand Dollar* farther down the wharf out of sight?

Her uncle's carriage stood parked beside his store. She hurried inside and heard voices in the back room. She entered as crates and sacks were being brought in from the dock. Uncle Rufus instructed men, who reminded her of John's crew, where to stack them.

He looked up. "There you are, just in time, Anna. We're about finished taking in this cargo. I'm checking off items on the manifest."

Jack, Rufus's clerk, stood counting barrels, crates, and thick grain sacks. He acknowledged her presence with a curt nod.

The storeroom, packed almost from floor to ceiling, emitted a strange odor. Anna's nose crinkled at the smell that reminded her of drying animal hides she'd observed on the plantation. "I heard the terrible blast down here last night, uncle. I'm so glad it wasn't near your store. What about...the *Sand Dollar*?"

A tall figure entered the dockside door. John Vargas walked in, carrying a paper-covered package he handed to Rufus. Two others followed him, lugging a long, rectangular crate, similar to a stack of wooded crates already in the room. He glanced at Anna, then spoke to the men in their bright-colored pantaloons stuffed in boots and puffed sleeve shirts with leather vests. "That's all, lads. Thanks for your help. I'll be back out to row with you to the ship in a few minutes. Send Thomas in to me."

Anna walked over to him, trying not to think about their interaction the night before. "Hello, John. Was the *Sand Dollar* damaged by the cannon shot last night?"

His muscular form looked fresh and striking in a blue waistcoat, white shirt, black pants, and boots. Two long pistols protruded in front from his sash, and he wore a dark bicorn with a rebel cockade on its brim.

He rubbed his bearded chin. "No. And it wasn't a blast from a cannon. Someone set fire to a case of gunpowder stored in one of the dock sheds."

The knot of worry in her middle dissolved. "I'm so glad neither Uncle's store nor your ship suffered damage. The blast awoke me, and I saw from the top balcony of our house that flames billowed up from somewhere in the wharf area."

His lips tightened. "Tories at work, no doubt. You agree, Rufus?"

Her uncle nodded and handed John a bag of jingling coins. "This is a good cargo, Captain. It'll be a lot of help to our cause. Wish I could reimburse you double this payment."

"Forget it, friend. You and I both know you won't make much money from this load when most of it"—he glanced over at Anna Grace and said in a lower voice—"will go to the patriots."

She stretched to her full height. "You might as well not look at me like that, John Vargas. You can trust me."

A smile played at the corners of his mouth.

A young mulatto man entered from the dock, carrying a sailor's bag over one shoulder. He wore a blue headscarf over his thick curly black hair and stood almost at tall as John. Muscles rippled across his shoulders and arms. The grin on his lips reached his glowing amber eyes.

"This is Thomas, the man we believe can be of service to you. Thomas, this is Miss Laurens."

The young servant nodded at her with respect. "Ma'am."

"Anna, will you have space for him at your townhouse?"

"Of course. Welcome, Thomas. Our Moses will love having you on the place, I'm sure, what time we're not here. And he'll find a room for you near his."

John motioned for Thomas to follow him to the door, where they spoke in low voices. Then the captain turned and gave her a quick perusal.

A blast of heat moved up her neck and warmed her cheeks.

He left, and the young man laid his bag down on a crate, then approached her and Rufus. "Just tell me whatever you want me to do. I'm glad to help."

Anna smiled at him, surprised at his careful English pronunciation.

Rufus patted his shoulder. "Glad to have you on board, Thomas. You can help us reload this cargo when the drivers arrive, so we might as well sit and enjoy a brief rest until then."

Within the hour, three wagons, each driven by a couple of rough-looking men, pulled up to the mercantile door. They wore buckskin clothing, heavy muddied boots, and fur hats. Their faces were a brawny reddish brown, as if they lived out in all kinds of weather, and several of their jaws protruded with chewing tobacco.

From behind the counter, Anna observed them troop into the store. The smell of grass and leaves and campfires entered with them. One of the men prepared to spit tobacco juice onto the dusty floor, but stopped when he caught sight of her.

He retraced his steps back outside, spat off the dock, and returned. He jerked off his raccoon hat. "Ma'am, I hope you'll pardon my bad habits. Didn't know a lady were present."

Rufus came forward. "That's okay, men. This is my niece Anna, and she's on our team now. We are so proud of what you patriots are doing for our cause. We pray the Lord will keep you safe and help deliver this cargo you're risking your lives to take to our boys and General Washington."

The drivers trooped to the back room, but soon returned, each carrying bags or crates they stacked close together in the wagon beds. Jack and Thomas helped with the loading.

When all the conveyances bulged with their cargo, a driver came up to Rufus, holding his fur hat in his hand.

"Sir, I can't tell ye how much General Washington and the patriots need these goods, 'specially the salt, beef, and blankets. They's facing a rough winter again, but we thank ye for helping lighten it."

Rufus lifted his hand as if to bless them. "God go with you and give you a safe journey."

The men walked out, climbed aboard the wagons, and shouted to the mules. The animals strained into their collars with the heavy load stacked behind them, then the conveyances moved with loud squeaks, rumbles, and stamping of hooves, across the dock into the street.

Jack shut the wide doors to the mercantile and went to stir the embers on the hearth. The coals roared back into flame, gradually spreading warmth through the December chill.

"Uncle, what did we send to General Washington? I think I saw guns in some of those crates."

He handed her the manifest with its check marks. She read the weapons listed, but also flour, salt, dried beef, salted fish, corn meal, blankets, rice, peas, and molasses. The beef and fish on the list explained the smells she'd encountered when she first arrived.

She gave the paper back to him. "I'm so glad we can help in this way. Do you need me anymore today?"

"Well, I've one thing I want to show you that we didn't send to the patriots." He pulled the paper-covered package John had given him from under the counter.

Anna watched him untie the strings and fold away the covering. She gasped. It was a bolt of the most gossamer pearl gauze she'd ever seen. She moved to caress the thin silk fabric. "Where did you get this?" Where did John Vargas stumble on—or steal—it?

"Well, don't mind if I tell you. I told him to see if he could find something your aunt might could use in her millinery shop. Think she'll like this?"

"Oh, Uncle Rufus. She'll love it. But...isn't this material expensive?"

He smiled. "It would be, but I'm not selling it. I'm going to give it to Reba. Thomas can carry it for you."

The boy hurried forward. "Be glad to, sir."

Anna Grace walked home, humming in the winter sunshine. What a wonderful man her uncle was. She slowed her step to glance at the young servant walking behind her, carrying the wrapped gauze in his hands and with his sailor's bag hanging from a shoulder. He must be close to her age.

"How old are you, Thomas?

"Fifteen, ma'am. Almost sixteen."

"Will you tell me what Captain John said to you at the door?"

He hesitated.

"It's all right. I promise you. I somehow think it was something about me. Was it?"

"Yes, ma'am, he told me to not let you go anywhere by yourself. That it's not safe...for a lady these days."

She took a deep breath and continued the walk to the townhouse. Should she feel pleased John was interested in her safety? Or indignant that he didn't think her capable of taking care of herself?

～

*J*ohn put the finishing touch—a frothy, white cravat—to his outfit of blue silk waistcoat and linen trousers as he stood in his mother's townhouse. He tied his unpowdered dark hair back in a queue and attached a black cockade to his tricorn.

His man dusted John's shoulders with his brush, though there was nothing to sweep away, and smiled. "As fine a looking gentleman as anyone could ask for, sir. Even if I sez so myself. You gonna be looking for a young lady at the ball?"

John grinned as Anna Grace flowed into his mind. Would she be there? "Maybe, my man, just maybe." But he was going to be quite late due to finishing up the docking of the *Sand Dollar*. She may have already gone home. But wouldn't everyone stay up to midnight at a New Year's Eve ball? He hoped so.

After walking to the stable, he saddled his trusty Marsh Tacky mount he kept here. At times, he docked his ship in the harbor to ride into the back woods and swamplands in search of Francis Marion and his friends who rode with him. Sometimes they gave him messages about British troop movements he relayed to the patriots in the city.

John whistled as he rode the fine stallion toward the New Years Eve soiree of his father's friend, Christopher Gadsden. John and his father had visited him after Gadsden's successful defense of Fort Moultrie. That victory earned the man the title of brigadier general in charge of the state's military forces. He'd also replaced Henry Laurens as Lieutenant Governor when Laurens rode to represent South Carolina in the Continental Congress in Philadelphia.

Everyone in Charles Town now recognized the man's name and power. John came to know the brave man best through his own association with the southern Sons of Liberty that Gadsden led, to the grief of the British.

John relinquished his horse to a servant at the well-lit home of the lieutenant governor and dashed up the steps. Boughs of greenery, lanterns, and bows of red and white ribbons, still in place from

Christmas, lined the side porch railings on all three stories. A huge wreath of fresh-smelling pine and forest eucalyptus hung on the heavy front door.

When admitted, he strode across the polished wooden hall floor into the parlor on the left, nodding at familiar faces who turned toward him as his boots clicked near. He walked to a table against a side wall still laden with food and drink, then took up a glass of punch.

"Well, I do declare, I have no idea who you are, sir." He turned to see a lovely, blond, young woman standing nearby. She gave him a coy smile. "You know you are quite late. And I thought I knew everybody in Charles Town. I must find Mr. Gadsden and have him introduce us."

She turned and searched through the faces about them, and then motioned to the host himself. Gadsden nodded to those around him and came forward. He was of mid-stature and gray streaked his hair, but he moved like a young man. He smiled at the woman, then at John.

The girl fanned her face and gave him a coquettish smile. "Sir Christopher, I don't think I know this late-arriving guest, and I'd like to make his acquaintance."

"Of course, my dear. This is my good friend Samuel's son, Captain John Vargas. He's one of our helpful patriot privateers. John, may I present Della Ravenel?"

He doffed his bicorn and gave her a brief bow. The woman was pushy and fake, and probably used to getting everything she wanted.

She curtsied but before she could utter a word, Gadsden pulled him aside. "I need to speak to you. Follow me."

John nodded at the astonished young woman, who frowned and fanned her face with fury. He followed his host to a small office at the back of the house. Pleasant escape from the woman named Della, but what did Gadsden have on his mind?

Gadsden closed the door. "Can't take but a moment from my guests, John, but do you have any news? I know you sail up and down our coast and have wise ears. And you keep in touch with some of

Marion's men when you can. You are one of our most important sons of liberty, trust me."

John fingered his bicorn. "Just whispers that the British are planning something big, but I understand their ships remain docked in the New York Harbor, or at least that's the last I've heard."

"Yes, that's what we've gotten wind of, too. But I believe we'll soon hear more news." He patted John's shoulder. "Right now, let's get back out to the ball and enjoy what time we have for such gatherings. I have a feeling more ladies than young Della are going to be looking for your attentions. So many of our good men are off fighting, either with Marion or the Continental Army." He grinned. "You'll have your pick, I daresay."

When John walked back toward the parlor, music coming from the ball room and the hum of conversation attracted his ear. Glancing in the room, he saw most of the crowd dancing. But when he shifted his attention back to the hall, he did a double-take when the sweet face of Anna Grace coming alongside another woman appeared.

Anna's auburn hair, swept up in curls, made her look more mature, and her porcelain countenance had the flush of health and the outdoors. Her dress of soft white satin embraced her tiny waist and trim figure. She wore a small patriot blue flower above one tiny ear. He sucked in a breath and smiled. Beautiful beyond words.

Anna turned and their eyes met.

He nodded and moved toward her. The other woman gasped as he fell in step with them.

Anna smiled and gestured to him. "Abigail, this is Captain Vargas. John, may I present Mrs. Abigail Hamilton Welch, my dearest friend."

He pulled aside enough to give her a quick bow.

Mrs. Welch nodded and smiled at him, then spoke to Anna. "Will you both please excuse me? Mama has asked me to get her another glass of punch and sandwiches before its time to go." She moved away from them.

*A*nna tried to calm the hammering of her heart at the sight of John in his blue waistcoat and snowy cravat. He was the most handsome man in the house. It was all she could do not to sound breathless when she introduced Abigail. And now her best friend had abandoned her.

John took her elbow as they entered the ballroom. "May I have this dance?"

Could she stand being near him in the dance? Would she be able to breathe and remember the steps? Before she could respond, Della Ravenel swept up and took John's arm. "Sir, after the way you and Mr. Gadsden deserted me, I believe you owe me a dance or two."

His smiling face froze. With tightened lips, he bowed, and led the woman onto the busy floor.

Anna Grace found a chair next to the wall and sat to consider the situation. Who did Della Ravenel think she was? And what did she mean he had abandoned her? Did he know her from some earlier experience? She closed her eyes to force away the troubling thoughts bombarding her mind. After all, she had no claim on John Cooper Vargas.

Her eyes shot open. Why was she even thinking about him when she needed to be remembering the man she was promised to, the man she'd known all her life? She let the handsome face of Burton Rand fill her mind, and she whispered a prayer for him and her brother fighting with Marion's men. *Lord, please keep Burton and Henry safe, and bring them home soon.*

When she opened her eyes, John stood before her. He reached down and took her hand, drawing her to his side. "Come with me, young lady, before anyone else interrupts us. Let's get something to keep you warm." He motioned to a servant who came forward.

"Please bring this lady's wrap." He turned to her for its description.

What did the man have in mind? According to the large, gold-trimmed clock over the mantle, it was almost midnight and the start of a new year, 1780. Flustered, she mumbled the color and fabric. The servant moved away and returned with it forthwith.

John led her out to the second-story porch with its lanterns hanging at each end.

Anna took a welcome breath of the cool, fresh air scented with the pine greenery tied across the banister. With the many candles in the house and such a crowd of people, the place had become stuffy. But she hadn't realized it until now.

He led her to the far corner of the wooden balcony and stopped.

She fingered the damp green garland on the balustrade and looked out at the moonlight flooding the courtyard below. Stars twinkled across the heavens. No evidence showed of the earlier rainstorm, other than the smell of dampness and the clean-washed garden below.

He touched her shoulder and turned her to face him. The bells of St. Michaels rang in the new year. The year 1779 died in the loud clangs, and a new year burst forth.

A gamut of perplexing emotions swirled inside her. What would the new year be like? And why did she allow John Cooper Vargas to bring her out to this deserted balcony? She tried in vain to call up Burton's face in her mind, but John was too close, his scent of spice and leather too appealing. And the ringing, echoing bells filled her with a strange sadness, as if this were a moment never to come again.

John spoke close to her ear. "You are the most attractive woman I've known, Anna Grace Laurens." He drew her into his arms. His closeness sent her pulses spinning. Weakness washed over her.

She tried to say something, but every word that came to mind seemed idiotic.

He looked deep into her eyes, and when his glance dropped to her mouth, her eyelids drifted closed. He brushed them with his lips and her heart stuttered. When his mouth touched hers, at first with gentle pressure, then with warm passion, a delicious sensation traveled through her and sent the pit of her stomach into a wild swirl. She groaned and awoke as if from a dream.

He lifted his head and whispered close to her lips. "Should I be stepping back from that fast kick you've got, young lady?"

She pushed away. "I've more than a kick, sir." She hated the breathless sound of her words. Slapping his bearded face took all her strength, and she almost collapsed when she struck the blow. Something was wrong with her knees.

He caught her and chuckled. But then released her after she grabbed the banister.

She searched for her normal voice and glared at him. "John Cooper Vargas, how dare you take liberties with me? I am...promised to someone else, and you might as well know it."

He cocked his chin. "Oh, you're engaged, Anna? Why is this the first I'm hearing of it?"

"Because...because the war stopped our official announcement, but Burton Rand and I have...planned to be together since we were children. He's fighting with the militia." She worked hard to catch her breath and speak with calmness, but she'd never felt so shaken in her life.

He lifted a brow and stepped back. "All right, if you say so. Heaven forbid if I've touched one of our patriot men's fiancée. But maybe Mr. Rand will forgive me for a New Year's Eve kiss at the stroke of midnight. What do you think?"

His smile infuriated her.

But before she could answer, the thudding of hooves, men shouting, and the squeal of wagon wheels rang in the courtyard below.

Anna's chest clenched as she leaned over the balustrade to see what was happening.

CHAPTER 7

Heroes are forged on anvils hot with pain.
~ L.B. Cowman

Foreboding filled Anna's heart. Soldiers, dirty, and ragged, slid off lathered, hard-breathing horses. Two wagons stopped behind them. Servants ran from the stables to assist the men and animals.

One man, with his cockaded hat off center, pointed back to the wagon where forms lay in disarray. He gave orders to the servants flowing from the lower floor entrance.

Anna Grace clutched her wrap closer and turned to find John gone. She hurried into the house and down the stairs to the first level parlor and to Abigail's side as the soldiers entered the hall with stamping boots.

As that sound made its way into the parlor, silence fell across the crowd of partygoers. When the bedraggled soldiers appeared in the doorway and stood looking around, ladies in their bright, expensive dresses stumbled back against the walls, gasping. Voices rose from among the guests, asking what was happening.

A woman's high-pitched tone cried out above the others. "Oh me, oh my." Anna recognized that cry—Mrs. Hamilton, Abigail's mother. She glanced toward the woman and saw her swoon backwards onto the settee. Those beside her fanned her face. Abigail left Anna's side and made her way to her mother.

The soldiers tramped into the middle of the room, dripping muck onto the polished wooden floor. Most wore raccoon hats, and all their soiled uniforms were damp, their boots caked with mud. Anna crinkled her nose at the smell entering with them, but she also blinked back tears. Anyone could tell these were mighty men of war who'd given all they had to make it to Charles Town through the British lines and ambushes. What could she do to help them? Could this be her brother or Burton's regiment?

A short, wiry soldier moved to the front, his hooked nose and narrow face giving him a homely appearance. Yet his flashing black eyes and stiff, erect manner commanded attention. Everyone quieted. He stood straight and bold in his soiled blue uniform, clutching his bicorn as he looked around the stunned faces. "Is there a doctor in the house?" His voice strong and commanding rolled over the occupants.

Christopher Gadsden pushed his way through his guests. "General Marion, you and your men are welcome in my home. I'll send for medical help right away." He turned to search the groups clustered about the room.

John strode up to him from the hallway. "Sir, I'll be glad to go for Dr. Jackson. I have my horse outside."

"Good." He gestured to Marion. "This is Captain John Vargas, one of our privateers. John, this is General Francis Marion of our state militia."

Anna's heart skipped several beats. This was the famous Francis Marion her brother and Burton rode with. She noted the respect that filled John's face as he nodded to the general.

The man's bright eyes flitted to the captain but a moment, then back to his wounded. "Go as fast as you can for the doctor."

John asked the servant at the parlor entrance for his hat and cloak and hurried away.

Gadsden turned to General Marion. "Bring your injured in, sir.

Place them on the rug near the fireplace for warmth. We'll do our best to help them and all your men."

The thud of boots sounded again from the hallway. The leader pointed and yelled in a strong, authoritative voice to the gathering, "Clear that doorway and around the hearth. Can you hear me?"

Guests scattered aside as two soldiers, wet and dirty as the rest, strode in carrying a stretcher on which lay a still form. Behind them in the hall, more lined up bringing wounded men. Groans flowed into the room with them. Anna's heart lurched in compassion. On the pallets lay men with blood on their shirts, and clumsy bandages on their heads, arms, or legs. As the third wounded man came in lying on a makeshift bed, she gasped in horror. *Henry.* Tears blinded her eyes.

Pressing through the other guests, she rushed to the fireside and dropped to her knees beside her brother. She leaned over and touched his pale cheek, ignoring the mud and blood that stained her ivory dress. He appeared unconscious, but his damp chest rose and fell with each breath. A tumble of thick, auburn hair, smeared with dried red stains, lay across his forehead. His militia uniform that had been so smart when he rode off in the long-gone summer was now ragged and wet.

"Oh, Henry." The words flew from her lips, and she put her fist to her mouth to squelch a sob.

Another cot approached behind her, and the leader directing the placement of the wounded glared at Anna. With a strained courtesy, he spoke to her. "Will you please move out of our way, ma'am?"

She stood and moved back. "Yes, of course. Sir, this man is my brother, and I'd love to take him home only a few blocks away, if you'll allow it."

He glanced at her but gave no response and went on about the work, laying a hand on first one shoulder, then another, whispering an encouragement to the soldiers who could hear his voice.

The entire ballroom buzzed with anxious voices. Servants crowded in and fluttered around, as if they needed someone to tell them what to do. Several of the older male guests walked about, encouraging everyone to remain calm. Two women sobbed in a corner.

Anna turned as Abigail pushed her way forward, her gentle face pale as cotton and full of compassion. "How I wish I could stay to help these poor wounded, but I have to get mother home. This has brought back my brother's death last year. She's so upset, she'll be sick." She looked over the row of cots. "I heard what you said. Is that Henry?"

Anna wiped moisture from her eyes. "Yes. You go ahead." She laid her hand on Abigail's arm. "Are you all right?"

"I'll be all right if I can get mother home as quickly as possible."

"Good. I hope to move Henry to the house for Aunt Reba's doctoring once Dr. Jackson sees him."

Anna moved to the side as guests asking for wraps flowed into the hall and out the front entrance. Carriages were being lined up in rows by the servants.

She found the settee vacated by Mrs. Hamilton and collapsed on it. John would help her. Until he returned and the doctor had time to examine Henry, she'd wait. Some of the tiredness pressing against her lifted. Taking a deep breath, she blinked back further tears and scanned the pallets of the suffering men. Surely there was something she could do now. But what?

A servant approached her and gave her the message that her carriage waited in the street. Dear Thomas. He must have wondered where she was when she didn't come out with the rest of the guests. She asked Gadsden's man to explain to him she'd be coming later, since her brother was among the wounded, and Dr. Jackson would need to examine him before she could bring him home.

Once all the stretchers from the hall found a place on the rug, the assisting soldiers hung back and stared with rolling eyes at the corner tables still laden with food and drinks. Scalloped oysters, wild duck, baked whiting, shrimp, smoked ham, tarts, jellies, cream-puffs, and a variety of breads and root vegetables lay out across the stiff, starched white tablecloths.

Christopher Gadsden gestured toward the banquet. "Men, please help yourselves. And there's more in the kitchen if this runs out." He moved to talk with Marion.

The soldiers scrambled to the tables and grabbed bread and meat in their soiled hands. They dripped gravy on their coats and dropped scraps on the floor as they pushed victuals into their mouths.

Servants, wide eyed and tense, scurried in and out with more platters. She tried not to cringe at the mess increasing around her. The poor men were half starved.

"Ma'am, could you git me a drink of water or anything wet. This fever's got me plumb dried out." A voice from the cots startled her tired mind.

Anna Grace twisted to see a young man with a leg wound, propped up on an elbow beckoning to her from the pallets. She smiled at him. Yes, relieving the thirst of the injured—she could do something to ease all the pain in the room. *Thank you, Lord.*

She stood, lifted the hem of her not-so-spotless ivory gown, and hurried to the end of one table and its punch bowl of golden, life-giving liquid. The soldiers in line grinned, and gave her room, and she filled a large goblet with the apple cider spiked with rum.

She returned, stepping around the pallets, to the man waiting. She handed him the large cup, and he gulped huge swallows, then passed it to her. "Thank ye, angel." He laid down with a sigh.

Another soldier next to him lifted a weak hand, and she moved to him, knelt down, and cradled his head so he could drink, too.

Other voices from the stretchers called out. "Angel, here. Give me some."

She refilled the cup several times until she met every need for a drink. She looked again at Henry and wished he were conscious and able to swallow. Taking the vessel back to the table, she stopped in her tracks when a familiar voice called from the doorway.

"Anna Grace."

She turned and dropped the mug as Burton Rand crossed to her in quick, long strides. He took her in his arms, and she didn't resist. Tears formed in her eyes, and the blanket of tiredness she'd been fighting made her feel faint. She laid her cheek against his chest. This must be part of his militia group. His heart beat steady against her ear. He was strong and well. For now.

When he lifted her chin to look into her face, a tear escaped. He kissed it away. "I was outside helping move the men from the wagons, my dear, then seeing about the horses. You're a sight to lift any man's heart, sweet Anna."

She remembered where she was and pushed aside from his embrace, but Burton kept his arm around her waist. Another familiar countenance in the doorway stared at her. John Vargas stood there with Dr. Jackson. When her eyes met his, a smile tugged at the corner of his thin lips, and he shrugged one wide shoulder.

Anna crossed her arms and moved farther away from Burton. She bit down hard on her lower lip, and endeavored to brush off a restless, irritable feeling. The emotion, she tried to convince herself, was due to the lateness of the hour, not the fact that John had seen her in Burton's arms and made sure she knew he didn't care.

The doctor hurried to the pallets with his black bag. John strode over toward Gadsden and Marion.

The militia leader's authoritative voice carried, pulling Anna's attention. "We know from our spies that the British are preparing a massive, combined land and sea attack against Charles Town under Sir Henry Clinton. They have sworn to turn the city into a pile of rubble and take every rebel captive. You have about two months to prepare."

Anna shivered and her throat went dry. Destroy Charles Town? How foolish for the enemy to think they could get through the patriot defenses. She swallowed and whispered a prayer. *Isn't that right, Father God?*

⁓

The next day John, with William Burns's help and the crew needed to man the sloop, rushed to finish outfitting the *Sand Dollar* and loading trade goods for the islands from Rufus's warehouse. Filling the hold were rice, indigo, and the desired pine lumber the islanders used to burn under huge boiling pots of sugar cane juice to make molasses. The merchant always kept back small portions of other items for the colony, in case the British succeeded in blockading the harbor—corn, leather, wheat flour. God willing, John would return with supplies for the town and Washington's army before the enemy closed off the port entry.

By the second week out, Anna Grace filled his thoughts as he stood on the quarterdeck. Why would she not agree to go to safety away from Charles Town? He'd tried to persuade her one more time before leaving the city, but she refused.

He'd met her brother and supposed fiancé. Once Henry recovered from his wound, he and her beau would, without a doubt, rejoin Marion's troop to battle the British in the outlying areas around Charles Town as they marched toward the colony. It would leave her and her aunt in imminent danger if the enemy threw up the blockade from land to sea like they planned. No one would be able to leave or enter the city. Residents would be at the mercy of British cannons from all sides.

He, of course, would do everything in his power to help the patriots defend the town, including bringing back as many guns, powder, and the much-needed salt and other supplies he could from the islands—or from ships he encountered and relieved of their goods. He smiled. British or Spanish vessels were open targets, in his thinking.

He headed toward a harbor in Jamaica that bordered his relative's sugar plantation. The place wouldn't be guarded by the British. His father Samuel's stepbrother, Joshua, managed the estate there and had promised to do everything he could to help the colonies with supplies.

"Ye think your relatives have gathered what we need to take back?" Lieutenant William Burns walked up on the quarterdeck. His soft Scottish burr, as always, sounded pleasant to John's ears.

"We'll see." He leaned over the railing. "Take a sounding, men. We should approach land soon."

"Aye, Captain," a voice hollered back.

Twenty minutes later, John eased the *Sand Dollar* into the Becket

Plantation dock, and a young boy on the wharf jumped up and began ringing a large bell. John gave instructions to William, who would oversee the crew while they took a gift of rum to the workers' village on the island. His men would have one free night before they'd have to unload and reload cargo.

Three of the crew kept guard on the ship with the promise of double pay on their return to port. His lieutenant sometimes had his hands full getting the men back on board, but so far, not a man had ever gone missing in any seaport. John smiled, thinking about the tough stance of his first lieutenant that could persuade any of the crew when needed.

Two mulatto armed guards, who looked more like pirates than plantation workers, sauntered down the path. The boy stopped ringing the bell. When they saw Captain John and the *Sand Dollar*, they lowered their weapons and nodded at him. He strode up the worn road past the warehouses to the sprawling plantation house owned by the Beckets, relatives he'd seen only twice, except for his Uncle Joshua. The armed men followed at a respectful distance.

Joshua Becket came down the steps, grinning. He reached out to John. "Good to see you, John. Can't wait to get news from Charles Town. The rest of the Beckets are in Kingsport for a few days, so you and I have the place to ourselves."

John shook the man's proffered hand as his uncle continued, "And it's just as well they're gone, as we have important business, don't we? But let's break bread first. Our Essie is the best cook in Jamaica."

John's glance passed over his father's stepbrother. Though approaching middle age and with a streak of gray in his thick black hair, the man was still handsome, lithe, and moved like a much younger person.

Later, over the meal of kitchen pepper rabbit, hominy, and okra, John brought his uncle up to date about the dire threat of a British attack against Charles Town.

Joshua looked at him with furrowed brows. "Are Samuel and your mother in the city or at Windemere?"

"I've taken them to Salt Marsh for the duration. I can rest pretty easy about them. But Grandfather Ethan and Grandmother Marisol wouldn't leave their congregation when I took mother and father. I hope to talk them into going to the island when I return." He tapped his fingers on the table. "If there's time before the British blockade the harbor."

Joshua frowned and stared. "You believe it'll come to that—a complete barricade of the largest southern port?"

John nodded. "Yes, Francis Marion and his agents have told us the British are leaving New York to launch a land and sea attack, the likes of which the colony has never seen. And that's why I must leave tomorrow and head back."

"Well, I'm happy to say, I've picked up some good supplies. They're stored in one of our warehouses. I believe you'll be glad to see them, want to walk out there right now? We still have a little daylight, but I'll take this lamp in case." He moved to a side cabinet and picked up a rusty lantern.

John stood. "Let's go."

They strode out into a Caribbean sunset that painted the sky in brilliant hues of pink, orange, and purple. When John stepped into the warehouse, with its musty smell of barrels, burlap, and stacked crates, a mouse scurried away behind a large container. His eyes widened at the supplies waiting for his ship's hold. Washington's army desperately needed the many sacks of salt. Crates of yams, barrels of molasses, and sacks of sugar filled another side of the space.

Joshua pushed further back in the warehouse. "Come and look at this bounty." He held up the lantern. Crates of muskets and several barrels of gunpowder stood stacked in the two rear corners.

John whistled. "Uncle Joshua, where and how did you come by this?"

"You never mind. Just know that I'm doing my part to help the colonies win independence from King George. Be sure and tell your father." He smiled and rocked back on his heels. "One day, I might want to return to Charles Town, and I want to see it just like I left it. I often dream I'm back there."

His voice turned wistful and John glanced at him, then away from the melancholy look on his uncle's face. If the man loved Charles Town so much, why did he ever leave it? Why had his father Samuel never explained that part of the story to him?

~

*A*nna walked up the stairs to Henry's room, a trek she'd made many times over the past weeks. February had finally come, and Henry seemed stronger each day. Prince loped up ahead of her, as usual. She knocked at her brother's bedroom door, and the dog barked and scratched at the bottom panel.

"*Entre*, whoever you are. *Personne ou animal.*"

She loved hearing his voice so much stronger. And, too, their Huguenot ancestry trait of sprinkling French into his conversation. As she entered, the air no longer smelled like a sick room.

Prince ran to her brother's chair. He laid the *South Carolina Gazette* he'd been reading on the bedside table and gave the dog the good petting for which the animal begged. The animal sat on his haunches, and his wagging tail thumped the oak floor, making a cheerful sound.

"I'm glad you've come, little sister. I've something to tell you." He leaned his head, with its thick hair almost the same auburn color as hers, on the chair back and stared at her through pale eyelashes. Where his wound had been on his head, he now wore only a small bandage, and that would soon disappear. He had shaved, and he wore his tan militia pants, blue shirt, and black boots.

She sat in the only other seat and inhaled a deep breath, dreading what she thought he was about to say. Would he leave so soon? He still needed to gain back more of the weight he'd lost since he joined up the past summer.

He gestured to the newspaper. "Editor Peter Timothy says he took a spyglass up to the steeple of St. Michael's Church yesterday to look out, and he saw smoke from hundreds of British campfires in the distance."

Anna trembled, but tried to hide it.

"Do you know what that means? It means they've landed, most likely on Simmons Island, and I've got to get back to help stop them."

She clasped her hands and leaned forward. "Oh, Henry, do you have to go? Are you well enough?"

He stood, walked to the window, and looked out between the drawn curtains. "Yes, I'm in far better shape than some of those out there who haven't gotten the good care you and Reba have given me. It's my duty, and I must be at it."

"When are you leaving?" She tried to keep the fear from her voice.

"Before nightfall."

She sucked in a breath. "That fast? Where will you go? Could you not stay in Charles Town with all the other soldiers who are here?"

He paced across the floor. "I must try to find my company and Colonel Marion, but I've heard he's left the city after he was injured."

She sat up straight. "How was he wounded, Henry? Who in Charles Town would want to hurt Francis Marion?"

He stopped pacing and ran his hand through his thick hair. "I've been told he jumped from a second-story window to escape a drunken patriot officer party after they locked the doors. He damaged his ankle."

Anna's brows knitted, and she opened her mouth to ask why he wanted to get away, but Henry continued.

"You may not know this, sweet sister, but Colonel Marion does not imbibe rum, wine, or any kind of liquor. None of us who ride with him do either if we want to stay in his brigade." He smiled. "His chosen drink for himself and his men is the old Roman army standby —water laced with vinegar."

Anna's eyes widened. "I like this man more and more. But if you can't locate him, what will you do?"

"I'll report to General Lincoln here and serve with the Continental forces in the city. But I think I know where Marion may have gone to recuperate. I do want to find him and my militia company, if possible." He grinned and came to stand in front of her. "I'm sure Burton Rand is wondering when I'll return."

She sighed. Dear Burton. She prayed he continued well and safe, wherever he was.

"There's one other thing I need to ask you, Anna." He stood a moment, looking down at her. "Will you give me permission to take Jolie? There's a severe shortage of mounts, and she'd be most useful to me." He hesitated. "I know it will be a tough decision for you."

Anna blinked back moisture. "Of course, you can have her, Henry. She always liked you. I'll feel better knowing you have a good mount like her to help you." She stood and turned away, determined not to let a tear fall. If she cried now, he'd think it was over letting Jolie go. But any tears she shed would be for him.

~

*R*ight after the evening meal, Anna and her aunt watched Henry ride away on Jolie with a warm coat and saddle bag filled with dried beef, peas, and hard bread. As he galloped down the street, he didn't look back.

"May the Lord keep him safe and give him and General Marion and our militia, and General Lincoln and the Continental soldiers here, the wisdom and strength they need." Reba's voice broke, and she pushed into the house.

Anna sat on the porch swing, swathed in a warm wrap as evening shadows lengthened. She no longer cared about the tears, finally letting them fall. She didn't even try to cover the sobs that followed. Would God keep Henry safe? He hadn't kept her parents safe. Henry and Reba and Uncle Rufus were the only close family she had left.

A footstep sounded nearby, making her lift her head and wipe her face. She sucked in a ragged breath at the figure before her.

Captain John Vargas stood at the steps from the street. He looked impossibly handsome in his thick blue cloak, bicorn, and black boots. His shining eyes lit his tanned face, shrouded in the gathering dusk.

He whipped off his hat. "Anna, why are you crying? Has anything happened to you or your aunt?"

She cleared her throat, but it didn't help her voice much as words tumbled out. "John Vargas, what does it matter to you that the British have landed on Simmons Island with hundreds of campfires, and their navy sails our way, and Henry, barely healed, has gone off to join with the militia, and Burton left months ago." Something very akin to anger flowed through her body and stiffened her back. She jumped to her feet. "All you have to do is board your sloop and sail off into the sunset while others risk their lives to save Charles Town." Her strident tone filled the air, surprising even her.

He stiffened for a moment, then came up the steps two at a time, and strode across the porch to stand before her. Too close, but she couldn't step backward because of the swing.

He placed his warm hands on her shoulders and gave her a shake. "You don't know what you're talking about, Anna."

She looked him straight in the eye. "Is that so? What part of my story is not true about you?"

His grip tightened. She tried to shrug loose, but he held fast.

His gaze drilled into her. "I'm here for one last try to get you and your aunt to come away to a safe place before it's too late. Yes, I know about what's happening, more than you do. Cannons will soon begin blasting into the city. Will you leave it?" He dropped his hands. "Will you *please* come with me? There's only a small window of opportunity left to escape." His voice held a pleading note.

She put her palms on her hips and glared into his face. "Will you give up? I am not leaving Charles Town. Aunt Reba and I are here for the duration. We'll help defend this city any way we can, help anyone possible, including today, giving my beloved Jolie to Henry to ride with the militia. What are you going to do? Anything? Or is that too much to ask?"

His burning eyes traveled over her face and stopped on her lips. Before she could move or say another word, he pulled her into his arms and kissed her, a hard, desperate kiss, the like of which she'd never dreamed. His mouth on hers was like the soldering heat that joins metals. Her head spun with the intensity of his touch, and her emotions whirled and skidded. When he lifted his head, her breath swooshed out of her lungs and her knees buckled.

He placed his arm around her waist to keep her from falling. Then he whispered in her ear, "Anna Grace, how I wish there was a little more *grace* in you than the beautiful, spoiled Anna part. You know next to nothing about me, but you've judged me as if you knew all." His voice sounded hoarse as he let her drop onto the swing.

"If you're determined to stay, then at least take some advice. Collect every pitcher and bucket in the home and fill them, some with water, some with sand. Put them all over the house—close to the walls, so you can get to them but not stumble over them in the dark."

A wave of apprehension coursed through her. "You believe we'll have fires in our house?"

"Yes, and take some blankets and drinking water down to your cellar. When the cannons start firing, you and your aunt and anyone else here should stay there." His words demanded, his voice harsh. "Will you do this? Start preparing right away?" His steady gaze impaled her.

She sighed. "I shall, if it'll make you happy."

He pushed his bicorn down on his head, stamped off the porch, and disappeared into the falling night.

Anna sat for long moments, the shock of his compelling presence and words holding her immobile. Her lips still burned from his kiss. A pain squeezed her heart. Was there any truth in what he said about her judging him? What did she know about Captain John Vargas, other than he brought the colony supplies from the islands?

He was different from her brother and Burton. In fact, he was unlike any man she'd ever known. Perhaps she'd let her fear over Henry leaving possess her and took it out on John. But never mind. Didn't he sail off in his sloop at every opportunity while others fought the enemy? And were they headed into great danger in the city, like he described?

Lying in bed later that night, she closed her eyes and tried to summon up Burton's handsome face. As sleep pressed against her eyelids, she gave up and slid down the slippery slope into the memory of John's astonishing goodbye kiss.

CHAPTER 8

*By laws of Nature and Nature's God...All men are created equal and
endowed by their Creator with certain unalienable rights.*
*~ From the Declaration of Independence that Washington read aloud to the
troops, July 9, 1776*

ohn strode down the street, shaking his head after
leaving Anna Grace. Even the daffodils and sweet-
smelling hyacinths waving in the evening breeze along
the street didn't attract his attention. Why had he kissed her? Again.

May the Lord forgive him for falling into temptation, but she had a
way of tempting and aggravating him at the same time. And she was
stubborn. With an effort, he forced her lovely image from his mind
and whispered a prayer. *Father, please keep Anna and her aunt safe. Help
her follow my advice to prepare.*

Before he reached the corner, an urgent voice called behind him.
"Captain John?"

He stopped and turned.

Thomas hurried to catch up with him. "Sir, may I come with you
wherever you're going?" Jamie and Belle's son was almost as tall as
John and thick with muscles.

John looked into his dark, stormy eyes. "Hello, Thomas. You're not homesick, are you?"

The teen lifted his chin and shook his head. "No, sir. I'm not. Just had a birthday, and I want to help stop the redcoats any way I can."

"So how old are you? Sixteen?"

"Yes, sir."

John clapped the youth on his firm, broad shoulder. "Would love to have you with me, but I need you much more here with Anna and her aunt. Even though they have several other servants, when the British bombard the city, things will get most dangerous here. I trust you more, my man, to help take good care of them and keep me posted."

Thomas hung his head. "Actually, they've only got Moses and Sadie Mae. All the others done ran off."

John sucked in a breath. "There, you see? Just two elderly servants." He repeated the instructions for preparing he'd given Anna. "They need your aid, and I can't tell you how much more peace I'll have knowing you're here protecting them. It'll free me to do what I've got to do. You'll be assisting me."

The boy stood up straighter, and his countenance lifted. "Aye, Captain. If that's my assignment from you, then I accept it and will do my best."

"Great, Thomas, and I want to keep you informed of my movements."

"You do, sir?" His dark eyes widened.

"Yes, you know where my mother's townhouse is, and you've met my man there. Reach out to him every so often. I'll leave any messages for you with him when I can."

"Sir, if I may ask, where are you heading now?"

John took a deep breath and leaned closer to the youth as if to share a secret. "Here's my plan. First, I'm taking my grandparents, now on board the *Sand Dollar* hidden in a nearby cove, to safety at the island. Then I'll return to hunt up Colonel Marion and determine how I might help him defeat the British. And I plan to leave my ship in the care of your father, Jamie." He removed his hand from the shoulder and stood back. "Now you know more about my plans than anyone, even my family. See how much I trust you?"

The boy smiled, and his white teeth gleamed in the darkness. "I won't tell anyone, sir, and I'll check with your man, like you told me."

John gave the young man a salute before he turned and strode down the dark street. Anna Grace would have at least one capable young man nearby to help.

~

*T*he next morning, Anna Grace awoke early, dressed, and headed down to the dining room. The fresh, nutty smell of coffee filled the air. Her aunt, along with most other patriots, refused to buy the over-taxed English tea now difficult to find in Charles Town.

Aunt Reba sat with her Bible beside her plate. "We need to live in Psalm 91, Anna, to keep our faith strong during these dangerous days. In fact, it would be good to read it daily and pray. Would you like to join me?"

She took a seat across the table from her aunt and folded her hands. "I'd love to."

After sharing the scripture, Aunt Reba prayed its promises. "Father God, Anna and I confess You are our refuge and fortress, our God, in You we will trust. We will not be afraid for the terror by night, nor for the arrow that flieth by day. Thank you for giving your angels charge over us and give wisdom for whatever we need to do to prepare."

Once they both finished the light repast, Anna pushed her plate aside. "Captain Vargas gave me advice about what we should do before...*if* the British fire cannons into the city."

After she told her aunt what he'd shared, Aunt Reba nodded. "Very good advice. We'll start getting ready today and have Thomas help."

They both stood, and Aunt Reba touched her arm. "There's one more thing I need to tell you—Sadie Mae and Moses left us. Their grown son, to whom your father awarded freedom, came by early this morning and asked if he could bring his parents out of the city to a hideaway some freed slaves had. I let them go. Do you think you and I and Thomas can take care of things for a while?"

Anna's heart lurched, but she forced her lips to smile. "Of course."

"Good, first let's get the shirts we've promised for this week ready for the patriots. I understand they have desperate need of them. Then we'll set up our house according to John's instructions."

Anna sat and worked alongside her aunt for three hours, until the cotton and linen clothing they'd started earlier for the patriot army sat, folded, and wrapped for Rufus to pick up.

She walked out the back door, past the kitchen garden, and to the stable. Thomas mucked out Jolie's empty stall, and a bucket of milk stood on a low table by their single cow's enclosure. He stopped his pitch-forking when she came near and explained to him the preparation they needed to do.

"Yes'm, I'm your man to help with this. Captain John told me about it."

"He did? When?"

"I saw him after he left the porch last night and we talked."

Anna's brows rose. What else did the servant see? She forced her face to calm and gestured to the brimming white liquid. "I'm glad you know how to milk a cow."

He grinned, picked up the container, and followed her to the house.

By noon, they had every bucket and pitcher they could find stationed throughout the home, filled with water or sand.

After a mid-day meal of corn bread, sliced ham, and buttermilk, Anna turned to her aunt. "Today I want to take a walk with Prince, with Thomas accompanying us, to visit Abigail. On the way, maybe I can see the siege works we've heard are being built. Do you think the British will be able to cross the barriers our patriots are erecting?"

"Let's pray not. I'm glad you're visiting your friend. Do check on her mother's health." She stood and looked at the food left on the table. "While you're walking by the battlements, see if you can discover where Rufus's son is serving. I understand he's with General Lincoln's Continentals, or the militia, helping defend Charles Town.

God bless him." She wrapped up a piece of ham and corn bread, then poured milk into a skin. "Give this to Warren if you spot him."

Then Aunt Reba reached for Anna's hand and prayed again for their safety and wisdom, and for all the patriots.

Anna donned her cloak and tied a lead to Prince. He barked with joy and danced around her. She and the dog, with Thomas behind them, started south toward Meeting Street. Near the bay they saw slaves with shovels and wheelbarrows building a sizable fortification from tabby, a mixture of ground oyster shells, lime, sand, and salt water. Others dug a huge ditch before the earthworks.

Anna walked past the work and turned up King Street. The sound of sporadic hammering dishonored the early morning quietness. Some merchants nailed boards across the fronts of their shops.

She reveled in the touches of spring along the streets and behind wrought iron gated gardens. Daffodils and hyacinths waved in the breeze, and magnolia blossoms in tall trees added their scents. Preparation for war seemed out of place. Who would want to destroy Charles Town?

The reality of the battle and imminent danger was imprinted on the faces of soldiers marching down the opposite side of the street, and a shudder ran down her spine. But they looked a hardy lot. Armed with muskets, fowlers, tomahawks, and knives, they appeared invincible. Only a few wore the South Carolina blue regular uniform coats with the white-edged buttonholes. Henry had told her military clothing was scarce. Most of the men had donned leggings and long hunting shirts dyed an assortment of colors.

The defense force whistled as she passed, but then eyed Prince and Thomas with her and went on about their business.

She discovered her cousin near the north breastworks, muddy and sweating in his work, helping build a fortification that would follow the bank of the Ashley River. He asked his superior officer's permission before stopping to come speak to her.

She managed a smile for him. "Hello, Warren. Aunt Reba and I are praying for your safety, and I've brought you something to eat."

"You have? Thanks so much." He wiped his hands on his britches leg and stepped aside to sit down on a log. She handed him the milk, corn bread, and ham. He opened the skin and drank the liquid in big gulps, and then wolfed down the food. "This was wonderful, Anna. I can't tell you how much I appreciate it."

Anna dropped her chin and blinked back moisture. Her cousin seemed half-starved. She glanced at the other workers casting envious glances their way. Were the patriots running low on foodstuffs?

He wiped his mouth with his sleeve and looked up at her, squinting against the sun. "You haven't seen my Tory brother anywhere, have you?"

"No, I haven't. Where is James supposed to be this time of day?"

Warren smirked. "Any time of day, my brother and his rich English friends spend their waking hours slouched in the Queen's Street tavern, just waiting for the British to come marching back into the city."

"Do you think they'll be able to retake Charles Town?" She tried to keep the worry from her voice, but it squeaked through.

"No, I'm here, and I plan to stay here with General Lincoln's forces to make sure they don't. We'll soon have a row of cannons encircling this city, aimed at Clinton's redcoats." He smiled, then stood and returned to his labor on the siege works.

When Anna reached Abigail's home, she opened the gate. Thomas took Prince and walked around the house to the back yard.

She approached the porch where her friend sat with needlework in her hands. Abigail looked up, dropped her embroidery, and stood. "I'm so glad to see you." She embraced Anna, and they sat side by side on the swing.

"How are you, Abigail? Sorry I haven't visited for far too many weeks. But you knew we were nursing Henry."

"Yes, how is your brother?"

"He's fine and already gone back to his company, wherever that is. I gave him Jolie, that's why I'm walking today."

Abigail's lips tightened. "I heard about the shortage of mounts." She clasped her hands in her lap. "We are living in changing, risky times. Mother worries we'll end up starving when the British surround the city and cut off all supply routes." She smiled. "But I know Who my trust is in, and He never fails His people."

"You haven't answered my question about how you are, dear friend. Is...everything progressing well with you and...?" She placed her hand across her own middle.

Abigail's smile widened. "Yes, it's my only consolation during these troubled times. And I know God will provide for me and...the child. I am showing, but I have full skirts which can still hide it."

Anna patted her hand. "Have you informed your mother? And how is she? Aunt Reba asked about her."

Abigail looked out toward the street. "No, I've not told her. She's almost to the point of losing her mind. I have my hands full trying to soothe and help her. The doctor says Mother is worrying herself to death. She's taking a nap right now, which is why I can come out to the porch."

Anna blinked. "Oh, Abigail. I'm so sorry things are hard. Now I know how to better pray for you. Might I share what you've said with my aunt? She's such a prayer warrior."

"I don't mind telling you and Reba at all. Father has gambled away most of our wealth and now stays drunk most of the time, so pray for him, too. Then there's the war."

Anna touched Abigail's hand. "I'm so sorry, dear friend, for your family troubles. But don't you think our good patriots will protect our city? On my walk here, I saw some impressive breastworks for defense and powerful-looking soldiers."

Abigail swiped at a tear that slipped down her cheek. "Forgive me, dear friend, for sounding like I've lost my hope. I haven't. I'm sure our God will see us through." She stood. "I'm so glad you came. Come in the house. We concocted a mint drink for mother that seems to calm her. And I like it, too."

Anna followed Abigail into their elegant hallway and to the back steps that led to a detached kitchen.

On the way, her friend spoke over her shoulder. "Do you still have servants? All ours have run off now, but one woman and her daughter. Father and Mother have fits whenever they notice their absence."

Anna sighed. "Same with us, but we do still have Thomas, who Captain John Vargas sent to us. The young man has been a real blessing."

They arrived at the kitchen, and Abigail went into their larder and brought out a silver pitcher. Soon they were sipping their cool mint drink.

Her friend lifted her brow. "Now, young lady, please tell all details about the handsome Captain John. I want the complete story. He didn't send you Thomas for no reason."

Warmth flooded Anna's cheeks. "There's nothing much to say. The last time I saw him, I chided him for sailing off in his ship instead of staying here and helping us win this war." She lowered her eyes as the memory of that astonishing kiss afterwards threatened to take her breath. That was one bit of news she wouldn't tell Abigail—or anyone else.

~

*J*ohn anchored the *Sand Dollar* in the bay near the Salt Marsh dock and glanced at his grandparents standing on deck.

"You are every bit as good a sailor as me or your father, son." Ethan, his step-grandfather, grinned at him. Once, his grandparents had told him the story of how they'd found each other and started a new life, overcoming much adversity, even baby Samuel's kidnapping. But his own father and mother's story and their run-in with Barbary pirates always held his interest the most.

The boy on the dock pulled the bell rope with brawny arms, and the loud peals sounded out over the island. Servants began running down the path from the plantation house in the grove of oaks.

As John helped his grandparents into the longboat, William Burns ambled up to him. "Sir, do you want me to stay here or disembark with you?"

"Come ashore for the night, you and the small crew we brought. Tomorrow we'll dock the ship as planned and release the men to go to their homes, and we'll be on our way to search for Marion's brigade and join if he'll have us." He stared into his lieutenant's face. "Unless you've changed your mind. Don't you have some family somewhere around Charles Town?"

"Yes, but they're too far away from the city to be in the bombardment. My brother and his servants stand prepared for whatever might come. And I can't wait to make the British pay for what they did to several of my friends."

Jumping on the dock, John smiled and hugged his mother and father, who'd walked out from the house. Then they kissed his grandparents. Happy chatter filled the air as the group made their way up the path to the island abode. Servants brought the trunks and baskets of goods that William Burns and the crew dispatched at the wharf.

John ate the evening meal with his entire extended family around the large oak table. Except for the war clouds gathering around Charles Town, it would have been the perfect gathering. Even though his parents and grandparents tried to make cheerful conversation, the continuing life-and-death struggle facing the patriots hung like a shadow on every face.

Later, in the library, his mother came to him as he sat reading one of the *South Carolina Gazette* issues he'd brought to his family from the city. "John, tell me about Anna Grace Laurens. Is she still in Charles Town?"

He cast the paper aside, stood, and paced across the pine floor. "I tried my best to get her to come here, both her and her aunt, but she refused. She is one stubborn young woman."

His mother's brows lifted, and a smile tugged at the corners of her mouth. "Obstinate and more beautiful than ever, is my guess."

How could she always read him? He walked to her and hugged her, bending his tall frame to do so. "You know I've never been interested in any woman since...Ruth. But there's something about Anna Grace Laurens I can't figure out. Is that why I can't seem to get her out of my mind?"

His mother patted his arm. "It's a good sign you're over Ruth, and that makes me happy." She turned to leave. "I hope you can stay awhile with us, but I feel in my bones you can't wait to get into the middle of the battle around Charles Town."

His father and grandfather entered as she left. Ethan sat in one of the leather chairs and picked up a newspaper from the stack John had brought.

His father came to stand near him at the fireplace. "Son, what's your plan?"

"Tomorrow I'll sail to Jamie's island and leave the *Sand Dollar* with him. It should be safe from British cannons. Then Burns and I propose to take a couple of horses and seek Marion's militia in the backwoods and join up for the duration."

"And there's no way we can persuade you to stay here?"

John looked into his father's face. "No, sir. I believe I'm supposed to do what I've told you."

"Reminds me of when your mother tried her best to talk me out of going to the Spice Islands. I knew I must go. What I didn't know was all that would happen during that venture."

"But God brought you back safe and sound, didn't he?" John smiled.

"Yes, and that's what we'll be praying for you and William Burns."

~

*W*hen the *Sand Dollar* reached Jamie's small farm, John assembled necessary supplies: blankets, two tin canteens, pistols, and holsters.

Belle, Jamie's wife, had sewed two burlap sacks into a rough semblance of saddle bags, and filled them with smaller packages of parched corn and peas and powder for their guns.

They secured the holsters around their waists, inserted the weapons, and mounted the horses Jamie led from the stable, saddled and ready, with the sacks tied behind the saddles.

He looked up at John and patted the thick chestnut neck of his mount. "We named this stallion Big Boy, and the mare is Prissy. Both are spirited, strong, and used to galloping across the bay bottom at low tide to the mainland. Just get there before it's too deep for crossing. We'll be praying for both of you, God's protection and wisdom."

"Thanks, old friend. You've been a great help." John reined Big Boy toward the dirt road, and William guided his horse behind.

As they galloped to the bay, he looked up into the spring sky at a dark cloud moving in. Neither of the mounts hesitated to enter the knee-high water, splashing John and William. His partner guffawed as the cool spray hit his face.

Lightning flashed, and pelting rain followed them as they entered the area northeast of Charles Town. They skirted around British sentries, who kept watch on major outlets. Their hardy mounts crossed low sand hills and swampy areas with the same energy. The downpour ceased as fast as it had begun.

They passed the first night in the ruins of a plantation and built a fire in the one standing fireplace to dry their clothing. So the flame didn't draw the wrong attention, they snuffed it out with sand before darkness fell. They tied the horses in the field so they could graze.

The following morning, they galloped through land that evidenced British soldiers' day-old campfires and destruction. Since they couldn't know whether a plantation or cabin was patriot or Tory, they avoided them all. They finished all the victuals in their packs and even plucked corn from fields still standing unharmed. When no food was in sight, they let their stomachs growl.

Toward evening, they reached farmland bordering the Black River and stopped to rest the horses. John motioned toward the river. "Scotch-Irish Whigs settled this area, and I've heard it's a patriot stronghold. Let's take a chance and see if it's still full of good friends."

They halted at a plantation on the banks of the tributary. The owner, a red-headed Irishman, held them at musket-point until they answered his questions. When he discovered two fellow patriots, he fed them a hardy meal of pork roast, sweet potatoes, and collards.

"Do you know Colonel Francis Marion?" John asked as they finished the tasty meal.

"Who doesn't know that brave warrior?" Their host picked his teeth with a broom straw. "The south would have little hope except for him and another like him, Colonel Thomas Sumter. The Redcoats call him a gamecock because he fights like one."

John had heard the name, but never met the man. "Do you have any idea where we might find Colonel Marion?"

"Now that's the one the British have tried in vain to catch. They've even nicknamed him the Swamp Fox because he evades them by riding right into the swamps. I heard he was up north, but he moves fast."

~

*H*ours later, John and William veered west to avoid a column of soldiers. Hiding in a canebrake, John managed a good look at the riders. They wore green coats and an unusual helmet made of leather and fur and a white plume. Could they be the notorious, cruel, British Legion, known as Tarleton's Raiders who gave no quarter in battle or in raiding and burning plantations? Bile rose in John's throat.

Riding north toward Kingstree, they discovered a horrific burned area five miles wide. At a crossroads, they stopped to speak to a man picking through ashes and blackened timbers.

The fellow paused to speak with them, and the sadness in his gaze was impossible to miss. "I'm the pastor of this destroyed Presbyterian chapel. Those horrid British soldiers claimed it housed a rebel camp."

John's lips thinned. "Do you know what officer led this attack?"

The minister's face blanched with bitterness. "His name was Tarleton, and they had specific orders they were pleased to recite several times. 'Disarm in the most rigid manner all persons who cannot be depended upon and punish them with total demolition of their property.' From here to Kingstree, everything's gone. They destroyed gristmills and smithies, and broke looms people depended on for a livelihood. The monsters even shot milk cows and bayoneted sheep." The man's voice broke.

John sighed. What solace could he offer? "Do you have information about Marion? We seek him to join his militia."

The minister wiped his face. "Thank God for Marion. He's giving us hope. We've heard he's in North Carolina, but also the swampland of the Waccamaw or Santee River. He moves so fast no one can keep up with him."

Riding on, John approached a forest so dense with pines and oaks only thin rays of sunshine slipped down between the trunks. Burns reined his horse behind him in single file.

The slow tread of the horses' hooves on the matted leaves and pine straw competed with the whistling and cawing of unseen birds.

"So many bird calls." William whispered behind him. "Something doesn't seem quite right."

They passed under the low limbs of an immense oak tree. John heard the unmistakable click of a musket cocking. A voice hidden in the branches above growled, "Stop your horses or breathe your last, lads. Your choice."

CHAPTER 9

I will say of the Lord. He is my refuge and my fortress, My God, in whom I trust. For He will deliver you from the snare of the fowler and from the deadly pestilence.
(Psalm 91:2-3)

*A*nna jolted awake one morning as sounds of booming cannon fire echoed in the distance. Dawn peeped through the curtains of her bedroom. She jumped out of bed, slipped on her robe and slippers, and entered the hall.

Her aunt strode up the corridor, her face stiff with concern. "I'm almost sure those guns are roaring from the harbor."

Together they climbed to the attic and opened the window that gave a view of the wharf. Anna pushed out her eyepiece. Vessels flying the English jack lay scattered along the eastern horizon beyond the port entrance. At least, twenty ships, maybe fifty—she couldn't tell how many because they kept moving, disappearing beyond the water line. Fort Moultrie cannons blasted toward the British men-o-war frigates, and their return fire exploded in the early dawn light.

A choking feeling pressed over Anna. How long could their small garrison hold back the mighty warships?

The same spyglass that revealed the enemy showed her a protective ring of guns pointed out from the city toward the sea. She swallowed with relief. Patriot cannons stood ready in the harbor to fire against any ship that might slip past Fort Moultrie.

Her aunt, who had her Bible in her hands, sank down to her knees. "We need to pray for God's angels to protect us. I learned yesterday that the king's men have landed across from the Ashley River."

As if to confirm her words, the sound of cannons firing from that western direction now added to the roar of guns from the harbor.

Anna pulled in her eyeglass and wrapped her arms around herself, refusing to give in to stark fear that tried to possess her. What if the British cannon shots reached into the city? To *their* house? The advice of John Vargas seemed wise beyond words. Buckets of sand and water stood along most walls of the townhouse. But why did this precaution fail to provide relief to her hammering heart and sinking feeling in her middle?

She dropped beside her kneeling aunt, who opened her Bible to Psalm 91 and prayed it aloud. "'I will say of the Lord. He is my refuge and my fortress, My God, in whom I trust. For He will deliver you from the snare of the fowler and from the deadly pestilence...'"

As the bombardment continued, Anna grew to hate the long days, with respite only as darkness fell. She sank into bed exhausted most nights, yet had nothing accomplished to show for the tiredness. Constant thoughts of how Henry and Burton fared in the militia plagued her. Outside communication ceased as the British surrounded Charleston and cut off all supply and communication lines into the city.

She dared not walk the streets now. Visiting Abigail was out of the question. Yet she prayed over and over. *Oh God, protect her and her unborn child, and her family.*

Her aunt's face, though calm, had thinned and showed lines that weren't there before. Uncle Rufus still dropped by weekly to give them supplies, but he had little news. His tight countenance also revealed the strain. Was his Tory wife gloating and just waiting for Charles Town to fall to the British? Anna gritted her teeth, imagining how her Aunt Merle and James stood confident that the city would soon be back in King George's hands.

Uncle Rufus showed up one evening at their gate with two soldiers carrying a cot as though it were a stretcher, with a form laying atop. Her uncle no longer used a carriage because the patriot army confiscated all the horses.

Watching from the window, Anna's heart fell to her slippers. Who lay wounded on that pallet? She ran down the walk to them, and her heart clenched at the sight of her cousin, Rufus's patriot son, laying on the stretcher.

Stress lined her uncle's face as he looked at her. "Warren's hurt pretty bad. I can't take him home to a Tory household. I could only think of your aunt nursing him best. Can we bring him in?"

"Of course." Anna swiped at a tear that slipped from her eyes as she glanced at the handsome countenance of her cousin, contorted with pain, and blood oozing from a leg wound. He lay on the cot unconscious.

Aunt Reba made a place for the boy in the downstairs bedroom and laid her hand on his forehead. "He's hot with fever, but the first thing we must do is curb the bleeding."

Uncle Rufus gripped his bicorn in his hands so tight, his thick, tanned fingers turned white. "Yes, I know. I've tried, but the boy's still got a bullet in him and it keeps breaking open."

His voice, hoarse with emotion, stung Anna's heart.

Her aunt's brow contorted. "You mean the army doctor hasn't taken it out?"

Uncle Rufus exhaled a hard breath. "That temporary military hospital is packed with men dying, and I couldn't find a surgeon who would come help him. Said others were more critical. The place was a little like hell, pardon my expression. I could see Warren would die if I didn't do something."

Aunt Reba turned to Anna. "Ask Thomas to go find old Doc Wilkins at the end of Queen Street. He's always had success getting bullets out, and I think the man's too old and loyalist to be working at the rebel military hospital."

Rufus took out a thick, yellow coin and handed it to Anna. "Give the doctor this with a promise there's another like it, if he comes to help right away."

She looked at the piece and blinked. It was a gold Spanish doubloon. Only the richest West Indies merchants traded with them. It would feed an ordinary family for a month.

She found Thomas at the rear door and sent him on the way. When she came back into the room, her aunt had managed to stop the blood flow on the thigh by placing a scarf above the wound and winding it tight, then loosening it every so often.

Anna pulled a chair near and fanned Warren's fiery face with the fan she kept in her pocket.

Doctor Wilkins arrived twenty minutes later, breathing hard. She met him at the door. He wore a black waistcoat, stiff white cravat, and a powdered wig. He carried a small, worn leather bag. A smell of toilet water, not medicine, emanated from him. She led him into the sick-room. He spoke to her aunt. "Your boy insisted I walk as fast as I could. Said it was a matter of life and death."

He glanced at Rufus. "So that gold doubloon came from you, sir? Hadn't seen one of those for several years."

"Yes, this is my son Warren. He needs a bullet taken out of his leg. Are you able to do this kind of surgery?"

The doctor examined his patient and rubbed his chin with its gray stubble. "I see you got the bleeding checked. That's good. Done lost count of how many bullets I've extracted, and I don't remember losing a single man."

Uncle Rufus released a relieved breath. "Just tell us how we might help."

The surgeon turned small, pale blue eyes on Anna as she once again fanned Warren's feverish face. "Young lady, you can take my coat and my cravat." He removed them as he spoke and handed both toward her. She folded and dropped her fan into her pocket, then took them. He reached up and removed his white wig, revealing his own wisps of thin gray hair. "Please be careful with my piece, it's fresh-cleaned and powdered."

Anna received it and sighed. Did the Tory expect her to curtsy, too? Well, she wouldn't. Not while Henry and Burton and many other patriots were fighting for their lives against the British and loyalists who were bringing chaos everywhere they could.

The doctor moved toward his patient but spoke to Rufus. "Sir, I'd like to ask that you go wait in another room, please. Fathers have never been a help to me. These two women will assist fine, and that young man who came to get me."

Thomas stuck his head in from the hall, and Anna motioned him in.

Uncle Rufus spoke to her aunt. "I'll be in the parlor. Let me know developments."

The doctor turned to Aunt Reba. "You have water boiling yet? I see you've got some sheets torn up for bandages and towels standing ready. And we'll need a bowl of salt solution."

Her aunt hurried out of the room, and Anna glanced at the surgeon and Thomas, and then took the fan from her pocket. She pushed damp locks of black hair back from Warren's face and wiped it with a cloth. Then she fanned him again. Heat rose in waves from the still form, and a fly buzzed above the bed.

The doctor tied a towel about his neck like a bib and another around his waist as an apron. He bent to examine the wound and Warren groaned under his touch.

Moisture gathered in Anna's eyes, and she prayed he'd stay unconscious. Once, a bullet had been extracted from a servant on their plantation. The surgery was done in the man's home above the stables, but the entire household heard the man's screams of agony, even far up the hill.

A shell crashed somewhere near them, rattling the windowpanes and shaking the floor.

Warren opened his eyes, dark with suffering, and looked up at the doctor. "I know the bullet's got to come out." His hoarse voice cracked. He glanced at Anna with apology. "Will you forgive me if I yell?"

Aunt Reba reentered the room with a basin of scalding water and a bottle of salt solution. "Warren, you holler as loud as you like. None of us will pay it any mind. We just want you to get well." She placed the items on the table next to the bed.

Anna wiped a tear and nodded. "That's right."

Her cousin closed his eyes and took a deep breath.

The doctor opened his bag and extracted some implements. He dropped them into the bowl of steaming water. One looked like a sharp razor, another large tweezers. He set tongs beside the pan.

She turned her head away.

"Young woman—" the surgeon began, mopping his forehead with his handkerchief.

She interrupted him. "Sir, my name is Anna."

He shrugged. "You will sit across from the bed and fan me so no flies will disturb me, and I'll have some relief from this heat." He spoke this as an order, not a request.

She did as he asked. Whatever it took to save Warren's leg. Why were the British so demanding and uppity? Her Aunt Merle's haughty face flowed into her mind. Thank God Uncle Rufus had brought Warren to their house.

Dr. Wilkins spoke to Thomas. "When I begin, you are to hold this man down. Put your knee on his chest, whatever you have to do to keep him from moving when I'm probing for the bullet. Do you understand?"

Warren's eyes widened, and so did Thomas's, and the two exchanged quick glances.

Thomas nodded. "Yes, sir. I'll do my best." He moved into a ready position.

The doctor reached into his case and pulled out a small block of wood. He looked into his patient's sweating face. "Young man, you will clamp your teeth on this so you'll not bite your tongue off by accident."

Warren accepted the piece with a shaking hand and placed it between his teeth. He clamped down on it and clenched his eyes.

Dr. Wilkins motioned to her aunt. "You will keep the blood swiped away as much as possible."

Aunt Reba nodded and grabbed a thick towel.

Anna looked at her cousin, with the wood block gripped in his mouth. She glanced at the basin of hot water and the doctor reaching for the tweezers with the tongs. She wanted to close her eyes, but didn't dare. If she did, she would faint.

The surgeon began to probe.

The patient's body lurched, but Thomas had his knee pressed against her cousin's chest to keep him on the bed.

Terrible noises erupted from Warren's throat and nose, not screams, but guttural, deep, agonizing sounds.

Tears flooded Anna's eyes and slipped down her cheeks. She glanced at her aunt, who swiped tears with her apron while dabbing at the bleeding that gushed with each probe.

A trail of blood flowed down from Warren's leg, across the mattress, and to Anna's dress pressed against the bedside. She moved back but kept fanning.

The doctor wiped sweat from his forehead with his sleeve, then probed again.

Warren spit out the wood block and bellowed in pain.

Oh God, help him find the bullet!

Dr. Wilkins's back arched. "Thank God, I've got it." He pulled the bullet from the flesh just as Warren passed out.

Her aunt had a hard task stemming the bleeding. But the crimson liquid was cleansing the gash as yellow infection flowed out with the blood. She grabbed fresh towel strips.

The doctor washed the wound with the salt solution, then put in several stitches. He bandaged the injury and told them the patient might sleep until morning. He gave instructions to feed him broth at first, and then go to more solid food.

Uncle Rufus came into the room as her aunt laid her hand on Warren's forehead. She looked up at the father. "Thank God the fever is going, and he appears to be resting."

Her uncle smiled and reached into his pocket.

Dr. Wilkins accepted the second gold coin and donned his cravat, coat, and wig.

He gave one parting remark, his face stiff and blue eyes blazing. "When will you rebels give up? You can't win over the king of England." He picked up his bag, turned, and strode out of the room and to the street.

~

*A*nna sat at table with her aunt finishing their mid-day meal of rice, ham, and collards. She touched her lips with her napkin. "I'm glad Warren improved and wanted to go home, but I miss him."

Aunt Reba nodded. "We'll pray the tension from his loyalist mother won't set him back.

A loud banging sounded at their front gate.

Anna stood and moved to peek out of the window. She saw Thomas stride around the side of the house from the stable toward the street.

Prince barked at the hall door with his ears alert. Anna pulled the dog away and shut him up on the back porch. Then she walked to the front door and swung it open. Her aunt moved to stand beside her.

Three soldiers in faded uniforms stood at the gate with a cart. They looked muddy and worn, but determined.

Thomas spoke to the men, and then scooted up the steps toward Anna and her aunt. "Miss Reba, these are patriots and they want to see the lady of the house. Says its orders."

Her aunt walked down to them.

The officer, a smallish young man, doffed his stained bicorn, revealing a shock of red hair. He stood straight, heels together, and he spoke in a clear voice. "Good day, ma'am, how do you do? I'm Lieutenant Brown and you're Mrs….?"

"Miss Reba Collins."

"We're here to collect foodstuffs for the army. General Lincoln has decreed all meat and salt in the city must go to the soldiers defending our fair town. We're here to check out your kitchen storeroom, and any animals you may have on the place. Will you show us the way, please?"

"But what…?"

"Orders, ma'am," said Lieutenant Brown. "Sorry, and we're in a bit of a hurry."

Her aunt clicked her tongue and turned. "Through here."

Though the man seemed polite, he meant business. Anna stepped aside as the Lieutenant and two privates followed her aunt through the hall and to the kitchen. Another soldier cut around the side of the house toward the stable. He wouldn't find any mounts there. All the horses were long gone.

Anna motioned to Thomas, and they moved into the house to follow the men with Aunt Reba.

Along the heavy brick walls of the storeroom, which helped keep the area cool, several barrels stood in a row. Above them, shelves gleamed with jars and canisters of various sizes. The air held a tempting spicy scent. One private sniffed with appreciation, but the lieutenant gave him a look, then turned and spoke to her aunt.

"Ma'am, we'll be grateful if you and"—he glanced over at Anna —"don't make a fuss. We want all the meat and salt you've got."

Reba stiffened and gasped.

The soldiers began taking lids off barrels to see what they held. They were opening every box and smelling the contents of jars and canisters. They moved past sacks of rice without examining them.

"The army's not interested in your rice," the Lieutenant remarked, as if to apologize.

Anna put her hands on her hips. Of course not. A colony made up of rice plantations would never run out of rice.

One soldier looked upward and whistled. "Thank God, we're going to have meat tonight." He dragged a chair from the kitchen into the larder and climbed on it to reach the smoked hams and cured sides of bacon hanging from the ceiling. He handed each down to the other soldier, who carried them to the cart out front.

Lieutenant Brown found a barrel filled with wrapped rounds of cheese, and another of dried beef. He spoke to Thomas. "Give me a hand with these containers."

Reba turned and left the kitchen area, shaking her head.

Thomas glanced at Anna.

She sighed and couldn't keep the despair from her voice. "I guess you must."

Thomas and the lieutenant pushed and rolled the barrels from the kitchen toward the front of the house, the wood making loud squeaking and scratching noises.

She placed her hands over her ears and wanted to shriek, *What do you expect us to eat?*

The private stepped off the chair and stuck the point of his knife into a burlap sack. Some white crystals fell out, and he put them onto his tongue, then whooped. "Jumping frogs, where in the world did you ladies get this much salt?"

Anna's lips thinned, but she didn't respond. They'd gotten it from Uncle Rufus, of course, who'd kept their needs well-supplied up 'til now. What would he think about this robbing of their larder, even for the patriot soldiers? A chill ran up her spine. Had they confiscated all his stored food, too? Would they all starve? And dear Abigail. Had they taken all her supplies?

Anna followed the soldier who carried all their salt out to the front walk. Their cow stood tied to the back of the cart, chewing her cud.

A suffocating sensation tightened Anna's throat, and she clenched her teeth to keep from crying out. How dare they take their only source of milk. Poor Daisy. Would they slaughter her?

The private loaded the salt onto the wagon with the other food-stuffs. He looked back at her one brief second, his face long and sad. "Sorry, ma'am. But you ought to see how bad we need supplies on the front lines. General Clinton and his eight thousand soldiers are moving toward us from John's Island. They done bragged they'd make us surrender or they'd blow us to kingdom come."

Trembling, Anna glanced up the street and saw other groups of soldiers bringing food from neighbor's houses. Women stood on various porches, some of them weeping or screaming threats. Others, like her, only looked on.

All she and her aunt had left in their larder was…rice. Could they live on it? Then she raised her chin and took a deep breath. They could do whatever they had to do. But could a woman expecting a child live on only rice? *Lord, please supply Abigail what she needs.*

When she returned to the house, Thomas knocked on the back door and Anna went to see what he wanted. To her delight he held a red hen under his arm.

He whispered, "I hid her under my bed, and that's not all. Come see. I heard yesterday that the soldiers would come, so I prepared."

She skipped down the steps and walked to the stables with him. He led her up the stairs to his small apartment. He opened a closet door, and a mother goat came strutting forth, bleating.

"Oh, Thomas!" After thanking the man, Anna flew to the house to tell Aunt Reba about the animals and how she'd prayed for Abigail and her unborn child to have the food they needed. They agreed the nanny and hen should go to Abigail, and they would have Thomas take them by night. But first, they sent him with a note, so Abigail would be expecting him.

Abigail sent back the sweetest note in response.

You've saved my life and unborn child. I've never dreamed how important eggs and goat milk could be. For weeks, all I've been able to get mother to eat are eggs. But the soldiers took our chickens, so perhaps you've saved her life, as well. Thank you, dear friends. We will make it through this.

Abigail.

~

*D*ays of only rice to eat, *unsalted*, brought on desperation in Anna. She ignored their rule of staying down in the cellar during the daily bombardment. When her aunt still slept on her pallet that next morning, Anna caught up her skirts and tip-toed up the stairs, grabbed her basket, and slipped into the back yard. Perhaps she could find some vegetables in the garden from the previous year.

Though time for spring planting, they had no servants to help and couldn't be outside to do what work they could manage themselves.

Cannons blasted in the distance and an occasional whizz flew overhead, but none seemed too close. Birds twittered in the trees bordering their property. She searched the once-neat rows of the back kitchen garden, now overgrown with weeds. Might she find a few carrots, onions, or potatoes still under the soil? They'd stripped the collards to their roots, cleaned and boiled them already. Thomas had even gone into the fields at the edge of town, when the battle seemed quieter, to look for wild greens. He'd helped find food every way he could.

She saw a green onion stalk sticking up in the bed beyond her and started in that direction. As she stooped to reach for the brownish green stem, a long screaming whistle split the air. An object flashed by her and struck the ground between her and the stable with such force that the surrounding earth rippled like a stone thrown into a pond.

Anna couldn't move as the air filled with earsplitting whistles. Thuds of cannon shots landing. Cries of panic.

Then the object that had landed beyond her exploded with a reverberating boom. The earth around her rose like a water fountain. Her face smashed into the onion bed.

CHAPTER 10

Resistance to tyranny is obedience to God.
~ John Knox

Anna's violent fall swooshed the breath out of her lungs. Choking and coughing up soil, she raised her head and wiped her eyes. Running feet and Prince's wild barking approached from the stable. A wet nose touched her cheek.

Thomas leaned over her. "Miss Anna! Are you all right?" He stooped and helped her stand, holding onto her swaying form until she stopped wobbling. She brushed the dirt from her muslin gown.

Prince kept up his barking and danced around her.

Aghast, she stared at the crater the shell made in their garden—a hole five or six feet across. If she had been standing in that spot, she'd be dead.

But she was not. She swiped the soil off her cheeks, and then wiped her hands on her skirt. She trembled, but she also experienced a sense of triumph. God had protected her life. "Thank you, Father, for protecting me," she whispered.

Thomas breathed, "Amen."

She leaned down to pet Prince. "It's okay now, boy. You can settle down."

More whistling noises, explosions, and people screaming and running in the streets grabbed her attention. Guns roared from every direction. What was happening?

The rebels must have refused to surrender, and the deadly attack had begun in earnest on the entire city of Charles Town, including the citizens and families. Now, innocent men, women, and children might end up cannon fodder.

Bile rose in her throat. British General Clinton was heartless. *Oh, God, help our militia protect Charles Town. Assist General Washington to defeat these monsters.*

Thomas touched her elbow. "Come, Miss Anna, let me walk you back to the house. Your aunt is probably wild with worry. I pray you both stay in that cellar until…whatever is going to happen, happens. I hear the rebels must soon surrender. That your leader even done left the city so the whole government can't be captured."

Tears mingled with the dirt on her face. Governor Rutledge had abandoned them? Who was in charge of Charles Town now?

As Anna entered the rear door, her aunt folded her in her arms. "Anna, my dear. I came to look for you and saw that terrible shot land in the garden near you. How I prayed you'd be spared."

The whistling sounds of cannons ceased, and a banging on their gate drew their attention. They hurried to the front of the house and saw Uncle Rufus at the street entrance. Aunt Reba met him there and drew back the bar to admit him.

"I had to come see how you made it through the last bombardment. Thank God you both look all right." He glanced around the residence and examined its roofline. "And it appears the house is intact."

When her aunt didn't mention Anna's close call in the onion patch, Anna decided not to share it either. Hearing the episode would only worry her uncle.

They walked back toward the porch, trailing behind Uncle Rufus. He glanced down the street where sounds of distress still echoed.

"I need to tell you Governor Rutledge has finally heeded General Lincoln's warning and left the city with three other members of the council. Christopher Gadsden is now in charge."

"What will happen next, uncle?"

"Several of us are going to talk to Lincoln. We believe we need to surrender and save the city. We've no food, little ammunition, and many wounded." He frowned. "Warren has even gone back to his unit, though he needed more time to heal. The pause right now of the bombardment is because Clinton has sent another order to surrender, and the army is considering it."

After he left, Anna and her aunt went back into the house and cooked the only thing left in their larder—rice. Anna forced spoonfuls of the unsalted grain into her mouth and made herself swallow. How much longer would this siege last?

She took her leftovers outside and called Prince, but the dog didn't appear. Now where could he be? Probably out hunting somewhere to keep from starving. He, too, hated the bland diet, and she couldn't blame him. He'd show back up in the morning, as was his usual habit. Sometimes he even brought a rabbit he'd caught. How welcome would that be?

After clearing the kitchen, she preceded her aunt down the cellar steps to their pallets. Tonight, if the temporary peace held, they should get some decent sleep. What would surrender be like? She clenched her eyes. What would happen to Henry and Burton...and a certain sea captain?

John Cooper Vargas's handsome tanned face and bright green eyes filled her mind, despite her efforts to blot them out. And her last words to him. Had she misjudged him? Was he doing something—anything—to help the colony's cause? He wouldn't be able to sneak in supplies through the bombardment. Why should she be thinking about him at all? He was not putting himself in harm's way. Not like Henry and Burton living in the swamps and fighting with General Marion's brigade. She sighed and flipped over.

"Are you all right, Anna?" Her aunt shifted on the cot beside her.

"Sorry, Aunt Reba. I'm fine. Didn't mean to disturb you."

The next morning, Prince appeared at the back door with a dead rabbit in his mouth. Anna started to pet him and take his offering, but he dropped into the grass, released the rabbit, and whined. She stepped out and stooped down to examine him, and her heart fell to her feet. He had a bleeding wound in his fur coat.

"Aunt Reba, come quick. Prince is injured."

Her aunt hurried down the steps, and Thomas ran from the stable.

The man knelt and felt around Prince's coat. His hand came back bloody. When he looked up at Anna, his eyes darkened. "Someone's shot him, more than once. It's a miracle he made it home. Perhaps they wanted the rabbit."

Reba did everything she could for the pet, but he died within the hour.

Anna couldn't stop the tears from flowing down her face. Prince *gone*, one of her last connections to her father. He'd brought the hound home as a puppy, and they'd been inseparable.

Thomas cleaned the rabbit and Reba cooked it, but Anna couldn't force a bite between her lips. Prince gave his life bringing them the offering.

~

*D*eep in the woods, John stiffened at the accusing voice above him and click of the weapon. He raised his hands and looked up into the oak on his right. William did the same. The tone sounded like a local, so John said, "We're searching for Colonel Marion's militia."

The man above them whistled a perfect imitation of a Carolina wren. Another sentry, wearing a stained, torn hunting shirt, dropped from a birch on the left.

John's stallion shied and reared at the sudden appearance. Behind him, William's mare snorted and pawed the forest floor.

The second man strode forward with a musket in his hand. "You found 'em."

"We're from Charles Town and we want to volunteer." John quieted Big Boy with strokes and whispers.

The first guard slid out of the oak. He was squat and as grubby as his younger counterpart.

The fatter man circled them, frowning, and spit tobacco juice to the forest floor. "You better be telling the truth, or you'll never see tomorrow's daylight. Git our horses, Jess."

The sentries led them farther into the forest, through several wetlands, and at last, to an encampment on the shore of a tributary.

After they dismounted, John gazed around. The camp held about seventy-five men, and they all appeared to wear homespun clothing about as grubby as the first two. But details were difficult to make out in the fading daylight, with smoke streaming from the many camp-fires. The rebels lounged in front of lean-tos with roofs of fronds, but turned to watch John and William dismount.

Francis Marion sat by his fire munching on a sweet potato. He looked as severe as John remembered him. The short officer wore a red coat, cleaned and brushed. His bicorn and infantry sword hung from a tree branch. The sentries whispered their report, and he sent them away, leading Big Boy and Prissy. Would they feed and water them?

Marion spoke to John. "We've met before."

"At Christopher Gadsden's New Year Eve's party."

"I remember." The man wasn't unfriendly. "You went for the doctor."

John turned as two officers stepped from the path. One he would not soon forget—Burton Rand, who had embraced Anna Grace at the same gathering.

Burton spoke. "I remember you, too. A sea captain, I believe."

John nodded.

Burton gestured to the younger man beside him, whose face John studied for a moment. Something about him tweaked his memory. "This is Henry Laurens. His sister, Anna Grace, was at Gadsden's, too."

That was it. Henry and Anna favored in facial countenance and auburn hair. The man lay wounded and unconscious at Gadsden's house, so John hadn't met him.

He extended his hand and Henry grasped it. His bronze eyes—the color of Anna's—flashed with intelligence and welcome.

John introduced William to him and added. "I'm glad to see you recovered from your wound at the first of the year."

"Yes, my sister and Aunt Reba were excellent nurses." He smiled.

The two men walked away, talking in muted voices.

Marion wiped his mouth on the cuff of his sleeve and gestured for John and William to sit on the low stones surrounding the campfire.

John's sword clanged as he sat.

Marion peered at the weapon and the guns in his and William's holsters. "What is a sea captain doing this far inland?"

He cleared his throat. "Sir, we've looked for you about two weeks. We want to join the militia. As you know, the British have Charleston harbor blockaded and the entire city surrounded. You were correct in the news you shared at Gadsden's. We had little time to prepare. I can no longer help the patriots with my privateering. So me and my lieutenant"—he elbowed William—"have come to join up."

"Yes, sir. That we have." His lieutenant eyed the food on the coals.

Marion glanced at him and pointed to the potatoes. "Help yourselves if you're hungry."

William reached for a potato and bounced it between his hands to cool it. "I believe we can be of service to the patriots, if you need two more brawny lads." He dropped the sweet potato on a rock and took a deep breath. "John Knox once said, 'Resistance to tyranny is obedience to God.' And we're determined to be obedient."

John smiled at his friend's Scottish burr and wise words that held the leader's attention.

Marion leaned back and studied Burns before he spoke. "We can always use more loyal patriots. And with excellent weapons like you men have." His lips curved up. "And I like that quote."

He turned to John. "Did you lose your ship to the British?"

"No, sir. I've got it hidden in a safe place."

"Good, we'll need it again one day when we drive them home to England."

John breathed easier. The man didn't say *if*.

～

*A*nna Grace stood at the attic window with her eyepiece focused on the harbor and the battle raging full force. Perspiration trickled down her back and beaded her forehead. She wanted to cover her ears from the loud blasts, but couldn't hold the lens and do so.

Fort Moultrie fired on the British ships sailing in. A shot hit home and burst into flames. She tried to feel pity for the English soldiers on the burning ship as they dove into the sea. Another vessel came to their rescue. Many other warships followed into the harbor with their English flags flying. Cannons roared, and soon every patriot vessel docked in the harbor exploded and sank in flames.

The poor rebels aboard those vessels. She choked back a cry and fought a black cloud hanging behind her eyelids. Tremors shook her frame so hard she dropped the eyepiece. Tears burned her eyes as she fled down the stairs.

Her aunt met her at the foot of the steps. "Where is that blasting coming from, Anna? It sounds so close."

She swiped moisture from her face. "The British have sailed into the harbor. Fort Moultrie couldn't keep them out." She gulped back a fresh downpour. "Those close blasts were our patriot ships being...blown up."

Her aunt patted her shoulder and wiped tears falling down her own cheeks.

She retreated with Aunt Reba to the cellar, and they stood clutching each other until their legs gave way and they sank onto a cot.

For hours, a furious bombardment of hundreds of British guns, from the land side and the harbor, showered bombs and red-hot shot over Charles Town. Screams and the smell of burning confirmed the onslaught ignited buildings and killed soldiers and civilians alike. Answering shots from Charles Town's own cannons grew slower. Were they running out of ammunition?

A few moments later, a loud explosion shook the house like a hurricane wind, or a tree falling on the roof.

Anna screamed. She and her aunt jumped to their feet. Had a shell hit them?

CHAPTER 11

This old fox, the Devil himself could not catch him.
~ British Military Officer Tarleton's description of Francis Marion,
November 8, 1780, as the state leader escaped into the swamp.

*A*nna grabbed her aunt's arm as the woman prayed aloud. "Lord, we place our trust in You. Send your angels to protect us."

Scurrying feet above drew their attention, and Thomas's face soon appeared down the cellar steps. "The back porch has taken a hit, but I think we can put the fire out with the sand and water you've got stored about."

The sounds of cannon blasts receded into a strange lull, but cries and shouts still clamored in the street.

Anna picked up her skirts and ran up the stairs with her aunt close behind her. They battled the pungent smell of burning wood and, alongside Thomas, grabbed up the buckets and threw their contents toward the flames licking across their porch.

At last, nothing but trickles of smoke rose from the embers that had once been their stoop. Anna sank into a kitchen chair beside her aunt, exhausted. Thomas went outside to check for any more damage.

A loud banging sounded on their gate, and Anna led the way to the front of the house.

Uncle Rufus stood at the entrance, and they hurried down to him. His face, etched in despair, lightened when he saw them.

He came through the entrance and wiped his sweating brow. "Thank God, you're not hurt. Charles Town just surrendered. General Lincoln and Brigadier General Moultrie are heading down to await Clinton's conquering army. Mark this day, May 12, 1780, for history. Charles Town has fallen."

Had the siege only lasted forty days? It seemed a lifetime. Emotion welled up inside Anna, and she no longer had the strength to hold it back. Surprised she had any tears left, she fell into her uncle's strong arms and sobbed.

❧

The next week, Anna found out what surrender meant to Charles Town patriots. Her uncle came by and told them what took place. He wore a jaunty, daisy-like chamomile blossom in his waistcoat buttonhole, but his haggard face told a different story.

He sat a box down on their kitchen table. "Surrendering our entire garrison was no quick or easy process. The surrender of two thousand, six hundred Continentals and three thousand militia took some time." He hung his head. "I loathed to watch our men, Warren included, march out to open ground and lay down their muskets and fowlers and cartridge boxes in front of the British army."

He took a deep breath and looked up. "But I would've hated more to see them wounded or dead and Charles Town further destroyed. We've got a lot of injured as it is."

"What will happen to Warren and the other prisoners, uncle?"

"The Continentals are being confined in barracks in town or on British prison ships in the harbor. But thank God they gave the militia boys the opportunity to sign a parole stating they'd never take up arms against His Majesty's troops again. Then they could go home. Warren's at the house, but he's pretty heartsick."

Her aunt pressed Uncle Rufus's hand. "We'll pray for Warren, and we're so glad he made it through without more injuries. What's in the box?"

Uncle Rufus smiled. "I've started negotiations with a British merchant I ran across on the dock who seems really interested in getting business up and going again. This is a little something for you and Anna and Thomas. Will have more later."

"Thank you, Rufus."

He took a deep breath and stood and then gestured toward the chamomile with its white petals and yellow center in his buttonhole. "Wondering why I'm wearing this when most patriots feel like we're in the midst of a funeral?"

Anna smiled. "Well, I admit I did wonder."

"The chamomile is a hardy rebel flower," he explained. "It thrives when trampled. Just like we will. And keep in mind, though Charles Town has surrendered, Francis Marion and his men have not, and will never surrender the rest of South Carolina. They continue to give the British, especially the hated Tarleton, all sorts of trouble. The man's even given Marion a nickname, the Swamp Fox." He doffed his bicorn and headed out.

Aunt Reba examined the box Uncle Rufus had set on the table. "Anna, look. Corn meal, cheese—and glory be—salt."

She looked at the needed food and smiled. But in her heart's eye she saw her brother Henry and Burton Ross riding with Marion, risking their lives daily. *Lord, keep them safe.*

~

*F*ollowing Marion's order to get ready to move two hours before dawn, John saddled Big Boy, with William and the mare Prissy alongside him in the darkness. The leader's words and admonishments the night before lay heavy on John's mind as he strapped the saddle and bags on the stallion.

Charles Town's over five thousand patriot soldiers had surrendered to General Clinton and fourteen thousand British regulars on

May 12 after deadly bombardment from land and sea. Marion told them that the continued Carolina resistance was up to them and other groups led by Thomas Sumter and Andrew Pickens. The broad plan was to surprise, harass, and disrupt British supply lines in South Carolina wherever they found them. And, of course, confiscate the goods and pick off as many redcoats as they could.

Had Anna and Reba survived the terrible onslaught Clinton inflicted on the city?

Marion had reiterated in strong words that his men would not plunder or burn Tory plantations or mistreat innocent civilians they might encounter. This differed greatly from what John had heard about Thomas Sumter's more aggressive methods. Gossip circulated that he promised to pay his recruits with loot taken from Loyalists. The British gave him the nickname, the Game Cock.

John mounted and followed the other riders along the riverbank at a slow pace. Marion led the brigade of seventy with his two officers, Henry Laurens and Burton Rand. He left thirty men to protect the camp.

"Where do you think we're going?" William's whisper came from behind.

John turned in the saddle to respond in a low voice. "Only the general and his two lieutenants know. But I suspect it's attacking a British supply line."

John smiled. Francis Marion kept his own counsel and plans of assault until the last moment. Deserters and volunteers arrived and went so often in the camp, the man probably never knew for certain whose side they were on until the actual fighting began, hence his secretiveness.

As the first streaks of dawn spread across the sky in the east, a smell of burning tripped across John's nose, and the flickering light of distant flames glowed through the trees.

The horses in front started moving faster, and sounds of distress echoed in the early morning breeze. They turned left into a field, and a nearby plantation house appeared surrounded by riders on horseback with torches. A man and several servants poured out of the home. The armed visitors dismounted, knocked the men down, and pushed their way into the house. Women screamed, raising the fine hairs on John's neck.

Marion pointed toward the house and yelled, "That's a patriot farm. Charge!"

The brigade galloped toward the besieged home. Shots rang out, and the man and two servants fell to the ground. The raiders poured out of the dwelling with items clutched in their hands. One cutthroat came out with a screaming girl thrown across his shoulder.

When the marauders saw or heard them coming, they threw their torches toward the house. The shattering of glass sounded, and flames lit up the early morning light. John shot two retreating raiders off their horses.

Burton Rand followed the rider holding the captive young woman, who no longer screamed, but lay limp across her captor's saddle pommel. Had she fainted or caught a stray bullet? John prayed the former.

Marion and half the men chased the cutthroats, while John, William, and other soldiers skidded off their mounts and began battling the flames. A woman and a boy of about ten ran out of the house and fell down beside the man who'd been shot. The victim lifted a hand to the woman's face as she wept and then dropped it back down to his side. Two servants ran out to help them. Other servants came from the barns and surrounding buildings with wet burlap sacks to battle the fire.

By the time they finally extinguished the flames, everyone in the group wore exhaustion on their soot-covered faces. The servants helped the woman shuffle up to the one undamaged rocking chair on the porch. The boy trudged behind her, and when he turned to stand by her side tears coursed down his cheeks. Two strong field workers picked up the man lying still on the ground and carried him up to the porch and laid him down near the woman and boy.

John's chest ached at the sight. There might not be much he could do for them, but he had to ask. He walked up the porch stairs. "Madam, we're part of Francis Marion's brigade. I'm so sorry about what's happened here." He stooped down to check the victim, and his throat tightened at the sight. Death marbleized the middle-aged man's face and blank eyes. He watched in vain for the slightest movement of the chest with its gaping bullet hole. None came from the pitiable form. Fighting the burn in his eyes, he took off his bicorn and stood, shifting his focus back to the woman. "My name is John Vargas. Can we do anything else for you before we leave to chase the men who did this? Did you recognize any of them?"

The woman wiped the tears still flowing down her cheeks with the back of her sleeve. "I knew some of them. They were Tory neighbors and riffraff that they picked up, heaven knows where. They've shot and killed my Tom, and that no-good Richard's taken Isabel." Her voice grew shriller with each word. "He's been after her the last two years. She's only seventeen. Please try to find her, sir, and bring her home." She lifted her hand and pointed. "Go after them. The servants will help us here."

The boy threw out his chest and swiped at the tears on his face. His dark eyes settled on John. "Please sir, I'll get my squirrel gun and go with you."

His mother shook her head. "No, son." She patted his small balled fist. "I need you here, Joey. You have to be the man of the house now." Her voice broke and fresh tears gushed from her eyes.

John strode to the stallion. All the other men and William were already mounted.

They galloped in the direction they'd seen Marion chase the raiders.

The sun beamed high and hot in the sky when they found the rest of the brigade beside a stream.

John dismounted and stooped to get a drink of water after the other riders. William offered to take Big Boy and Prissy downstream to drink.

Marion sat on a rock beside an oak, surveying his troops. "That bunch of Tories and scavengers won't be repeating this morning's work any time soon. Most all are dead or wounded." He glanced at John. "How did you leave the house? Get the fires put out?"

John walked closer. "Yes, sir. We did. The man they shot died. Left a mother and son about ten, and the daughter carried off. She said the raiders were Tory neighbors and lowlifes who joined them."

He looked around for Burton Rand. The lieutenant was not in the group.

Marion took a deep breath. "We're missing only Rand. I believe he'll rescue that girl, if I know Burton. Thought we'd just rest here a bit. Give him time to get back, and if he doesn't come soon, we'll go looking for him." He leaned against the tree and closed his eyes.

Within the hour, Burton Rand rode up with the girl held in the circle of his arms in front of his saddle. He'd given her his blue waistcoat to cover her thin gown. Had she been kidnapped out of her bed?

The tears dried into streaks on the young woman's countenance didn't conceal her beauty. Blond, windblown curls caught the sunlight and framed her sweetheart face.

John raised his brows at the sight of her held close in Burton's strong arms.

Rand reined his horse in and stopped before Marion. "Sir, it's my idea to take this young lady home. Do I have your permission? This is Isabel Thompson." He gestured to his leader. "May I present Colonel Francis Marion?"

Marion looked up at his lieutenant, then at the girl who turned wide, sky-blue eyes on him, then back to Burton.

The adoration in the girl's face toward Rand was hard to miss.

She faced Marion and took a deep breath. "Sir, I owe my life to this gentleman, and I thank God you and your men came when you did. My family are patriots, every single one of us, even my ten-year-old brother, Joey." Her voice shook with emotion, but the words seemed to tire her. She leaned her golden head back onto Rand's shoulder and sighed. He adjusted his arm around her, and redness crept up his neck.

Marion appeared to have trouble keeping a straight face. "By all means take the young lady home, Rand, and then come back to our camp we left this morning. You do remember the way there, right?"

Burton raised his chin and looked over the bright head pressed against him. "Uh, yes, sir. I do. I'll rejoin you before nightfall."

Henry came forward and handed his water skin to Rand, who offered a drink to the girl, then drank himself. He reined the horse around and trotted out of the camp without looking back.

As soon as he was out of earshot, the men standing about, who'd been quiet and watching the exchange, slapped their knees and whooped.

Henry Laurens walked up to him and William and smiled. "Burton seems to have all the luck. This isn't the first pretty damsel he's rescued. But it's the first one I've seen him tongue-tied over. What do you bet he won't be back to camp before dark?" He kicked at a stone and strode away.

A dart of anger pricked John. Was this the way Burton acted when supposedly engaged to someone as precious as Anna? If so, he'd like to kick something, too.

Marion gave the order to march, and John mounted with the rest of the men. Anna Grace filled his mind, her red hair, lithe, curvaceous form, and her temper. God protect the man who tried to kidnap her. And how would she respond to the scene he'd just witnessed with her beloved Burton Rand?

When John arrived with the brigade back at the camp in late afternoon, a loaded supply wagon stood in the shade.

One of Marion's men sitting on the driver's seat explained as they rode up. "Found this wagon waiting down at Nelson's Ferry. Had a servant in fancy livery who told me it was for Marion's men, so we were happy to relieve him of it. The man had a high-stepping horse tied to the back, and he took off on it."

Marion looked over the barrels and sacks stacked on it. "Who sent it? Did he say?"

"Yes, sir. He said a rich widow by the name of Ruth Garfield Edmonds. Said she'd been married to a Tory who lost his life in the battle for Charles Town, and now she wanted to aid the patriots."

John was in the process of dismounting, but when the man spoke the woman's name, he grabbed hold of the saddle so hard to steady himself that Big Boy grunted and nudged him.

Baroness Ruth Edmonds.

He forced surprise off his face before turning around. So Ruth had not abandoned all her patriot senses when she discarded him and married Edmonds. Bile boiled up in his throat at the memory of their last conversations—arguments about independence. With her eyes blinded by the offer of marriage to a baron, she gave no heed to him at the time. Maybe something he'd said had stuck.

That night, John enjoyed a good repast with Marion's men. Supply wagons were said to be few and far between. One reason being no one could find the partisan leader's hideouts. The militia hunted for meat and lived off the land when they ran across fields of sweet potatoes and corn. They baked both among hot coals, and the two staples kept well in saddle bags.

After the meal, John lay on his woodsy pallet he'd made and battled thoughts of Ruth. But even when he let them come, Anna Grace's lovely face kept replacing his childhood sweetheart's. About midnight, a horse's repetitive steps and the low squeaks of leather rubbing approached the camp in the darkness. He grabbed his musket and crept to the edge of the clearing. A lone rider, leading a horse, walked quietly toward the encampment. Where were the guards stationed in the outer perimeters?

He aimed his gun and stepped out of the shadows. "Halt."

Burton Rand lifted both hands and grinned. "Just me, Vargas. Returning from delivering Isabel to her family."

He lowered his weapon and returned to his pallet. The man was already on a first name basis with the girl? Fast worker.

～

*D*ay fell into night and rose again with its southern heat more times than John could count as he fought with the Brigade through the long, hot summer. He experienced many campaigns and skirmishes near the Santee River, the Black, and the

Pee Dee Rivers. Much of their time, Marion played cat and mouse with the hated British officer Tarleton, who was determined to stop the elusive rebels who robbed their supply lines. The cruel leader and his regiment burned and sacked plantations and towns as he tried to track Marion's men without success.

In the fall, Marion set up an almost impregnable hideaway on Snow's Island.

One morning, the man stood on a rock and addressed his brigade. "Men, I'm going to release you for four days to check on your families. If you're not back by high noon on the fourth day, we'll move on without you. I encourage you to return, we need every one of you. Be careful. See if you can pick up any intelligence on the movement of the enemy. We've a lot of work to do to hinder the British from taking all of South Carolina. Let's show them what makes us Southern patriots impossible to defeat."

A great shout erupted from the men, with John and William joining in. Four days off. He knew exactly where he had to go.

He and his friend saddled up amid excited talk and jests among their compatriots. Even the two horses sensed the excitement and stamped their approval.

William hesitated before mounting. "I think I'll go along to the in-laws near Kingstree, see how they're surviving. I can almost taste that good cooking of my sister-in-law on the back of my tongue. Where you headed, captain? I'd be glad to have you accompany me."

John took a deep breath and mounted. "I'm heading to Charles Town."

William's brown eyes widened as he settled in his saddle. "You're sure, lad? Going back there is beyond dangerous, with fourteen thousand British soldiers occupying the city."

John held the reins tight as Big Boy champed at the bit. "The Lord will help me. I need to check on something."

William nodded and grinned. "Or *someone?*"

CHAPTER 12

I only regret that I have but one life to lose for my country.
~ Twenty-one-year-old Nathan Hale, hanged by the British as a spy.

*A*nna awoke with the distinct feeling she should visit and check on Abigail and her mother. Had they made it through the bombardment, and now the influx of British soldiers? She dressed quickly in the dim light of the autumn morning coming through the window and headed down to the breakfast room.

Her aunt sat at the table with a cup of herbal tea, reading her Bible. "Good morning, dear. I thought it fine for you to sleep in a little, but here you are. Didn't you rest well, or was it too quiet?" She smiled.

Anna poured herself a cup of the hot brew and placed a piece of toast and a small chunk of cheese on a plate, then sat. "I slept well, but feel in my bones I need to check on Abigail." She took a bite of bread, then a sip of tea.

"I don't know whether it's safe, dear, with all the soldiers in the streets."

"I'm concerned for her. She's not too far from her confinement, and there she is with a sick mother, an often absent father, and only two servants." She pushed another bite of food into her mouth.

"Would you go with me? And Thomas could follow for protection. I do believe we need to visit her." She finished her toast and cheese.

Her aunt sat up straight and touched her lips with her napkin. "Well, maybe it's the Lord telling you there's a good reason. I'll get my walking cane and shawl and meet you at the front door."

Anna smiled and hurried to the back entrance to call Thomas. He came forward, and when she told of their errand, he retrieved a thick stick he had propped next to the door. She ran to her room and donned a thin green cloak and hood.

Walking down the cobbled streets beside her aunt, with Thomas close behind, she swallowed a lump in her throat, seeing again the damage to her beloved town. The entire city looked tired and sick. Palmetto trees stood shorn of their top plumage. Some homes had roofs knocked in by cannon shots, which still lacked repair. They had to walk around fallen garden walls. Piles of bricks and broken glass lay scattered about corners. British flags waved from most windows, and in every space imaginable, redcoats camped, like a rash spread over the town.

When soldiers passed close to Anna, some whistled and made lusty remarks. But as soon as their glance lit on her aunt's stiff countenance, backed by Thomas's thick-muscled glaring presence, they grew silent and stepped aside.

Loud sounds of revelry echoed from taverns as they passed, and they hurried onward toward Abigail's.

At the corner of Broad and Meeting Streets, they passed the statue of William Pitt with his left arm gone and the broken place on his shoulder gaping like an open wound.

The sidewalks, filled with movement, revealed people of all types and descriptions. They passed two women squired by British officers in white trousers and smart forest-green coats. The two soldiers stopped, doffed their hats, and bowed to Anna and her aunt, somewhat unsteadily, as if they'd been drinking.

She followed her aunt's example and did not acknowledge the greeting.

The older of the ladies with high, powdered hair and painted face, turned to them. She thrust out her chest with its deep cleavage displayed. "Well, I never. Don't these high and mighty people know they've been conquered?" She spit on the hem of Anna's skirt.

Thomas banged his stick on the cobbled stones and his nostrils flared.

The woman's eyes widened, but her soldier escort grabbed her arm and the four of them stumbled away laughing.

"Pay them no mind, my dear," her aunt whispered. "They're women of the street and the soldiers are drunk."

When they reached their destination, Abigail, pale as alabaster and large with child, met them at the gate and opened it wide. "Thank God, you've come. I prayed you would."

Anna hugged her, allowing for her friend's full waist. "What has happened, dear friend?"

"Father has been shot and killed in a duel...and Mother...is...I do not know what to do for her and neither does Dr. James." Abigail swallowed a sob.

Aunt Reba took her hand. "It shall be well. We're here to help. Stop any fretting. Remember your little one."

If Anna had not appreciated her aunt's wisdom and steadying presence before, she did over the next hard hours with often-whispered thanks to God.

Her aunt took the responsibility of the house in mourning, the nursing of Abigail's mother, and the instructions to the two servants, a mother and grown daughter. The doctor gave little hope of the woman surviving another day. Her heart, he said, was just giving out.

Mrs. Hamilton passed away in the early morning hours. Anna and Aunt Reba had urged Abigail to get rest for herself and unborn child, and she'd acquiesced. Then they sat by Mrs. Hamilton's side until the end.

Aunt Reba stood and pulled the sheet over the woman's stiff face. "She's at peace now. We give praise to God." She turned to Anna. "Let's go to the spare rooms and lie down until daylight, then we'll tell Abigail and help with the preparations."

After discarding her clothing down to her chemise, Anna sank into much-needed sleep in the borrowed bed.

Sunlight peeping through the window awakened her. She dressed with haste and walked toward her friend's room. From downstairs, the sounds and smells of breakfast filtered up to her ears and nose. Aunt Reba and the two servants were already getting the day started.

She gave a gentle rap on Abigail's door and opened it. Her friend sat by the window with her Bible propped on her extended abdomen. She looked up and wiped a tear escaping down her cheek. "Mother's gone, isn't she?"

Anna walked to her and knelt beside her chair. She took her friend's hand. "Yes, she's well and happy now, Abigail, if you believe that book you're holding."

"I do believe it. It's just all happened so fast. First father, now mother." She blinked and laid her cool fingers on Anna's shoulder. "But you've been through more than this, losing your parents like you did. We're both orphans now, I guess." Tears flowed down her pale cheeks.

Anna stood and pulled a chair near. "Dear friend, I've thought this out sitting beside your mother's bed last night, and Aunt Reba is in full agreement. You must come to live with us. Close up this house. Move in with us after...the funeral. Will you think about it?"

Abigail straightened and a small smile touched the edge of her lips. She removed the Bible, took Anna's hand and placed it on her protruding middle. "Do you feel it? He...or she has been active every day now for some months."

Anna marveled at the feathery movements of the child. "I do. Oh, Abigail, you've got a new life to plan for. Do you know when your time is? From the looks of you, it can't be long."

"I think I must be about eight months along."

Anna stood and clasped her hands. "That close? See, you must come to us as soon as possible. Your confinement could start any time."

$\sim$

*A*nna stood on curled dead leaves and crushed seashells beside Abigail in the small group on the narrow cemetery path. The sky overhead turned darker by the minute. She prayed the storm would hold off until the simple graveside double service of Mr. and Mrs. Hamilton took place.

Since the battle of Charleston and its surrender, short graveside interments had replaced the longer funeral services held inside sanctuaries. To every patriot's horror and anger, the British had turned most non-Anglican churches into stables for their horses.

Abigail's family plot stood in a corner of First Presbyterian's gated cemetery. Weather-worn stone statues and faded markers covered the entire yard except the space around the two open graves. One rock wall beyond lay in shambles from a cannon shot. Even the roof of the large church had a tarp spread over damage to a gable. The smell of mold and fresh-turned earth permeated the air.

Anna looked up in the trees beyond the walled enclosure while the minister read the familiar scriptures. With the first rumble of thunder, the bird chatter ceased in the tall overhanging oak limbs. A burst of lightning broke over the solemn assembly, and Abigail shuddered. Anna took her hand and held tight.

The minister glanced up at the sky, then to the assembly, and finished his remarks in short order.

He moved through the group, smiling and nodding to Abigail as he extended his hand. "Please let us know anything we can do to help you, Mrs. Welch. You have our deepest sympathy. I will be by to see you later in the week."

Anna opened her mouth to say Abigail would be at their house, but the man moved away, weaving through the few bystanders on the path and out of the cemetery.

She pulled her friend to their carriage and helped her climb in. Her aunt had already seated herself inside. The storm broke moments after they found their seats in the conveyance. Sheets of rain fell, enveloping them in a cocoon.

Anna whispered a prayer of thanks that Rufus had found a horse to pull the conveyance. Otherwise, they'd been walking. And that would've been impossible for Abigail, so big with child, with or without a rainstorm.

$$\sim$$

*J*ohn slipped up the stairs in the stable to Thomas's room about midnight. He gave a tap on the door and waited a moment, then gave two more, and whispered, "It's John Vargas."

The door opened, and the mulatto stood there with a musket in his hands, the whites of his eyes showing. He blew out a breath. "Oh, captain. I'm so glad to see you." He lowered the gun and pulled the door wide.

"How are things here?" John entered and sat where Thomas motioned, in the only chair in the small room.

The young man leaned the weapon in a corner, lit a candle, and perched on the edge of his cot. "It's okay for now. We made it through the bombardment, and Mr. Rufus is bringing us food again since the surrender. What have you been doing, sir, if I might ask?" The youth's eyes brightened with interest.

"Riding with General Marion. He gave the men a four-day leave. How is Anna...and her aunt?"

Thomas smiled. "Those two are the proper stuff, sir. We've been through some rough times, but *through* is the important word." He took a deep breath. "You want to hear about some of it right now?"

"No, what I wish to do is see Anna."

Thomas's eyes widened again. "But they all gone to bed in the big house, sir. And I need to tell you, there's some other folk there, too. Miss Anna's friend, Mrs. Abigail, done come to live with them, and her two servants. Those two, a mother and daughter, are in the servants' attic. But worst of all, two soldiers been garrisoned in the townhouse. They're on the third floor, I think, and Miss Anna and her aunt and friend are on the second. But I don't think I can get a word to her for you in the middle of the night like this. Who knows if them soldiers are even asleep?"

John took a deep breath. "I know about the soldiers garrisoned here." But no matter what, he would see Anna Grace Laurens tonight. Some way, somehow. "Do you know which room and window belongs to her?"

"That I do, sir."

"Well, come on. Time's a wasting."

John waited for Thomas to pull on a shirt and pants and follow him from the stable to the back of the house. Dim light from the moon sailing between clouds shrouded them in shadows.

Thomas pointed to Anna's window on the second story.

John picked up a pebble and threw it against the glass. With his third effort, candlelight glowed around the edges of the drapery.

∾

*A*nna sat on the edge of her bed after lighting the torch and frowned. Whatever was hitting her window? Perhaps a wounded bird?

When the tap came again, she arose, slipped on her robe, and opened the curtain. Seeing nothing in the darkness, she raised the window and leaned out.

Thomas stood in the yard, his broad shoulders barely discernible in the darkness.

"What is it, Thomas? Do you know what time it is?" Her whispered words floated down on the warm evening air.

"There's someone to see you, ma'am."

A man stepped from the shadows into the dim light emanating from her candle in the window. He looked up at her and grinned.

She gasped. John Vargas.

Turning back into the room, she tried to still the hammering of her heart and think what to do. How dare he come at midnight to her house and demand to see her? And with soldiers on the floor above. If she refused to receive him, would he cause a ruckus and rouse the men, as well as her aunt and Abigail? Both of them needed their rest.

And he would be arrested.

Leaning back out, she whispered to Thomas. "Bring him to the front of the residence and into the corner parlor. Please be as quiet as possible."

She closed the window and stepped into the first dress her hands landed on in her closet. Glancing into the mirror at her mussed auburn locks fanning around her shoulders, she shook her head. No time to do anything to her hair. What could the fellow expect from a midnight call?

She tiptoed down the stairs to the parlor with her hand shading her candle flame. A good piece of her mind was what the man deserved. But why was her breath catching in her throat?

He stood as she entered and closed the door.

She swished past him and placed her light on the mantle, then turned to face him. "Sir, I hope there's a mighty good reason for this nocturnal visit of yours. I only came down because I was afraid you'd wake the household and the soldiers."

He strode close to her. In the dim light, he had the pleasant scent of the woods about him, the smell of earth and leaves and pinewood campfires like she and her father had built when she was a child. How could a sea captain have this kind of scent?

"What if I just wanted to see you?" His gaze, soft as a caress, disarmed her.

Her heart jolted and her pulse pounded. She stepped back and tried to breathe. He projected an energy and power that attracted her like a magnet.

He moved in and drew her into his arms.

She was powerless to resist the warmth from his frame that enveloped her.

"You'll never know how I prayed for you to stay safe during the bombardment." His voice next to her ear and his nearness made her senses spin.

This couldn't be happening. Yet it was.

He cupped her chin and captured her mouth with his own. A delicious shudder heated her body. Without making a conscious decision to do so, her arms slid around his thick neck, and she melted into his embrace. The kiss deepened until her knees would no longer hold her. But he held her in his own powerful arms.

He lifted his head and stared into her eyes. Then he smiled and moved apart from her. She dropped into the nearest chair and tried to slow her breathing.

He sat across from her, leaned forward, and then whispered, "Now down to business."

She gazed at him, trying to clear her brain. What on earth could he mean? And how could he possibly think straight after that kiss?

"I've done some checking about the two officers you have garrisoned here, Lieutenant David Palmer and Captain Richard Waring. Am I right? These are their names?"

"Yes. How did you know?"

"Don't worry about that. Do you remember telling me once you'd like to become a spy for the patriots?"

Anna sat erect, her heart tripping with interest. "But how—?"

"Palmer is not so important. But Waring is. He has the ear of General Clinton, being the son of a friend of Clinton's, and often hears marching plans in advance. He likely will receive the orders to march with Clinton into the back country and destroy patriot strongholds, hoping to occupy the rest of South Carolina. What a blessing it would be for us to know where he's going ahead of time."

"Who is *us*?"

"Marion's Brigade. I'm riding with them now. Didn't I tell you?"

"No, you never told me. Do you see my brother Henry?"

"Every day."

"How about Burton Rand?"

"Him, too, most days. But don't expect to see either of them back here soon with fourteen thousand British troops occupying the city."

Anna sank back into her chair as she considered his words. Now his fresh, woodsy, campfire smell made sense. "Why did *you* come? Isn't this most dangerous for you?"

"Because of the important business I'm trying to enlist your help with." He smiled, showing even white teeth. "And, like I said, I wanted to see you, make sure you'd made it through the bombardment."

Anna swallowed and took a needed breath. "So you want me to listen to whatever I can of Captain Waring's conversation. And do what with the information I might gain?"

"Give it to Thomas. I'm going to tell him how to pass news on so it will reach the place it'll do the most good for the patriots." He pulled a folded sheet from his vest pocket. "Here are secret ways you can relay the message, in case the British intercept them. Guard this with your life. Best to memorize them, then burn this."

She took the piece, opened it, and skimmed a recipe for hidden writing and a list of code symbols. Then she refolded the paper and placed it in her skirt pocket. "So this is what you've been doing all these months?"

"It's what I'm adding to what I've been doing to help the cause. We've got to turn this thing around somehow."

Anna looked at his handsome animated face, and couldn't summon a single image of Burton Rand. How she had misjudged this man.

He stood. "I've a journey ahead of me after I instruct Thomas."

She rose and stepped closer. "Where are you going, John?"

"I can't tell you that. The less you know about my part in this, the better." He pressed her shoulders with his muscular hands. "Please be very discreet, Anna. Tell no one about this, not even Reba or your friend living here. Do you understand? This is most dangerous work."

"I think I comprehend, and I'm glad to do what I can."

Lines creased his forehead, and he dropped his hands and clenched them into fists. A muscle worked in his strong jaw as he looked aside in the dark room, beyond the cameo of flickering candlelight embracing them. Was John going to change his mind? Take back everything he'd said. Tell her to forget it because the role was too risky?

He took a sharp breath. "It's so dangerous, I wouldn't be here enlisting your help, except for what's at stake. Knowing where Waring or Clinton might head can save many patriot lives, maybe even help save the rest of South Carolina from British control." He swallowed and looked deep into her eyes. "But I must warn you, precious Anna, spies are being hanged by both sides these days. Are you sure you want to do this?"

She squared her shoulders. "Of course I am. Who would suspect a woman of having the nerve or skill to do this?"

He kissed her forehead then turned away. She followed him to the hall where he slipped out of the house without a sound. Her heart ached, watching him go.

With her candle in hand, she made her way back up the stairs and down the hallway toward her room. She hesitated at Abigail's door and leaned against it, listening for any sound or movement. The birthing of her child could begin any day or night, and she didn't want her friend to go through a single pain alone.

"Good *early* morning, Miss Laurens. I thought I heard someone in the hall down here. What are you doing up at this time of night?"

She almost dropped the candle, and her mouth dried up like a potsherd. Turning, she met Captain Waring's suspicious scrutiny.

CHAPTER 13

*I do hereby solemnly promise in the presence of Almighty God to bear
allegiance to his present Majesty, King George The Third, and His
Successors, Kings of Great Britain, to be a true and faithful servant and to
strictly observe and conform to the Laws of England without any
Equivocation, mental Evasion, or secret reservation whatsoever."*
~ *Oath of Allegiance required in Charles Town after the British recaptured
the city in 1780.*

*A*nna swallowed as best she could and sucked in a breath,
praying Captain Waring couldn't hear her pounding heart.
He must know how to move without a sound. She'd heard nothing of
his approach from the third floor. How long had he been near?

The man stood before her, half dressed, with only a wrinkled shirt
and trousers and no boots. That answered for his soundless steps.

His hard, dark eyes raked over her in the dim glow of the candle.

She drew her robe tight at the neckline. "Sir, you startled me. I was
checking on my friend whose baby is due any time." She gestured to
the door, keeping her voice low. "This is Abigail's room."

His cynical stare bore into her, and he strode closer, leaned toward her, and sniffed. "You smell like…hmm…the fresh outdoors. Have you been outside?"

She stepped back and thrust out her chin. "Of course not. At this hour? Please, move. I must get to my room."

"I'll go. But keep in mind where my room is, little lady, if you want to check on me some night. You'd be most welcome."

The smoldering lust in his eyes sent a chill up her spine. His thick lips curved into a smirk before he turned away.

He moved like a shadow up the stairs and disappeared on the landing. How she wished she could've slapped his face for that parting remark.

Entering her room, she locked her door and leaned against it, trying to get her breath to return to normal. How could John's fresh woodsy scent cling to her? She closed her eyes and smiled, treasuring his embrace and smell.

Then she blew out the candle and dropped into bed, whispering a prayer. *Lord, bless and protect John and all Marion's men. Help me be wise as a serpent and harmless as a dove in the assignment given. Give me at least one good piece of intelligence to serve our patriots.*

〜

*T*he next morning while dressing, Anna heard boots stamping down the two sets of stairs, and she sighed with relief. Thank God she wouldn't have to face Captain Waring after the confrontation last night. She'd hate to have to answer any more questions.

The officers left early to report to their superiors housed in the finest homes in Charles Town, or to their troops camped in the city or its outskirts. Lt. Palmer had shared their daily schedule with Anna and her aunt when they first arrived. He assured them he and Captain Waring desired to be as small a bother as possible to the household. They only required morning meals and late dinners, no mid-day meals. The lieutenant, unlike the captain, displayed gentlemanly qualities.

Anna smiled at the mother and daughter servants of Abigail as they replenished the eggs, grits, and bacon on the buffet. "Thank you, Naomi and Esther. Has your mistress been down yet?"

"No, ma'am. She's complaining of a backache and said she'd stay abed longer," Naomi responded.

Esther, a lovely mulatto like Thomas and about the same age, returned Anna's smile.

Aunt Reba arrived in time to overhear the servant's words. She glanced at Anna and cocked her chin. "Today, we will keep a good check on the mother and baby to come. This might be the beginning."

By midafternoon, Abigail suffered in strong labor pains. Anna and her aunt collected everything in readiness for the midwife's arrival— hot water, linens, butter, and an herbal tea to ease the pain.

Tears gathered in Anna's eyes with her friend's deepening groans. Why did birthing have to be this difficult? Abigail gripped her hand so hard when the pains came that Anna almost wanted to cry out herself. When her friend released her grip, Anna sponged away the beads of sweat popping out on Abigail's forehead with a cool, damp cloth. Aunt Reba kept the cool washcloths supplied and water hot in the kitchen fireplace.

The midwife arrived and went to work.

Before midnight, the lusty cries of a fine baby boy announced his entrance into the world. An exhausted smile slipped over Abigail's face.

Anna, overcome with awe at the birth of a child, whispered a prayer of thanksgiving to God that both mother and child seemed well.

The midwife handed the little one to Aunt Reba while she tended to Abigail.

After bathing the child in warm water, and rubbing olive oil into his skin, her aunt wrapped the little one in a soft blanket. Then she kissed his forehead, and handed him to Anna. "Give this wee one to his mother."

Anna's heart overflowed as she looked at the tiny being, perfect in every way, with his miniature hands balled into miniscule fists. He pressed one to his mouth and made a sucking noise. His thick black hair lay in ringlets around his head. She'd never held a newborn before. "Oh my goodness, he's so precious." Wonder and love swept through her as she handed him to his mother.

After the midwife helped Abigail begin nursing the child, the exhausted mother took the time to study her babe. She unfurled one of his tight fists. "Anna, these are Philip's hands in miniature. Look at this hand span and strong fingers."

Anna smiled. "And the hair. I believe it's his same shade, from what I remember of your husband."

Her friend patted the dark curls and smiled. "Yes. It's unbelievable. Philip's color and curly locks."

"Have you thought of a name?"

Abigail's expression grew wistful. "Philip Hamilton Welch."

~

Uncle Rufus came by the next day to share some news. His furrowed brow alerted Anna to the seriousness of the information.

Aunt Reba led the way to the parlor, and her uncle shut the door, and then sat across from them. "It's been announced that everyone will have to sign a loyalty oath to King George before they can engage in business or hold a job of any kind. Christopher Gadsden and about forty other rich men who don't have to hold jobs refused to sign. Colonel Balfour arrested them all and put them on a ship to the British fort in St. Augustine." Her uncle's gruff and angry voice reverberated through the room.

Her aunt clasped her hands in her lap and asked the question on the tip of Anna's tongue. "Rufus, have you signed the pledge?"

"Yes. No choice. I must keep the mercantile trade going strong." He looked around as if to make sure the chamber was empty, and he lowered his tone further. "Not only for my family and yours, but for all our patriots."

"So, you're saying I must sign it, too, before I can reopen my millinery shop." Aunt Reba's voice rose.

"Yes. And, Anna, you must sign it as well to help in Reba's shop or the mercantile. Their office for the oaths is on Queen Street."

Her aunt sighed and stood. "Well, there's no use putting it off. I do want to reopen as soon as possible, now that it's cooler autumn weather." She turned to Anna. "Let's go now."

As Uncle Rufus showed himself out, Aunt Reba and Anna hurried up the steps to prepare to leave. First, Anna settled Abigail and the babe for a good rest with Naomi and Esther keeping happy watch over them. Then she picked up her reticule from the dresser, tied on her bonnet, and descended to meet her aunt at the front door.

Thomas accompanied them as they made their way through town to the Queen Street building where the British had set up offices to receive the oaths.

A tired-looking older officer showed them to a side room where two redcoat soldiers lounged at desks. He directed Anna to the younger man.

In an impeccable red uniform, he took one look at her and sat up straight, then adjusted the silver gorget hanging at his neck in place of the popular cravat.

"Miss, are you ready to take the king's protection and resume any former employment?" He spoke with a confident voice as his eyes flickered over her with appreciation.

Anna lifted her chin at the insolent man. "I am, and so is my aunt here with me."

The man glanced at Reba and then directed her to the other officer's desk.

He took up his quill and turned back to Anna. "What is your name?

"Anna Grace Laurens."

He scratched something down in a ledger in front of him.

"Now lift your right hand and repeat after me."

Anna did as he asked—but slid her left palm into a pocket and crossed her fingers.

"I, Anna Grace Laurens, do hereby solemnly promise in the presence of Almighty God to bear allegiance to his present Majesty, King George The Third, and His Successors, Kings of Great Britain, to be a true and faithful servant and to strictly observe and conform to the Laws of England without any Equivocation, mental Evasion, or secret reservation whatsoever."

As Anna echoed the man, Aunt Reba repeated the same words at the other desk.

The officers gave each of them a slip of paper they were to show if questioned about their loyalty. She tried not to grimace as she folded it and placed it in her reticule.

On the way home, they stopped at Aunt Reba's millinery shop. Her aunt instructed Thomas to pull the boards down protecting the front window, and then she unlocked the door.

Anna followed her inside, where a musty, unused smell greeted them. Everything seemed in order, but the tables and cloth-covered head models for the hats boasted gray layers of dust.

Aunt Reba scanned the area and put her hands on her hips. "Tomorrow I'll come and get this place cleaned up." She ran a finger over the main countertop and shook her head.

"I'll help you if Abigail and Baby Philip don't need me." She smiled every time she thought of the precious baby who had baptized their house with a special joy.

"Hello-o." A female voice called from the doorway.

Anna and her aunt turned to face a visitor.

An aristocratic woman in a beautiful cream satin day dress and exquisite hat atop her high powdered hair stood staring at them. "Are you opening for business? I saw your sign earlier." A heavy scent of lavender flowed into the shop as she stepped inside and gazed about. Disappointment flickered across her face. "I'm in need of some new hats."

Her aunt walked forward. "I am Reba Collins, the owner and milliner, and I will be open for business by the end of the week. This is my niece, Anna Laurens. Are you looking for something special in color or fabric?"

The lady gave Anna a cursory glance, then turned her attention to her aunt. "Gauze, my dear, French silk gauze. And green is the color for Charles Town these days."

Anna tightened her lips. The Tory choice. When Marion's men and General Washington's continentals succeeded, that would change.

Reba smiled at the woman. "I have some hats completed at my home I'll be bringing in as soon as I clean the shop." Reba walked to the counter, dusted off her appointment book with her handkerchief, and took up a quill. "Shall I make an appointment for you to come by and try on my new creations? How about Friday around eleven?"

"Delightful, my dear. That will be in plenty of time for the officer's ball coming up."

"Your name?"

The woman drew back her shoulders and lifted her chin. "Mrs. Henry Balfour. My husband is Colonel Balfour, the City Commandant." She smiled at Anna's intake of breath and adjusted her silk shawl with its golden filigree edging. The fine work caught a beam of sunlight from the window and sparkled.

"So you see why I must have the best, my dears. If I choose your hats, others will follow to your shop." She retreated to the entrance, her skirts rustling, but she turned back at the door and raised her brows. "Have you taken the oath?"

Reba sighed. "Yes, we both have."

"Good." She stepped outside and entered a gleaming carriage in the street, with green liveried servants manning it and two sleek bays harnessed to pull the rig. The conveyance rolled away with the horses stepping high and their tails lifted behind them.

~

*A*s John rode into the encampment and greeted William, a delicious smell of roasted meat permeated the air around his campfire.

The Scot's face broke into a wide grin. "So you actually made it into Charles Town and managed to get away without getting arrested, did you, my lad?"

"I told you the Lord would help me."

"You did, and I prayed, but it sorely tested my faith, I can tell ye. And how about the lassie you went to check on? She made it through the bombardment?" He squatted down and stoked the campfire where he had a rabbit roasting on a spit. "Don't know why I'm asking. Your face would be as long as the Santee River if she hadn't."

John took a deep breath of the pleasant smell of roasting meat and grinned. He sat down on a rock beside William, as Anna's face slipped through his mind, her beauty made more striking by her courage. "Yes, she and her aunt survived with only a little damage to their property, but Charles Town is a wreck." He shook his head as those sad images took over.

"See many redcoats?"

"Like ants running over a fallen apple. Made me think of the *Sand Dollar* after we went through that battle off the coast of Africa with the two pirate ships. Remember their number and the harm we suffered?"

William turned the spit. "Sure I do. And you need to recall how we got it all repaired to better than new."

John appreciated his friend's faith, but he had to share another troubling thing. "One of the saddest things I saw, and you will not like this either, was what's happening to churches that are not part of the Church of England. The rotten British are making hospitals out of a few and stables out of the rest, even St. Michael's and First Presbyterian."

"You don't say." William's quiet tone was thick with pain.

"One of the most unfair things I learned is that any plantation owner who doesn't sign the oath of loyalty will have his house and land confiscated and sold to Tories for a pittance, or awarded to them as a prize or reward."

As if he'd heard enough for one sitting, William gave the meat another quick turn, and then lifted it off the spit. "You ready to appreciate my offering as cook, or do you want to talk all night?"

John smiled. Better to enjoy the evening meal.

～

*O*ver the next weeks, John fought with Marion's brigade at strategic river crossings. At Nelson's Ferry, they strangled the British supply line running from Charles Town to Camden. At several outposts, they lay in wait and surprised soldiers, which gained them supplies, ammunition, and even a valuable medical chest. And they managed to escape Lieutenant Banastre Tarleton's angry pursuit, often by retreating into the Santee swamps.

After successful clashes with the king's men at Black Mingo River and Tearcoat Swamp, many new volunteers poured in to join the partisan brigade.

Francis Marion held an almost mystical power over his militia. Although the man lacked physical presence—he was short and wiry, and without a magnetic personality—his men regarded him with awe. Part of their esteem came because of his success against the British, which bred respect. But it also had to be his gravity and seriousness of purpose, along with his steady, consistent character that caused most to follow where he led. The man was considerate of the sensibilities of others, and he kept his temper under rare control.

The man had bristled with anger a few days earlier when he discovered two of his followers had burned and plundered a Tory house, something Marion detested and had forbade. He told the guilty parties to gather their belongings and leave, yet did it without yelling or cursing. He dealt with the situation with only a few words and an icy glare.

A few days later, a report came that Camden had fallen to the British and many patriot captives taken. Marion's face had blanched, and several of the men cursed under their breath.

The blow that news brought was softened when John's Charles Town servant brought a piece of intelligence Thomas had passed to him from Anna. When he first heard it was from Anna, his gut wrenched. Had she put herself in danger to obtain it? He'd never forgive himself if anything happened to her trying to gain important facts. But apparently, she had managed to pick up the information at her aunt's millinery shop from two Tory wives' conversation. General Cornwallis, who had replaced Clinton over the Southern army, was marching under escort one hundred and fifty Camden prisoners down the road to Charles Town harbor to be detained on prison ships.

He informed Marion, and the entire brigade set out to rescue the patriots. In a stealthy night attack, the men approached the escort's camp. The fight lasted a matter of minutes. Before the astonished British guards had time to react, two of their number were killed, five wounded, and twenty taken prisoner. The brigade lost no men, and were able to set a hundred and fifty patriot captives free and confiscate many muskets.

Not long after, Francis Marion sent John with Henry Laurens on a mission to collect any intelligence they could about the movements of British troops into the interior of the state.

Now, their second night out, a freak storm broke just as they neared an old barn. Lightning lit the sky amidst the heavy downpour.

"Let's get inside!" Henry jumped from his mount and grabbed for the barn door.

Normally, they would skirt around the outside of the structure before entering, but they might be struck by lightning if they didn't get under shelter.

John helped pull the door wide…and nearly yelped at the musket aimed at his chest. An entire contingent of redcoats clustered in the building, with a long row of guns aimed at him and Henry.

John grabbed for his pistol, but a shot rent the air.

Shouts sounded as a blow struck him backward. Pain gripped his shoulder, and the swarm of redcoats rushed them. He was jerked up and spun around in the darkness and rain.

They dragged him inside the barn and finally placed him beside another man. His shoulder throbbed like a knife had been plunged into the flesh.

The soldiers threw Henry down beside him, and the man moaned as the men chained them together, then fastened them to the prisoner beside him. There was a whole row of people fastened together against this back wall.

One of the soldiers—a major, by the insignia on his coat— turned to another. "Here's two more for the harbor prisons. Wonder if we'll get a reward for every rebel we bring in?"

John shuddered as stories about the deadly British prison ships flowed across his mind. He pushed his handkerchief into the wound on his shoulder to staunch the bleeding while his thoughts spun.

Henry was working over his own arm, where blood seeped through his coat. He glanced up at John. "You all right, old man?"

"Yes." Then John lowered his voice. "We've got to think of some way to escape. Few survive the prison ships."

CHAPTER 14

Treason of the blackest dye was yesterday discovered. General Benedict Arnold who commanded at West Point, lost to every sentiment of honor, was about to deliver up that important post into the hands of the enemy. Such an event must have given the American cause a deadly wound. Happily, the treason has been timely discovered...affording the most convincing proof that the Liberties of America are the object of Divine Protection.
~ George Washington, September 26, 1780.

*A*nna swallowed her surprise when Lieutenant Palmer followed her to the parlor instead of heading up the stairs after the last meal. He and Captain Waring usually left early in the mornings for duty and retired soon after the evening repast.

The soldier stood in the doorway after she entered, twisting his white-trimmed tricorn. He cleared his throat. "Miss Anna, I would like to ask you if you'll accompany me to the officer's ball next month? I hope I'm not being too forward." He pulled his cravat looser around his neck.

"Oh, thank you for the invite, sir. But, I'm sorry, that wouldn't be possible." Why would she ever want to attend a ball of loyalists gloating over and celebrating their retaking of Charles Town?

Disappointment overshadowed his hopeful face.

She softened her tone and added, "You see, I have a great deal of responsibility here. I don't have the time it would take to prepare for a ball or keep the late hours it would entail."

He ducked his head. "I understand. Just thought I'd ask." He turned and hurried up the stairs. His boots stamped up to the third floor.

That night before she fell asleep, her mind did a somersault. What had she been thinking to turn down this great opportunity to listen to British conversation from their top officers? She punched her pillow. Tomorrow she'd inform the lieutenant she'd changed her mind and would be delighted to accompany him to the ball.

The day before the event, Aunt Reba put the finishing touches on a lovely new gown of gossamer peach satin studded with rosettes and bows, from fabric Uncle Rufus bought from a British merchant.

Helping Anna get ready the next day, Abigail's maid Esther turned Anna's thick, auburn hair into cascades of curls. Then, leaving a few loose curls to dangle to her shoulders, she piled the rest of the ringlets high on Anna's head and added a late rose bud from the front garden.

Before donning the gown, Anna slipped on a chemise, a stay, and then a hoop and two layers of petticoats. Her skirts blossomed out from her like a lovely flower. She donned satin slippers, pulled on white gloves, and picked up her matching wrap and sequined reticule.

Lieutenant Palmer's eyes bulged when he caught sight of her descending the stairs.

She smiled and, at the gate, took his extended hand, then stepped up into Uncle Rufus's borrowed carriage. Aunt Reba pushed and patted her bouffant skirts in around her, then closed the door, and they were off at a fast trot.

They arrived at the large house on Meeting Street that General Clinton chose as his residence. Lanterns lit the drive, and servants in green livery stood at attention to help arrivals disembark.

Anna took a deep breath and pulled her shawl up on her shoulders against the cool late November air. She pressed the one patriot blue rosette she'd insisted on for her gown, set in a row of peach ones near her waist.

The Clinton butler announced their arrival in a loud, bored voice. "Lieutenant David Palmer and Miss Anna Grace Laurens."

Heads turned in their direction for a moment, and heat climbed up Anna's neck. She glanced around at the officers and extravagant dresses of the women milling about in the ballroom. These leaders were the enemies of her country. She forced her face to serenity and smiled and curtsied as the lieutenant introduced her to other guests.

Captain Waring appeared at her left and gave a low whistle. His beady eyes devoured her. "Here is Charles Town's freshest flower, ready for the picking."

Lieutenant Palmer's nostrils flared, and his lips tightened. But he stood at attention to his superior officer.

Waring's escort, Della Ravenel, glared at Anna and leaned to whisper something into the captain's ear. They both laughed. Whatever her words, they seemed to work. After a quick wink at Anna, he turned and walked away with the woman clutching his arm.

The genuine test of Anna's resolve came when Palmer introduced her to British General Clinton in his dress uniform of striking red and blazing white. He wore a curled, creamy wig. How could she keep from betraying her strong dislike for the man who had bombarded Charles Town and taken so many patriot prisoners?

"Laurens, you say? I recognize that name. One of Charles Town's prominent families—at one time." His pale blue eyes scanned her up and down. "Palmer, you've captured a true southern belle." He laughed. "See that she remains loyal to His Majesty and she'll live a long life." He perhaps had already had a bit to drink, for his penetrating voice carried to those around them.

Nausea roiled in Anna's stomach, and it took all her will power not to give a heated retort.

A distinguished woman in luxurious attire, sparkling diamonds at her neck, and high powdered hair came near to Anna and drew her aside. She leaned to whisper to her while Lieutenant Palmer continued to talk with General Clinton and his aid. "My dear, don't look so panicky. You're not the only patriot here."

Anna turned to the woman's placid, lovely face. Had her dislike of the general showed so much? A trickle of concern shot up her spine.

The woman smiled, and her emerald eyes danced, as if they were discussing fabrics or the latest hair styles. "I'm Ruth Garfield Edmonds, dear. And we have to make the best of what's happened, for the time being. Contact me if you need help." She pressed a card into Anna's hand and whisked away, waving to another couple.

Anna placed the piece in her gown pocket. Who was the elegant woman? Could she be trusted?

After several dances with Lieutenant Palmer, and two with Captain Waring—who kept breaking in and holding her much too close—she pleaded for a breather. The lieutenant, his face stiff, nodded his head to the captain and took her elbow. He steered her toward the corner table spread with various finger foods and a huge urn of apple cider. She placed an iced petit four on her thin china plate and a cucumber sandwich wedge.

Palmer led her to a hall settee, away from the crowded ballroom, warm from its many candles and people.

She sighed and took a deep breath. "Thank you, lieutenant. I needed this break."

He smiled and bowed. "I'll return with our drinks in a moment."

Soon, he handed her a silver goblet with General Clinton's coat of arms pressed into it, then sat beside her.

She lifted the cup to her lips and took a thirsty sip. Instead of the sweet, refreshing apple cider she'd hoped for, the alcohol inside stung her lips and throat. She lowered the drink and placed it on a side table.

Palmer glanced her way and apologized. "Sorry, I should've known it would be pretty strong by this time of the evening. Let me see if I can find you something else." He arose and disappeared down the hall.

She remained still and leaned her head back against the wall. Voices from a room behind grew louder. When General Clinton's excited, penetrating voice spoke, she pressed her ear closer.

Words drifted through. "Benedict Arnold... And later, a place called Kings Mountain, and Blackstock's farm."

147

Those sounded like a man's name and places, but what did they mean?

Her escort returned with a cool glass of a minty drink, and she smiled and satisfied her thirst. "Would you mind if we leave now, Lieutenant? I'm exhausted. And it's almost midnight according to that clock." She gestured to the large timepiece in its cabinet on the opposite wall.

"No, ma'am, I wouldn't care at all." He stood, and she took his arm.

When they arrived at the house, he helped her from the carriage and walked her into the hall, where Aunt Reba had left a lantern burning.

Anna stopped at the foot of the stairs. "I'll say goodnight here. I have some things to finish before I retire."

He bowed. "May I say, I enjoyed your company?"

"Thank you, Lieutenant."

He turned to ascend, but glanced back. "And I add to that. You were the most beautiful lady at the ball." He paused a moment. "And I want to tell you, I like your city and this area a lot. Wouldn't mind settling here sometime."

Anna smiled, and he hurried up the stairs. At least one British officer was an authentic gentleman.

She walked into the parlor and sat, gathering her thoughts and energy. She moved to the desk and wrote the words she'd heard through the wall at General Clinton's on a piece of paper, then slipped it into her pocket. After placing her wrap around her shoulders, she lit a candle and headed out the back entrance to the stable to give the note to Thomas. Who he passed her missives to, she had no idea. John had told her it was best for no one to know much of the chain, just the next person to whom they were to pass their information.

When she entered the stable, Thomas startled her at the bottom of the stairs to his room. His eyes blazed in the candlelight. "Miss Anna, I'm so glad you came. I have bad news. Captain John and your brother Henry have fallen into the hands of redcoats. They're imprisoned on the British prison ship in the harbor." His whisper lay like lead in the icy darkness.

She found it hard to breathe. *Henry and John on a prison ship?*

Heavy footsteps echoed from the yard, and Anna covered a gasp. That must be Captain Waring. She blew out the candle.

Thomas moved into the shadows under the stairs, and she hid in an empty stable, trying her best to keep her gown from making a swishing noise. Shivers slipped down her spine.

Captain Richard Waring appeared in the entrance without his coat or hat. He stopped and reached to balance himself on the corner frame. "Come, come, my sweet Charles Town blossom. I saw you slip in here. Where are you? I know you've got a lover. I saw him the other time he was here. And I'll make quick work of him." His husky, rambling voice revealed he'd been drinking. He pulled his sword from its scabbard and swept it through the air, then fumbled and dropped the blade. He laughed and came farther into the stable.

Sheer black fright swept through her and blasted at her reasoning. *Henry and John on a prison ship and now this man to deal with.* She fought the weakness washing over her. If she gave into it, she'd faint.

The captain stopped near her hiding place. "I know you're here, my lovely. Don't hide from me. I just want to steal one kiss."

She swallowed hard and stepped out from the stall into his full view. "Yes, I'm here, and yes, I have a lover. But he didn't show up tonight, so please let me pass." She picked up her skirt as if to whisk past him. Her breath came in short spurts, and her heart lurched in her chest.

He caught her arm and pulled her hard against him. Stumbling backward, he fell onto the hay piled in the corner, with her in his arms. Laughing, he pressed her tight against him. "Now that's better. We can be real cozy, so relax."

She struggled, but his strength, though half drunk, shocked her. He flipped over, and she lay a prisoner pinned under his hard, muscled form. Panic welled within her as he forced her face to his and pressed his mouth against hers. She fought and pushed at him to no avail. He tore her skirt. She screamed, and he hit her.

A dark figure moved above the major's body. Thomas swung a shovel against the captain's head. A skull-cracking, terrible sound erupted from the forceful whack, and the captain fell aside without even a groan.

Anna sat up and stared in the darkness at the fallen man lying so still beside her. Something warm flowed onto her hand, which was still pressed on the barn floor near the major's body. She gasped, jerked it up, and wiped it on the hay. The smell of blood sickened her.

Thomas helped her stand, and she stumbled up and leaned against the stall door to catch her balance and breath.

Another figure entered the barn. Lieutenant Palmer stood outlined by moonlight in the entrance.

Thomas stiffened, his muscles bulged, still gripping the shovel.

A new round of fear rose in Anna as she stared at him. What would happen now? Would Thomas be hung for killing a British officer? A sob slipped through her lips as the emotion of it all caught up with her.

Palmer walked to the captain's body, stooped down, and felt his pulse. Then he rose and turned to her. "He's dead, but don't you worry, ma'am. I can see what happened, and it's not your fault or your man's."

Thomas threw down the shovel and took a ragged breath.

The Lieutenant glanced at him. "You had to protect your mistress." He turned and paced in the corridor for several moments. "Let me think what we should do."

Anna forced her sobs into silence and watched him moving back and forth. What would he do? Have her and Thomas shot?

Palmer stepped over toward her. "Ma'am, I urge you to return to the house. Act like nothing has happened. Tell no one." He turned to Thomas. "Your man will help me dig and bury the captain right here in the barn. Then we'll talk about what to do next."

She expelled a long, hoarse breath. Would he really take care of everything?

He handed her his handkerchief, and she wiped her wet face with trembling fingers.

"Can we trust your man to keep silent about this?"

Thomas, the whites of his eyes showing, nodded his head. "Yes, sir. You can."

Anna cleared her throat and whispered. "He will tell no one."

"Then go and get some rest. I'll stay here a little, tomorrow after breakfast. Will you walk in your garden with me?"

Anna, still struggling to breathe, commanded her heart to resume its normal beat. "Yes, of course."

She stepped around the body of Captain Waring and ran out of the barn, into the house, and to her room. Her satin slippers made little sound. She hurried to her chamber bowl and pushed her hands into the tepid water and scrubbed them. She fought the urge to throw up. When she stepped out of her gown and petticoats, she dropped onto her bed.

A murdered British officer in her barn and Henry and John on a prison ship.

She pressed her face into her pillow to silence the sobs erupting from deep within.

❦

The next morning, she and the Lieutenant walked in the garden, then sat on a bench shadowed by Aunt Reba's favorite rose trellis with still a few red buds in evidence.

Thank God her aunt left early for her shop and had not been at breakfast with Anna, or she'd have asked about Anna's tired countenance. Or wanted a full description of the ball. That party seemed a lifetime ago.

Palmer spoke first. "One thing in our favor, ma'am, is that after a party of the sort last night, it's not looked on unfavorable if some officers don't show up for a day, or even for two. But after that, a soldier threesome will hunt for them until they're accounted for. I'll do my best to explain that Captain Waring never returned to your house, but I expect they'll end up searching the place."

Anna appreciated his use of *our,* as if the terrible problem was his, as well as hers. The man's kindness astounded her.

~

*O*fficers did come three days later, but they searched the house and walked through the stable, then left.

But why did Anna still feel she and Thomas were in danger? And how could she ever hope to rescue Henry and John from the prison ship in the harbor? These thoughts plagued her, the latter even more than the first.

The following day as she prayed, she remembered the card the lady patriot had given her at the ball. She found her peach gown stuffed in the bottom of her chifferobe and drew the card from the pocket. The note she'd written to give to Thomas came with it.

She read the name on the woman's card, *Baroness Ruth Garfield Edmonds,* and the street address. The way to the house would be an easy walk for her.

After the mid-day meal, Anna pulled on leather walking shoes from her closet, a warm cloak, and a bonnet.

She called Thomas, and after handing him the note from the night of the ball, she asked him to accompany her. He followed her a reasonable distance behind, but close enough to alert the soldiers they passed not to become interested and try to accost her.

At the front gate of the impressive townhouse, she rang a small bell on the post. An energetic young man dressed in spotless black and white livery came from the entrance and bowed.

"I'm here to see Baroness Edmonds. Please tell her I'm Anna Grace Laurens."

He hurried inside, then returned within minutes and threw back the bar. She followed him up the high steps and into the warm recesses of a parlor. A fire blazed in the tall marble hearth.

Ruth Edmonds stood next to an ornate mantle in a lovely lavender morning gown. She moved forward and took Anna Grace's hand. "I'm so glad you came." She gestured to a rose-colored sofa and then, after ordering tea, sat across from Anna in a brocade chair. "I have tea twice a day. Can you enjoy a cup?"

She nodded. How she'd love to taste it, not having had any English tea since the war began.

The brew came in an exquisite blue china set like Anna had never seen. She accepted her cup when offered. "This is a lovely setting."

"Thank you. I picked it up my last trip to Europe before these...aggravating hostilities started."

Anna drank several sips, then moved from genteel conversation to the main issue at hand. "Can you tell me if it is possible to rescue someone from the prison ship in the harbor?"

Ruth's brows rose, and she smiled. "You don't waste words, do you? I'd say it's possible, but not at all easy."

"How should one proceed?"

The woman, carrying her cup, rose and walked to the window, then glanced out. "I am expecting a visitor within the hour, and we must finish this conversation another time. But first, tell me who is it you wish to rescue?"

"My brother Henry and Captain John Vargas."

Ruth Edmonds dropped her cup. The blue china shattered on the polished wooden floor and splashed warm brown liquid on the hem of her gown.

CHAPTER 15

These are times that try men's souls...Tyranny, like hell, is not easily
conquered. The harder the conflict, the more glorious the triumph.
~ Thomas Paine

John groaned and fought his way up a long, black tunnel.
He awoke cold, lying on hard damp boards. A rat scurried
across his chest, down his leg, and dropped to the floor.
He reached up with his right hand to rub his eyes and wrinkled his
nose at the sickening odor as he remembered where he was. In the
Charles Town harbor on the British prison ship *Torbay*.

Moans and curses flowed through the putrid air of the dark hold
packed with prisoners.

"Welcome back to the living, John—if we can call this horrid place
that."

He turned to the nearby familiar voice. Henry Laurens sat beside
him, a sad smile creasing his dry lips.

Great thirst pierced John's throat and mind. He could find no
moisture in his mouth to swallow, and sudden heat flashed through
his body. Dragging himself up to a sitting position, he groaned aloud
as gusts of fire singed his left shoulder. The bullet still in there must

be causing infection and fever. Henry had helped him keep it wrapped tight to stop the bleeding.

"How long have we been here?" His voice came out weak and cracking.

"Three days to my count, but I can't be sure as we're in darkness so much. I think it's now morning on the fourth day, if that bit of light escaping around the hatch is any sign." He turned to examine John in the shadows. "How are you making it? Maybe the ship doctor will show up soon, if there is one."

"I woke up again, so I'm surviving."

"That's the way. Today is the day for bread with the soup, I think."

John closed his eyes and tried to take deeper breaths of the putrid air to clear his mind. Bread with weevils, foul water, and soup inedible to most, except the starving. They must get off this ship or they'd die.

As if his thought of death unleashed that specter's power, the hatch opened and a harsh voice called down, "Rebels, hand up your dead."

Henry stood. "Let me check on our mates." His arm, grazed by a bullet, still held its wrapping of the stormy night in the barn.

In the light from above, John made out two other prisoners with less serious wounds moving about the packed hold, reaching down and checking those who lay still and silent.

Three British soldiers crawled down steps. One kept his musket aimed for any insurrection, while the other two noted the ones who had died during the night. They kicked their stiff bodies and directed Henry and his helpers to hand them up to others waiting above.

Four bodies thus lifted from the hold would soon end up overboard into the Charles Town harbor. John gritted his teeth. Lack of fresh water, food, and medical help resulted in deaths each night.

He closed his eyes as his head swam, and blackness crowded from the edge of his consciousness. He must pray before that darkness took him. *Father God, please send aid.* Then he started thinking the words of a scripture he'd learned at his mother's knee.

The Lord is my shepherd; I shall not want.
He maketh me to lie down in green pastures;
he leadeth me beside the still waters.

He restoreth my soul: he leadeth me in the paths
of righteousness for his name's sake.
Yea, though I walk through the valley
of the shadow of death, I will fear no evil:
For thou art with me.

~

*A*nna hurried to dress and reached for her warmest cloak to walk to Ruth Edmonds for their next meeting. The woman had promised to find out everything she could about the prison ships in the harbor. Two weeks had passed since they'd talked.

She dropped by Abigail's room, bent and picked up Baby Philip, then gave him a big kiss on a rosy cheek.

"What are your plans today, Anna? You seem excited." Abigail stood next to a table folding cloth nappies and baby clothing.

"Trust me, something most important which I cannot talk about. But please pray, my friend, that all goes well."

Abigail nodded. "I will."

Anna donned her cloak, then skipped down the stairs and out the gate.

Faithful Thomas followed her as she made her way down the streets to the baroness's house.

Christmas boughs of holly and ivy lined the porch railing, and a large, pine-smelling wreath with red ribbons adorned the front entrance.

Ruth led her into the familiar parlor, and Anna removed her cloak and gloves. She warmed herself for a few moments by the blazing fire, then sat.

As they sipped tea, the woman spoke. "I've found out some very disturbing things about the prison ships. It's an absolute shame how the patriot prisoners are being treated."

Anna's heart lurched, and she placed her cup back on the table. "Did you...find out anything about my brother Henry or John Vargas? Are they...?"

"They are still alive, my source has assured me. But we must make a plan to get them rescued as soon as possible."

Anna swallowed fear that threatened to close her throat. "Are either of them injured?"

"They both had wounds, but they are surviving. However, they need medical care and decent food and blankets, now that it's winter."

Tears gathered in Anna's eyes.

Ruth patted her hand. "I've talked with some powerful women in the city who are ready to do something for the prisoners, especially for Christmas. What do you think about a late Christmas Day visit with food, good water, and blankets for them?"

Her heart leapt with hope. "Oh, Mrs. Edmonds, can this be possible?"

"I think so. I'm organizing it myself." She leaned forward. "But my idea is for you and maybe old Doc Jones to go aboard with the goods. And can you get a message to Marion that a rescue attempt would be best on Christmas Day when few guards will stay on the ship?"

Anna couldn't breathe. "Yes. I believe I might."

"You, of course, will take charge of John Vargas, since his wound is the serious one, and get him to help. Do you know of a safe place to take him?"

Anna nodded. *Salt March.* Could she somehow bring him to his parents' hideaway? She left the house beaming with new hope.

Aunt Reba assured her she'd be praying for the success of the rescue. And when Anna gave Thomas a note for Marion's men, he pledged his full support in the venture. She would help Henry and John, and many other captives, too.

~

Christmas Day dawned overcast and cold, which, to Anna, was all the better. Most of Charles Town would be inside beside their hearths, celebrating the holiday. And soldiers without family in town would be in the taverns imbibing for hours.

At five o'clock in the evening, she filled a basket with bread, cheese, two thick wool blankets, and flasks of water, then donned her warmest cloak and hood. Thomas accompanied her to the harbor, carrying a separate package with two warm cloaks.

A cart waited near Uncle Rufus's mercantile, just like Ruth Edmonds told her it would be. Piled with food, water, and blankets, the sight made her heart sing.

Instead of old Doc Jones, Rufus, appeared. Without words, they walked around back to his dock and the roomy longboat tied there, bobbing in the tide. He and Thomas loaded the food and blankets onto the boat, then she, Thomas, and Rufus boarded. They rowed out to the *Torbay*.

A red-coated soldier looked over the railing, pointed his musket, and called out to them. "Halt, who are you?"

Rufus stood and waved, then read aloud the paper giving them permission to bring the food and blankets aboard, signed by Commander Balfour himself.

Anna smiled at how fast the soldier lowered his weapon. Ruth Edmonds had taken care of every detail.

With Uncle Rufus's help she sat in the deck swing and the soldier above lifted her aboard. The terrible smell of the ship assailed her nose, and the sight of men almost skin and bones sitting or lying along the deck, clutched at her heart.

Rufus and Thomas sent up the food and blankets, and then boarded to help with the distribution. Anna blinked back tears as the men reached for the water jugs first, and then the food with hearty thanks. They ate and drank like starving people. She walked down the row of prisoners twice, and wanted to cry when she could not find Henry or John among them.

When she asked a guard if this was all the captives, he pointed down the hatch. She climbed down the steps into semi-darkness and into a most awful stench and brittle cold, but her heart leaped when she saw Henry first, then John lying beside him.

Making her way over to them, she reached out, and Henry gripped her in a hug. He gave no evidence of being wounded, although he was much thinner. He bent down and prodded John, who appeared unconscious.

Anna stooped beside him and muffled a sob at his pitiful condition. He'd lost weight, too, and a bandage with dried blood on it covered his left shoulder.

"John." She pressed his hand. "I'm here to take you away."

He opened his eyes, and they seemed lucid for a moment. "Anna?"

"It is I."

He reached his good arm out to touch her hair that had escaped her hood. "You're a beautiful apparition."

She took his hand in hers and pressed it. "I am no ghost."

He stared at her as if he still wasn't certain she was real.

Henry leaned down. "She's real, John. Let's get you up and see what's happening on deck."

Henry placed his arm under John and helped him sit, then stand, being careful not to jar his injured shoulder.

John still stared at Anna as if he expected her to disappear.

She gave them the cloaks she'd brought, and then moved to the hatch and called for Rufus and Thomas.

As they got John up on deck, a shout sounded near the rail. Angry voices, then a gunshot split the air.

Anna bit back a scream as she hovered beside John and Henry, with Thomas and Uncle Reuben crouching in front of them.

More shots volleyed back and forth. Then a host of men clambered over the rail to board the ship, dressed in deerskin and fur hats.

Within minutes, the ship guards laid down their weapons. The militia tied up the British soldiers and dismantled the bell they would've rung for help, then threw it overboard.

"My friends from the brigade." Henry called as he looked across the deck. He laughed and shook hands with several of the newcomers. "God bless you men, good to see you." He turned back to Anna. "How did you manage this, dear sister? I'm well enough to rejoin with these great rescuers, but you must find John some help."

"Yes." Her word came over her shoulder as she was busy helping Rufus and Thomas get John off the *Torbay* and down into their boat.

William Burns hurried toward them, then gripped John's hand. "Well, me lad, you're in excellent hands now and on the way to mending, no doubt. I'm going with you." He smiled at Anna and assisted John into the swing, then began lowering him into the longboat. When John was settled, William skittered down the rope himself into the small vessel.

Before leaving, Anna turned toward Henry, who came and gave her a powerful hug. "Take care, dear sister, and get my friend John well. If anyone can do it, you are the one to see to it. An old surgeon got the bullet out of his shoulder, but pain and fever indicate infection." He looked into her eyes. "I've heard your name from his delirious lips many a night. Is there a returned regard from you?"

She took a deep breath. "Yes. But I don't know what you can tell Burton."

He laughed. "Don't give a second thought to Rand. I believe he's found another interest."

Another interest? So Burton's declarations of love for her had flown away with the winds of war. A tinge of sadness tripped through her but only for a moment. *I wish you well, childhood friend.*

Henry gave her a last embrace and hurried to the leaders of the brigade disembarking on the other side of the ship. Every prisoner able to walk joined them.

Once seated in their skiff, Anna opened her basket and placed a flask of water to John's parched lips as William held him up. Her heart ached at the sight of him so sick. He drank several gulps, and then leaned down against her in weakness. She got a piece of cheese into his mouth and then some bread. He washed it down with more liquid.

William and Rufus pushed the oars with ease across the water draped in lengthening evening shadows.

It was several minutes before she noticed they had arrived back at the mercantile dock, but neither her uncle nor Thomas attempted to help John or her out of the boat. Mist hung heavy over them.

"Uncle, what's...?"

He grinned at her. "Thomas and William are going to help you get John to his parents' place, where they can nurse him back to health."

With that, he uncovered a small sail and mast hidden in the dinghy's bottom. After lifting the sailing piece, he secured it, and then stepped up on the dock and waved.

Could it be possible? Could a longboat make it across the waves over the distance to Salt Marsh?

The little sail caught the wind, and the vessel took off with Thomas guiding it. Anna ceased wondering how the craft would stand on its own in deep ocean waters.

As the cold December night settled down on them with its damp sea breeze, she found more blankets in a gunny sack in the boat's bottom. Her uncle's forethought, no doubt. John sighed when she placed another blanket around him, and spread a second covering over her own and William's legs as well. After she tossed one to Thomas, she pulled her hood over her head to block out the chilly breeze and lifted John's, almost covering his head as William held him on the seat.

"That's a good lassie. Don't you go fretting any. The Lord is going to take care of us this Christmas night." The man's Scottish burr and confidence reassured Anna.

A soft amen came from Thomas's direction.

Heading out of the moonlit Charles Town harbor, covered by God-sent mists, in the smallest sailing vessel she'd ever imagined, Anna fell into a dreamy state. She gripped John's hand and continued to hold it when his grip relaxed, and his head slipped down to her shoulder. Would she ever forget this Christmas night sailing to Salt Marsh from the harbor?

A prayer rose from her inner being.

Thank you, Lord God, for helping us rescue John and Henry and the other patriots. Please keep Henry safe as he rejoins Marion's militia. Could you also help us make it to Salt Marsh with no confrontation from the British? And bring full healing to John.

CHAPTER 16

I like the dreams of the future better than the history of the past.
~ Thomas Jefferson

 nder cover of darkness, the longboat slipped out of the
Charleston Harbor into the open sea. They passed within
yards of British man-of-war vessels that arose in the mist before
them, bobbing in the tide like ghost ships. Their scant or drunk
holiday crews never gave an alert or shout as their small sailboat
glided by. Thanks be to God.

Anna must have dropped off into slumber, because the next time
she realized anything other than the biting cold, someone called her
name. Opening her eyes, she saw streaks of pink, gold and azure
painted across the eastern horizon.

"Miss Anna, we'll soon be at the dock. Are you all right?" Thomas
smiled at her.

She shook herself and inhaled a deep breath of the bracing air.
"Yes, and thank God, we're almost there. I hope you mean Salt Marsh."

"That's what he means, ma'am." William spoke, still holding the
blanket close over John, who leaned against his shoulder.

Anna reached under the wool coverlet and found John's hand. Her heart plummeted at its coldness. Her eyes flew to William's. "His hand...is so cold."

William pushed the hood back from his friend's face, showing the color in his cheeks and his breath making steam in the freezing morning air. She breathed a sigh of relief.

"Don't you fuss, miss. John's a sturdy lad. It'd take more than a bullet in the shoulder to put him down. He's just a little chilled like the rest of us."

The next few minutes, Thomas guided the boat toward a dock shrouded in weeds. How did the youth find it in the early light? A large farm bell hung from a wooded cross board secured between two poles. In the distance, an imposing house appeared through the morning mists.

Salt Marsh? John's parents' hideaway?

Thomas tied the vessel to the wharf and stepped out. He picked up the swinging mallet and hit the signal.

Anna jumped at its loud peal, and then laughed. How wonderful to be somewhere a little noise was all right.

A black man and woman soon ran down the path to the dock, with others following.

Thomas spoke to them, and they helped lift John from the boat. William assisted, keeping the blankets around his captain.

She tried to stand, but found her legs cold and stiff. She stamped her feet and swung her arms until her limbs gained strength. The black woman reached down to help her onto the dock. Her smile warmed Anna, and she tried to fall in beside her and follow the others up the trail to the house. But somehow her head didn't seem right. The narrow walk, the trees and the people, faded from her sight, and she slid to the ground.

Thomas's cry of "Miss Anna!" was the last thing she remembered.

*A*nna stretched and took a deep breath. How wonderful to revel in warm blankets, dry and safe. But all her muscles ached as if she'd done tremendous physical labor.

The older black woman standing beside Anna's bed spoke the minute she opened her eyes. "You've slept a long time, young lady, and you're going to be fine. You just need a little rest and lots of good soup. I've done made some for you and John and the others who come down the ocean coast in the middle of winter. You all got too cold." She gestured to a steaming bowl sat on the bedside table.

Anna smiled as memories surfaced. "You are Mammy June?"

"Yes'm, that's who I am, and I 'members you, too. Seems like we done this one time before." Then the woman's coffee-colored face broke into a most wondrous smile that lit up her elderly countenance and white teeth like sunshine.

Anna glanced up at the bed's scalloped canopy, trimmed in an embroidered ruffle that matched the blue damask curtains at two tall windows. A luxurious rug covered most of the floor she could see.

Sitting up, she allowed the servant to place a tray with the soup on her lap. The warm goodness was just the thing her body needed, and she spooned every drop of the delicious broth into her mouth.

As she finished, a knock sounded at the door, and a woman with blond hair streaked with gray entered. She swished over to the bed in her yellow gown and took Anna's hand. "Thank you, thank you, my dear, for rescuing and bringing our John home." Tears brightened her azure blue eyes.

The warm touch seeped through Anna. The touch of a mother. "Well, I did have quite a bit of help. You are John's mother, I believe?"

"Yes. Georgia Ann Vargas. We have been bombarding heaven for his rescue ever since we learned they'd captured him and put him on a prison ship."

Anna sat up. "How is he? Will he be all right?"

A tear escaped down Mrs. Vargas's cheek, and she pulled a lace handkerchief from her sleeve to dab at it. "He's going to get well. But I don't mind telling you, I am shocked at the weight he's lost, and there's a strong infection at his wound site."

Mammy June cleared her throat. "Ain't nothing our doctoring and the good Lord can't make right."

Mrs. Vargas glanced at her and smiled. "You're correct, dear friend. It may take some time, but I'm sure our son will soon recover. Thank God he's home. Now if you'll excuse me, I'll go see how everything, including dinner, is coming along."

She and Mammy June left, and Anna swung her feet from the bed, donned a robe, and walked out onto the balcony. A beautiful sight greeted her. Tall oak trees covered in hanging gray moss swayed in the wind. Beyond them, an outline of a white sandy beach stretched across the horizon. As she listened, the soothing swish of waves splashed against rocks, and the cries of a lone seagull floated on the cool, damp December breeze.

When a maid came with a pan of water and a cloth, she bathed and dressed in a borrowed green gown sent from Mrs. Vargas. She followed the young servant down the stairs and to a large dining room with a table spread for dinner. The seated men rose as she entered.

"Here she is. Anna Grace, I want you to meet John's grandparents, Ethan and Marisol Becket, and you know his father, Samuel." Mrs. Vargas gestured to them as she spoke.

"Great to meet you, Anna." Ethan Becket gave her a warm smile..

His grandmother stood and hugged her. "How grateful we are you could devise a way to get our grandson off that prison ship."

"Yes, we certainly are," John's father echoed.

"I didn't make the escape plan. I just walked it out. We had several great helpers." She gestured to William. "This man has been a real blessing to John, both before and after the capture."

He ducked his head and grinned.

"A kind woman in Charles Town set up the Christmas Day rescue. I just followed instructions." Anna sat at the table beside John's mother.

Mrs. Vargas unfolded her napkin in her lap and turned to Anna with her brow furrowed. "A sympathetic woman in the city? Of whom do you speak?"

"Baroness Ruth Garfield Edmonds."

Mrs. Vargas gasped, her face paled, and the napkin slipped from her clasp to the floor.

A servant standing nearby replaced the cloth and retrieved the one dropped.

Anna looked around the table at the faces turned toward her. "I assumed she knew your family. Do you know her?"

John's father answered her question. "We do. In fact, she and John grew up together. If she had a hand in the rescue, then we certainly thank God for her help." He motioned to the servants to begin serving.

Grew up together? Why did Ruth never mention that fact? Anna wiped the surprise from her face and smiled. "That explains it. She wanted to help her childhood friend."

When the servants came to serve her, she took small portions of roasted chicken, squash, peas, and cornbread. But the beautiful face and elegant figure of Ruth Edmonds filled her mind. How close were she and John? Why did she not mention her childhood spent with him?

~

*J*ohn threw the covers off his fevered body. He looked above him at the familiar canopy and around the room he knew so well. *Salt Marsh.* How had he escaped the prison ship?

Jumbled memories of William and Anna holding him on a longboat bench floated through his mind. And the bitter cold and darkness for hours. He closed his eyes and willed some of that coolness to come back now.

The door opened, and a figure entered, then made a swishing sound toward his bed. The tinkle of water came from the bedside table, and a cool compress landed on his forehead. He arched into it and took a deep breath of relief.

"John, it's me. Can you hear me?"

His mother's voice, full of concern, broke through the fog. He wanted to answer but couldn't seem to make words come forth. He moved his hand, and a smaller soft one took hold of his.

"Father God, in Jesus's name, I command this fever to go. Thank You for bringing healing to John from this infection. Please show us whatever we need to do to help him."

Someone else entered the room with a heavier tread. Voices spoke. Why couldn't he answer and let them know he was all right? He thrashed his legs in annoyance.

The sheet came back over his body.

"Oh, Mammy, what can we do? Is he worse?" A sob echoed above him.

"No ma'am, he ain't worse. It's just that fever working its way out. We done what needs doing, now we just needs to let the herbs we put on that wound and in the broth we feeding him do their work."

John slipped away into blackness.

Sometime later, a loud voice awoke him, and he opened his eyes and looked about. His mother, father, grandparents, Anna Grace, and Mammy June stood around his bed, holding hands with their heads bowed.

His grandfather's strong, pastoral voice filled the room. "...Father God we praise and worship You as the one true God. We come boldly to Your throne room of mercy and grace to ask Your help. Jesus, our Great Physician reach Your hand down and touch John. Your word says in Psalm 103, 'Bless the Lord, O my soul, who forgives all your iniquities and heals all your diseases. Who redeems your life from destruction.' Let this mighty promise now break forth for our son and grandson. We trust his healing is coming, so we thank and praise You. Amen."

Other voices repeated the amen.

He joined in. "Amen."

Gasps came from those around his bedside, shifting into grins all around. He returned with his own smile.

His mother bent down to him. "John, dear son, how do you feel?"

"Well, I'm tired of this bed, I can promise you that. How long have I been in it?"

His mother looked at Mammy June. "Is it…should he…?"

"He should do whatever he feels like doing." The servant reached for John's hand and helped him sit up. "You been in this bed for three days."

He swung his legs to the floor and fought dizziness. He shook his head and took deep breaths.

Mammy patted his shoulder. "Just take yo' time now, sir. Sit there a while until more strength comes."

The others around the bed clapped and praised God. Anna swiped a tear from her cheek.

When he gained enough power to stand, both his father and grandfather took hold to help stabilize him. They assisted his steps to a chair, and he sank into it.

He looked down at the wrinkled tan knee britches covering his legs. "Where are my clothes?"

The women left the room, and he dressed with the aid of his father and grandfather.

The first meal he had with the family proved tiring, and he fell back into his bed for a nap. The image of Anna's lovely, radiant face at the mid-day meal filled his mind as he fell asleep.

MARCH 1781

*O*ne cool, spring evening, Anna walked in the garden, which covered an acre on the left side of the big house. Not even the bright yellow daffodils and rows of crocus with splashy colors that lined the path could still the worry in her spirit. She wanted to pray, but felt more like screaming.

Why would John want to go back to Marion's militia so soon? He had regained some strength, but not all his former weight. Let William return if he wanted to. But hadn't John done enough? His mother's plea the night before marched across her mind, and she agreed with it.

Someone stepped behind her and pressed broad hands over her eyes. She gasped, and the scent of rawhide and spice flowed across her nose.

John.

He dropped his hands and fell in step beside her, wearing his militia shirt, hat, and boots. "Hello, beautiful lady in our garden. May I join you?"

She looked at his strong face and square chin, now almost back to its normal width and color. He'd spent some days the past few weeks with his father and servants on the rice fields, preparing for a new season.

She stopped and put her hands on her hips. "John, do you really believe you should rejoin the militia so soon? Didn't Morgan's victory at Cowpens mean the war has turned and will soon be over?" Anna had rejoiced with the entire household when that news reached them in February. "Yes, that was a decisive win, and we thank God for it." He glanced away from her frown. "But there's still much to do to win our independence. The war is not over." He looked around the garden. "Even Salt Marsh will not stay safe forever if we don't do what we can now. The British are confiscating plantations of patriots and selling them for pittances or giving them to Tories, if they don't burn them."

He turned back to her and put his hands on her shoulders, studying her. His gaze pierced in a way she couldn't look away from. "What kind of man would I be to stay here enjoying the quiet, the good food," he smiled, "and seeing you every day, when other fine men like Henry and Burton and all Marion's soldiers, and Morgan's and Sumter's and General Pickens's forces are still risking their lives daily to win our independence?"

Anna stamped her foot. But she also knew when to give it up. She shrugged off his hands and moved down the path.

He followed beside her.

The weight on her chest pressed harder as she forced herself to accept what she couldn't change. "When will you be leaving?"

"William and I will leave in two weeks."

"How about Thomas? I heard he wants to go."

"I will do everything in my power to get him to stay home."

"How will you find the militia? Don't they stay on the move?"

"We'll search until we discover them." He stopped on the path. "Anna, I would like for you to remain at Salt Marsh. Charles Town is much too dangerous for any patriots now. I've heard of two women of excellent reputation, unmarried sisters named Saracen, who were arrested and put into the dungeon under the Exchange, packed in a cell with common criminals. The trumped up charge? Suspected of sending out rebel information. You'll be safer with my family here. Will you promise to stay until I return?"

She sighed. Should she remain after he left? She answered him with the question still warm in her mind. "Did your mother tell you that Ruth Edmonds helped make your escape from the prison ship possible?" She searched his face for a sign of his thoughts.

His lips thinned. "Yes."

"Well, why would she do that? What was your relationship with her? I only know that your father said you grew up together."

He took a deep breath and gestured for her to sit on a nearby bench. He sat beside her, his face stiff.

"Ruth and I were once...engaged, but she chose to marry the baron. That's the beginning, the middle, and the end of the story." His green eyes softened, and he smiled at her. "Of course, I'm grateful for whatever she did to help our escape. I was surprised to hear it, as most of our heated arguments were about her loyalty to the king."

He stood, pulled Anna up with him, and swept her into his arms. His hat fell off, but he didn't reach down for it.

Her heartbeat raced, and she tried to throttle the dizzying current rippling through her. His closeness, so male, so bracing, thrilled her.

"Let's not waste any time we have left thinking about loyalists, and you haven't answered my question. Will you stay at Salt Marsh?" The warmth of his gaze caressed her face, making it hard to think about his words.

She managed a breathy response. "Is there a good reason I should?"

"There's this reason." His whispered words moved close to her face, his warm breath feathered her cheek. "Will you marry me, Anna? Now, before I return to the militia? My grandfather can marry us."

Her heart imploded with joy. "Yes, but now? Like, this week?"

"As soon as possible." He reached inside his coat. "I don't have a ring, but my grandmother gave me this to give to the girl I want to marry." He pulled a lovely ruby brooch from his pocket and held it out to her.

Anna took it as her mind raced through all that was happening. She traced the V scrolled in beautiful golden filigree across the top with her finger. "Does the letter stand for Vargas?"

"No, it stood for her maiden name, Valentin, but for us it will stand for Vargas."

He drew her into his arms and touched her lips with his own, and then pressed his mouth hard against hers. The kiss sent the pit of her stomach into a wild swirl, and she curved into his embrace.

"John, Anna?" A voice echoed down the path from the house.

He released her, and she sank onto the bench as his mother came around the bend in the trail.

She eyed them both before speaking. "Sorry, if I've interrupted anything, but John, there's a man who has arrived asking to see you. He looks like he's come a long way." She glanced at them both again, raised her brows and then added, "Have you two anything to tell me?"

Heat climbed up Anna's neck.

John grinned and stooped to grab his hat. "Mother, I've just asked Anna to marry me, now before I go back to the militia, and she's agreed. Do you think grandfather can marry us?"

His mother smiled. "I don't see why not, if you're both sure."

He plopped the bicorn atop his thick black hair. "We are." He gave Anna a warm grin and headed up the path.

As the tap of his footsteps faded away, only the twitter of birds sounded around them. Georgia Vargas was studying her, and Anna met her gaze and took a deep breath. So much had just happened, she could barely contain the jumble of emotions spinning inside her.

Married. John had proposed…and wanted to marry right away. Before he left. Or had she been dreaming? She pinched her arm to make sure.

As his mother approached and sat on the bench beside Anna. The reality of his leaving settled over her with a great weight. John would leave right after they wed.

Tears rose up to sting her eyes, and she didn't have the strength to hold them back. How could she let him go?

John's mother patted her hand. "I've known you love my son and that he loves you. But we can't keep him here, can we? Not when there's a war to be won." She handed a handkerchief to Anna.

Anna used the cloth to clean her face.

Georgia turned a kind glance on her. "John is our only child, and I love him like I love my own life. Over the years, I've learned in my worst anxieties about him when he pursues dangerous paths, that there is only one thought that can comfort me and quiet my worried soul."

Anna reached for the hope the woman offered. "What is it?"

"He belongs to God, not to me or to Samuel, and God loves him better than we could ever love him. He can protect him when we can do nothing but pray. That is the reminder that brings me a measure of peace." She patted Anna's hand. "Besides, may I remind you we now have a wedding to plan?"

Anna smiled and wiped away the rest of her tears. Yes, they had to get ready for her marriage to the man she loved with all her heart. She was not dreaming.

"And don't misunderstand when I say we can do nothing but pray. Prayer is a mighty weapon, and it can work miracles."

Anna nodded, meeting the woman's gaze. "I witnessed that when your family gathered and prayed for John when he was so sick."

"John told me he'd planned to ask you to marry, and to make Salt Marsh your home. Will you stay with us when he goes back to the militia?"

Anna took a deep breath. "If you'll have me, but I want to do my part. Tell me anything I can help with."

Georgia smiled. "Of course, we'll find something. Helping me keep this garden clear of weeds is a needed job." She stood and held out her hand. "Come, let's see what this stranger wants with John. We may have our prayer task cut out for us."

Anna rose to walk alongside her.

They proceeded up the path as the last rays of sun flickered over the garden and enveloped them in purple shadows.

Entering the house, John came out of the parlor toward them. The stranger with mud-splattered clothing stood behind him in the doorway with his hat in his hand. William Burns stood next to the visitor. Both men nodded a greeting to Anna and Mrs. Vargas. Their faces looked stiff and something else. Apologetic?

John's eyes, dark and shadowed, sought Anna's, then his mother's. "I have news. Francis Marion has sent for me and William to come as soon as possible. He has some special plans coming up, and he needs every man."

Anna's breath caught in her throat.

He placed his strong hands on her shoulders and looked into her face, his lips tight. "I'm sorry, dearest, but we must leave tonight as fast as we can pack and our visitor can get a decent meal and exchange his horse. We will take the barge across to the mainland."

His mother glanced at her before responding. "If you must go, son, our prayers will be with you. I'll send a servant to alert your father and grandfather."

Anna tried to stop tears from gathering in her eyes, but without success. He was leaving tonight. Not only would there not be time for them to marry, but she would have to say goodbye to him. What if this was their final farewell? As the tears blurred her gaze, she turned and fled to her room.

Somehow, she made it back down the stairs two hours later to bid farewell to John. He stood alone at the bottom of the steps, dressed in his militia garb and gear. He gathered her into his powerful arms, and his scent of rawhide, musket oil, and fresh clothing enveloped her. His lips found hers and burned a memory into her heart, bursting with love and anguish.

He lifted his head, and she looked up into his green eyes blazing with emotion. "Do you know how much I love you, Anna Grace?"

She wanted to speak, but only a sob escaped her lips, so she nodded, and pressed her head to his chest. His heartbeat drummed against her cheek.

"God willing, I'll come back to you, and we'll celebrate our marriage, and maybe the birth of a new nation at the same time." His voice broke, and he released her, turned, and strode out the front entrance. His heavy boots and sword clanging at his side filled the empty hallway with their familiar final sounds.

She followed to the doorway and watched him jump onto his horse and wave to his parents and grandparents standing in the circle of light from the porch. Thomas smiled from his mount. So he was going, too. Good. He and William would both help watch out for John.

As all four men galloped away into the enfolding darkness, a tear plopped down Anna's cheek. She folded her arms around herself and whispered a prayer. *Lord, bring him back to me safely. Please.*

CHAPTER 17

What I can do for my country, I am willing to do.
~ Carolina Sons of Liberty leader, Christopher Gadsden, 1776

Through the rest of spring and middle of summer, Anna did her part around the plantation house. The constant labor helped relieve her mind from worry about how John was faring in the war for independence. She kept his lovely engagement brooch on a ribbon around her neck.

John's mother, grandmother, and Mammy June taught Anna much about the management of Salt Marsh, showing her many work tasks, and which servants had certain responsibilities. She learned about the seasonal cycles of a plantation household.

Standing in the kitchen alcove one morning, Georgia told her, "In the fall and winter, the slaughtering of hogs and sheep take place, and we salt or smoke the meat to keep through the summer. Have you ever seen that done?"

"No." Anna had been too busy riding horseback at home when her own mother supervised such labors.

"Of course, right now in spring and summer, our big job is growing, harvesting, and finding ways to store vegetables and fruits, along with some candle and soap-making."

Anna took a deep breath. "I'd like to try my hand at the latter."

Under Mammy's and Georgia Vargas's supervision, she did, indeed, manage a few decent candles and bars of soap. She saved one of each in her room to show John.

Later that week, she helped pickle vegetables and fruit with vinegar and salt, and spread layers of peas on a pallet to dry in the scorching sun.

One day, John's mother showed her the account book in which she recorded all the labors by date when completed. She even kept track of when she opened a barrel of flour or broke into a loaf of sugar, and which hams fed the family, and which the rice field workers received.

After closing the record book, she looked at Anna and smiled. "Salt Marsh has a secret entrance and exit I want to show you."

Anna's heart tripped. "A secret way in and out?"

"Yes. Come with me." Mrs. Vargas picked up a lantern and two pair of gloves, and then started down the long first-floor hall.

Anna followed to the far end where steps led downward. A door stood in the wall at the bottom. Why had she never noticed it before?

John's mother unlocked the door with a key from the ring at her waist, and they entered a modest bedroom with a bunk bed, table, two chairs, and a fireplace with a narrow bookcase on one side, and stacks of wood on the other. The meager light came from a miniature barred window set high in the wall.

The woman placed the lantern on the table and sat in a chair. She motioned for Anna to sit. "Did you ever hear of the Yemassee massacre?"

Anna placed her hands in her lap. "It was an Indian uprising, but it happened long before I was born, so I know little about it."

"It was a terrible time for the colonists. I was a child of about three, so I learned much of the story as I grew up. The Indians had their tomahawks and scalping-knives, and guns provided by England's enemy in Florida, the Spaniards. They would come upon outlying plantations, corner the poor family in their rooms, and slaughter every living soul, including children. Many horrible stories filled the conversations for years."

"What a terrible time. How did your family escape?"

"My father saved our people by fleeing to Charles Town. After the Indians were subdued, many plantation owners decided to build secret exits from their houses, an escape route, in case anything like that ever happened again. Remembering those stories, I asked Samuel for one here when we built Salt Marsh. Let's put on these gloves before we proceed." She slipped her hands into a pair and handed the other to her.

Anna's heart thudded in her chest as she drew on the work gloves.

Mrs. Vargas stood, locked the bedroom door, and then walked to the fireplace. On the same side as the bookcase, she reached up to a certain brick, high enough to be cool to touch even with fire in the grate. She pulled the brick away. Behind it, in the recessed area, Anna caught a gleam of metal.

John's mother pointed out two levers, and Anna stood on her tip toes to see them. "The right pedal will unlock the passage, the left one, close it." The woman turned the first lever, and the bookcase beside them swung open with a soft grating sound.

Anna jumped and gasped. A musty, cool, damp scent flowed into the room.

"We have to keep all these hinges well-oiled." Mrs. Vargas moved to pick up the lantern from the table, then she entered the secret passage. Anna followed her through to a landing, which also had two gears set in the wall.

After Anna stood on the landing with her, the woman moved a lever and the bookshelf door closed behind them. She started down steps into what looked like darkness, lit only by her lantern. "Follow me, but watch your step. There is a rail on both sides of the wall you can hold onto if you need to."

Taking an excited breath, Anna gathered her skirt in one hand and reached for the bar with the other, then started down the steps. Heavy wooden beams braced the ceiling as it slanted downward. Narrow gratings above her head admitted a little light and air. Brick walls soon changed to rock while they descended.

As the gratings disappeared, the darkness increased. Except for Mrs. Vargas's lantern, their walk down would be in total gloom. The little sounds of their rustling skirts and work shoes magnified in the descent. Even her heartbeat sounded thunderous. Anna kept hold of her skirt tail and the side rail until they arrived at the bottom. They walked some distance down a hallway, no longer going down but straight ahead.

"We're almost to the end." The woman's serene voice carried back to Anna and brought a sigh of relief.

Farther up the tunnel, beyond the lantern's reach, the darkness turned to gray, and then became dim light. A new grate in the ceiling, admitted daylight, revealing another set of stairs going upward.

She followed Mrs. Vargas up to a landing with a set of levers. The woman pulled one down, and a thick door swooshed open in front of them. Anna took a deep breath of fresh air, laced with the damp scent of a river and lush greenery hanging around the entrance. The sounds of birds and rippling water refreshed her spirit after the dark tunnel.

John's mother picked up a stick beside the entrance and pushed the vines and fronds aside to allow them to pass on a path to the edge of a stream. She poked the dry limb on the ground as she walked and gave a little laugh. "I'm hoping this stick will drive away any snakes."

They arrived at a fast-flowing stream. The woman pointed beyond some undergrowth. Almost hidden among the grasses, a rowboat with two oars lay bobbing on the river's edge, tied to a low-hanging tree branch.

Mrs. Vargas pushed damp hair from her forehead and turned to Anna. "So now you see. Here is our secret escape route if we ever need it. The stream is only big enough for a small boat. It won't allow ships. It runs into the larger river, which flows to the mainland. John still loves to use this passage home to surprise us sometimes."

The way back somehow seemed shorter, now that it was familiar.

*S*cant news of the war for independence reached the island, and when it did, the intelligence was most often weeks old. John's father received a partial copy of a newspaper with both good and bad reports and shared it after dinner one evening. "Light Horse Harry Lee and Francis Marion's men laid siege and took British Fort Watson, and also Fort Motte and Granby. But Lt. General Cornwallis defeated Washington's own choice of a leader for the southern army, Major General Nathanael Greene, at the Battle of Guilford Court-house. Cornwallis is now marching north to corner and defeat Washington's bedraggled army." He finished reading and dropped the worn paper aside. "Well, we at least know how to better pray."

Anna gulped back tears. Was the war lost already?

One sultry afternoon in late August, while the men worked down at the rice worker village repairing cottages, Anna sat with John's mother and grandmother in the kitchen alcove, shelling peas. The bell from the landing pealed, loud and anxious.

The young black boy who kept watch at the bell ran up the back steps into the kitchen alcove, out of breath and the whites of his eyes showing.

"Missus, soldiers in red coats and a lady have landed at the dock. They starting up the path to the house."

Sounds of shouting and men's voices giving orders flowed up from the harbor.

Mrs. Vargas stood, shook out her apron, and headed to the front door. Marisol followed, and so did Anna.

British soldiers, twenty or thirty of them in their red and white uniforms, muskets, and tall black hats, marched up the path from the dock.

Field and yard servants dropped their rakes or hoes and muttered until the sounds of their words became a loud hum.

Anna cried, "Oh Lord have mercy on us."

John's mother spoke to the tall butler standing at attention on the porch. "Gideon, please send word for Samuel and Ethan to come as fast as they can."

The servant moved to do her bidding, and within minutes, the two men she'd sent for rounded the corner of the plantation house —just as the troop and entourage stopped on the front lawn. Father and son strode up the steps to stand with Georgia and Marisol. Anna stood just behind them, trying to breathe and blinking back moisture. Servants from the surrounding fields, garden, and buildings huddled in groups around the home, on the steps, and on the piazza. One servant woman began to cry, pressing her apron to her eyes.

Anna scanned the group, her gaze moving back to the expensively dressed woman amid a dozen servants in their black and white livery, guiding two loaded carts behind the soldiers. Her mouth fell open when she recognized the woman.

Ruth Garfield Edmonds. A younger man she didn't recognize walked beside the woman, in a green satin waistcoat, white breeches, and ruffled white cravat. Both of them wore white powdered hair or wigs. Ruth's was in a high, elegant style, with a gauze hat matching her rustling gray silk dress.

A British officer with a captain's insignia moved from the front of his men and came to stand in front of the bottom step of the plantation house. He held a large official document with a red seal in his hand. He wore tall headgear and white shoulder straps crossed in front of his red coat. His coat tails hung behind to his knees. His white doe skin breeches disappeared into high, gleaming black boots.

He looked up at the gathered family on the porch. "Who is the owner of this plantation?"

John's parents stepped forward, and Samuel spoke. "We are, sir. I am Samuel Vargas and this is my wife Georgia." He placed his hand around her waist. "What is your business here, Captain?"

Anna thanked God for the calm, dignified voice of John's father and the gentle expression void of anger or fear on his and Georgia's faces.

The leader stiffened in the presence of their gentleness and opened the document with the red seal. He read aloud.

"Know all men by these presents: In the name of George the Third, by the grace of God, the king, and John Cruden, Commissioner of Sequestered Estates for his majesty's province of South Carolina..."

Anna's heart sounded like thunder in her ears. Was she having a nightmare?

"...In consequence of the powers in me vested by the right honorable Earl Cornwallis, this plantation, is confiscated and sold, the owners having given aid and comfort to traitors during the insurrection. The estate known as Salt Marsh is hereby declared the property of his majesty's loyal subject, Baroness Ruth Garfield Edmonds."

Anna gasped and covered her mouth with her hand.

Samuel and Georgia both looked back at the woman behind the soldiers, then clasped each other's hands.

John's grandparents watched, but uttered no sound.

The captain walked up the steps, and the family moved with him from the porch to the parlor.

Ruth Edmonds and the young man with her joined them. She acknowledged Georgia and Samuel with a slight nod of her head, and introduced the young man as her brother who they might remember, Frederick. Then their eyes roamed about, as if inspecting their new property.

Anna stood by the hall wall, trying to be as quiet as a rose petal on the floor, fallen from a vase of flowers, but she couldn't control the spasmodic trembling within her. Her chest felt as if it would burst. The British actually thought they'd won the war, definitely the South, with the defeat of General Green at Guilford Courthouse. And Marion's men? Had they conquered the militia, too?

Outside the windows, the wailing of the Negroes, most of whom had only served Samuel and Georgia all of their lives, rose in volume.

The captain told Samuel he'd have to leave the horses, sheep, and all the farm animals in the pasture, and all furniture and accouterments in the house. And the slaves must stay as well. The family could pack their personal clothes only and should be ready to exit the island the next morning.

He cast somewhat kind eyes on them and added, "I'll be happy to carry your people on my ship wherever you want to go."

Ruth Edmonds stepped forward like a queen. She cast a lace hand-kerchief toward Georgia and Samuel, and a weak smile creased her porcelain face. "Don't worry, I'll take good care of this beautiful house, and you may each take one slave of choice."

She looked at Anna, standing still as a statue. "Captain, this girl is a visitor. She is not part of this family. Are you, my dear? She may stay if she likes."

Bile rose in Anna's throat and threatened to choke her. She knew she must speak. She'd hate to ever see Ruth Edmonds again, much less live with her. But no words came forth in her jumbled mind or to her mouth. She turned and ran from the room as tears plopped down her cheeks.

In her bedroom, she began pulling dresses from the wardrobe and piling them on her bed. She moved in jerks. Her limbs felt made of wood. A knock sounded at the door. Thinking it might be a servant bringing her trunk, she sighed and called without turning, "Come in."

Georgia hurried into the room and locked the entrance behind her. She came to Anna's side and took her hand. "Anna, you must stay."

"Oh, ma'am, I just can't. How could that woman do this to your family?"

Georgia's face looked as stiff and pale as the tabby walls around the plantation. She repeated in a low, urgent voice. "Please stay, Anna. John doesn't know Salt Marsh has been taken. He might come back through the secret entrance before we can get word to him. What if he met up with Ruth or her brother or some British soldier in the hall?"

She gasped and sank onto the bed amidst her dresses. He'd be taken prisoner, or even shot on sight as a rebel.

"You can ask Ruth for the room I showed you with the secret entrance. She'll never want to put one of her guests in that small bedroom."

Of course she'd have to stay. And, no, Ruth Edmonds would never want to put a guest in the tiny, separate space at the end of the hall.

She looked up at Georgia, and her eyes filled with tears. "I'll stay if...she's still willing." She peered around her comfortable, well-appointed bedroom. She'd miss it, but it had to be done. "And I think you're right. She'll be glad to have this room available and give me the other one."

Georgia stepped close and hugged her.

Anna pulled back to look into the face of the woman she'd come to love. "Is the war a hopeless cause?"

"No, I can't believe it is. We've prayed too much, my dear, for freedom, and so have many others."

"How can you keep faith? I mean, you're losing the lovely plantation you and your husband dreamed about and built. And where will you go?"

"We have another plantation, and if that's no longer standing, we have many friends who will take us in, including members of Ethan's church. So don't worry. God will take care of us. I want to ask Mammy June to stay with you. Would that make you happy?"

"Oh yes, but...will she let you leave without her?"

"I think so when I tell her I'm depending on her to keep things moving to the best of her ability, since Gideon is going with us. She'll bring some stability by her presence, and help the other heartbroken servants be able to serve under their new masters." Georgia swiped a tear that slid down her face, and a tremulous smile touched her lips. "And Mammy will be a wholehearted support to you and John if he appears. She loves him as much as we do, and she is the only servant who knows about the secret exit."

She and Georgia had prayer, and the woman left, her back straight as an arrow.

Anna went to the wash bowl and cupped water over her face, dried it, and then headed down the stairs to find Ruth Edmonds. God help her know what to say and how to speak it without rancor. How could the woman have done this wicked thing against John's family?

CHAPTER 18

Who but God could have ordained the critical arrival of the French fleet to
assist in the siege of Yorktown?
~ Yale President Ezra Stiles, May 8, 1783

$\mathcal{A}$nna found Ruth in the parlor examining her new possessions. A maid stood nearby, her head bowed. The woman held a vase in her hand, which she rotated, smiling as she spoke to the servant. "This must go upstairs to my bedroom, the one the owners are exiting." She handed it to the servant, looked up, and saw Anna standing in the doorway.

"Yes, dear girl. What do you want? Packing to go? Or have you changed your mind?"

Anna clasped her hands in front of her and lowered her head. "I've decided to stay, if the offer is still open."

Ruth smirked. "I expected you might, and the offer is still available, but you'll have to vacate your upstairs bedroom. I'll need it for guests."

Anna relaxed. This was going to be easier than she'd thought. "That's fine. If you don't mind, I'll be glad to take the small room at the end of the hall. I doubt you'd like to place a guest there."

Ruth's brows lifted. "Really?" She picked up the side of her satin gown and swished forward, with her owner keys clinking from a chain around her waist. "Don't think I've seen such a room. Come, show me."

Ruth took one look at the small space and smiled. "You're right. I'd never put a guest here. The room is yours." She whirled around in the middle of the floor. "You know you can be a help here with whatever tasks need doing. Can you make gauze hats half as good as your aunt?"

Anna sighed. "She has taught me much, and I do like the work."

Ruth moved to the doorway. "Good. Make a list of whatever materials you'll need, and I'll supply them with the colors of gauze I prefer. Meanwhile, please move your things here and clean out your former bedroom."

She walked to the door and then turned back. "I can see you're wondering about my loyalty now to the King, and you may also be surprised why I've chosen to live here on this secluded plantation instead of Charles Town." She flicked a silk handkerchief in the air. "I'm on whichever side wins, and it looks like King George is winning. But the city is now crowded with, not only soldiers, but Tories who've left their plantations because of the battles. Not to mention a lot of riffraff who sleep on the streets. I hate crowding. You've made a wise choice not to go back."

Anna dared to ask a question while Ruth was in her expansive mood. "Do you have any news of my Aunt Reba or my friend Abigail and her baby? Are they all right?"

Ruth shrugged. "I really don't move in their circles, but I can say I saw them both in my last visit to your aunt's shop." She touched the exquisite hat on her head. "And I daresay they looked fine to me, and busy. And a servant played with a baby, a boy, I believe, who chortled the whole time I was there." She swung out the door and up the hall.

Anna pressed her burning eyes. Dear Aunt Reba, Abigail, and little Philip. How she missed them. *Father God, please continue to take care of them in occupied Charles Town. Help John and Henry stay safe, and help me do whatever I can here to stay in peace and sanity.*

◈

*S*eptember arrived with its cooler breezes, and trees around the plantation exchanged their green leaves for gorgeous garments of red, orange and yellow. The fall sights should have encouraged Anna's heart. But the change of season made her feel more lonesome. She spent her days making hats for Ruth and her guests, and even helping serve at large dinners when needed.

She found it becoming more difficult to deal with the amorous advances of Ruth's wastrel brother Frederick. He'd paid little attention to her at first, but that had changed.

One evening, he opened her door without knocking and entered with a sly smile, as if he had every right to enter her chamber. He stumbled up to her and tried to pull her into his arms. She smelled liquor on his breath. She pushed him aside and ordered him from her room, but he didn't budge until Ruth's sudden appearance and angry command convinced him. He turned tail and crept away like a whipped puppy.

From then on, Anna kept her door locked, even in daytime. And she took her walks in the garden when she knew he was sleeping off a drunk.

Mammy June approved her locking her door, and together they came up with a special knock she'd give when she came to check on Anna or bring her a tray. Ruth had made it plain, Anna was not welcome to take dinner with her guests, and that suited her well.

"Now don't you go unlocking this here door for no one, except you hear this sound." She gave two fast, then three slower knocks. "There's too many gentlemen's roaming about this house, and most of them is up to no good. And, of course, if that Miz Ruth comes, you'll recognize her loud voice coming down the hall telling off them maids of hers."

Anna smiled. Mammy could always lift her spirits.

One morning, Anna returned from her walk in the garden and reached to open her door. It opened in front of her, and her heart clutched as she imagined Frederick lying in wait for her.

John's welcoming face stood in the opening—a smile lighting his features.

Her heart loosed its tension and soared, racing through her so fast she grew light-headed. John. Here. Finally. She managed enough presence of mind to put her finger to her lips.

He held out his arms, and she went into them, relishing his wonderful strength as she drew him back into the room. He pulled her tighter into his arms and planted a fervent kiss on her lips which sang through her veins and sent the pit of her stomach into a wild swirl. She hated to leave his embrace, but she had to step away enough to close and lock the entrance.

Then she turned back to him, trying to catch her breath. There was much he needed to know, but first, she drank in the sight of him. His tall lanky form, leaner than before, yet still strong and hearty. And she breathed in the fresh woodsy scent clinging to him and his deer-skin shirt. Glancing at her table, she smiled at how he'd cleaned up her breakfast, most of which she'd left on the tray.

She pulled him as far away from the door as possible before speaking in a low voice. "John, do you know that your parents have been evicted and this plantation sold to a loyal Tory?"

"What?" His face contorted and his green eyes blazed. He balled his fists and paced across the small room. Then he turned back to her. "But why didn't you go with them?" His face stiffened more. "I can't believe my mother and father left you here with a bunch of Tories."

Anna's brows lifted. "Surely you understand. What do you think would have happened to you just now if you'd walked up the hall right into the hands of Tories or soldiers? I thank God He brought me back from my walk in time."

John's face softened. He came to her and placed his strong hands on her shoulders. "You stayed here for me?"

She nodded, and he drew her into his arms. She reveled in his male closeness and breathed in the unique scent that was his alone.

A sharp knock sounded at the door and a voice spoke. "Anna, I may need you tonight to help serve at dinner, so be ready if I send for you. I'm having important guests."

Anna pressed her finger to John's lips. "Yes, ma'am. I'll be ready." She listened for the retreating steps before removing her hand.

A frown creased John's face. "Who was that?"

"The new Tory owner. Baroness Ruth Garfield Edmonds."

John stiffened. "I thought I recognized that voice, and I can't believe it. You told me Ruth helped my escape from the prison ship. And I saw one wagon of supplies she sent to Marion's men months ago."

Anna took a deep breath. "She is a chameleon. She plays to both sides, whichever one seems more likely to win at whatever time."

He drew her close again. "Is she treating you like a servant? I'll not have it."

Anna shook her head. "I'm fine. I try to please her, stay in the background, listen, and keep my door locked."

He smiled and lifted her chin. "You are a wise woman for your young age, sweet one." He brushed her lips with his own.

A thrill ran up her spine. His embrace seemed so good, so right, she wanted to press closer to him. But she forced herself to push away, turning toward the small table to clear her senses. They were alone and in her bedroom. She must use the wisdom he mentioned.

She offered him a chair, and he sank into it and sighed.

"I will go down and make sure Mammy fixes a tray for you. What are your plans now that you know our situation?"

His glance traveled over to the corner cot.

Was he tired? Of course, he'd be weary from his stressful trip to Salt Marsh through enemy lines, and he probably travelled most of the night. "Why don't you take a nap while I'm gone? I'll lock the door, and you won't need to answer any knock if one comes. I'll have the key to get back in."

He smiled and took a deep, tired breath. "I do need to rest before I start back. But I must leave soon after."

She made the room neater, pulled the curtain across the small top window, and headed to the door. Glancing back, she saw his head nod and his shoulders droop. With a groan, he stood and moved to her cot, then dropped down on it. Without another movement, he fell asleep, if his gentle snores meant anything. She prayed no one could hear him if they ventured down the hall.

Anna found Mammy in the kitchen alcove, helping prepare the mid-day meal. As soon as she could get her aside from the other workers, she told her about John.

The woman's full lips tightened and she nodded. "You have nothing to worry about young lady. I'll take care of that fine man good and proper and prepare food for him when he's ready and more to take when he leaves us. You warned him to stay in the room?"

"Yes, he's asleep right now from travelling all night. I'll go pick peas while he rests."

~

*E*arly that evening, Anna opened her door with her key, and Mammy preceded her into the room with a well-packed tray of food and a knapsack for later.

Anna closed and locked the bedroom door.

John opened his eyes, sat up, and smiled. "I could eat half a side of deer, Mammy."

The servant nodded and placed the food and sack on the table. "I ain't never seen you when you wasn't hungry, young man."

John arose and sat at the table. He eyed the slab of roasted meat, peas, and a fresh loaf of bread. After saying a quick blessing, he took a deep drink of water from the skin Anna placed nearby.

She sat beside him, watching and loving every movement he made as he dropped the napkin in his lap and tore a chunk of bread off the loaf with his broad hands.

Mammy, standing by, put her fists on her hips and spoke to John with her eyes flashing. "You know you can't stay here tonight, don't you? It ain't fitting, even if you is engaged. And ain't no other safe room anywhere on this plantation."

John stopped, with a knifed piece of meat headed to his mouth. He looked from the servant to Anna. "Of course, I know that, Mammy.

I'm heading out as soon as twilight falls. Got to get back to the militia."

Mammy nodded. "Just making sure." She reached down and patted his shoulder, grinned, and left.

Between mouthfuls, John told Anna good news of the war. "The French are helping us. Early this month, their Admiral De Grasse defeated the British navy and secured the Chesapeake Bay."

"Is that important?" Anna tried to grasp the news, but her mind kept turning over the fact that their moments together would end with the meal. And John would return to war—and great danger.

"Yes. It means we've got Cornwallis's army isolated at Yorktown in Virginia. The British fleet cannot sail in past the French ships to help them. It's a very important fact. Washington's army marches in that direction as we speak."

He finished the meal, wiped his mouth with the cloth napkin, and dropped it on the tray.

His face turned serious, stiff. He looked at Anna, and a sadness in his darker green eyes caused a sharp intake of her breath. Had something terrible happened that he'd not shared until now?

"What is it, John?"

"Anna, I'm so sorry. I have bad news that I've put off telling you until the last minute."

Her heart hammered in her throat, which had turned dry. "Is it about...Henry?" She could barely breathe as she waited for his response.

"Yes." He stood and pulled her into his arms. "He died a hero, Anna. And Marion was the most upset I've ever seen him when we brought his body into camp. He thought so much of your brother."

An ache pressed hard on her, blurring her vision, clouding her mind. "But...how?"

"We attacked a British patrol near Kingstree, and Henry did some amazing things before one of their bullets hit its mark. We defeated the British and took their supply wagons. The success would've never happened without Henry's fast thinking."

Dear Henry. It hurt to breathe. She blinked back tears.

John held her close, and she laid her head on his chest, listening to his heartbeat. "Where is he...?" Her voice cracked, and tears flowed down her cheeks.

"We buried him in a little wood near Kingstree and marked the spot." He pulled her face up. "I'll be able to find the exact place, and when this is over, we can move him to your family cemetery, if you'd like. We had a carpenter among us, and he made a strong oak box for him to rest in."

She nodded, and he drew her closer.

"It will not be long now. I believe the Lord is helping our new nation come to birth, though the birth pangs are still painful. Will you wait here and pray and not give up?"

"Yes." She breathed through her tears.

Then he lifted her chin and kissed her—a deep, tender kiss.

When he finally pulled back, daylight had disappeared through the small high window, and they stood in shadows. He released her, and she lit the lamp.

Picking up his knapsack of Mammy's food and the skin of water, John opened the secret exit and, after a final lingering look at her, disappeared into its depth.

When the door slid back into place as a bookcase, silent because of the oil she had used on the hinges, Anna fell onto her cot and sobbed. *Dear Henry.*

In addition to the sorrow, other thoughts plagued her. Would John make it back safe? Would he and Marion's men follow Washington's army to the distant place called Yorktown, Virginia? She pushed her face into her pillow to muffle her sobs.

~

*A*nna waited and prayed and tried to keep hopeful through the rest of September and October. The myriad colors of leaves came, then dropped to the ground from the trees where she walked, when she could believe Frederick was sleeping off his drinking or otherwise engaged. The evening air now laced with a chill made a wrap necessary on her strolls. She enjoyed the scent of the last roses holding on before the killer frost to come.

One November morning, she walked through the first frost glittering like diamonds on the grass. Feeling the chill air through her thin wrap, she soon went back inside and to her room before her slippers became soaked with the icy moisture. As she sat on the edge of her cot, she heard a dull noise a long way off. She looked up at her small window and listened. The sound came nearer until she heard it clearly, a rippling of thuds. She stood up, and her breath caught in her throat.

It could only be the hoof beats of many horses.

From somewhere outside, she heard a servant woman's scream. Voices and running footsteps sounded through the house and echoed down the stairs. Anna left her room and hurried downstairs, then followed Ruth Edmonds and the household staff out the front door to the wide porch.

A band of about fifty men on horseback, making the noise of twice that number, galloped into the yard. Handling their horses with great skill, they formed half circles, five or six deep. A raiding party?

Anna hung back, trying to decide if she needed to run and hide. Field hands came striding up from the back of the plantation and hung about in groups, pointing and mumbling.

Anna eyed the riders' strange clothing. One man had on a green coat like a Tory. Others beside him wore coats that had once been red, but re-dyed to brown, some purple, with patches of red showing through. Others wore clothing in tatters, with breeches of homespun or deerskin. Some wore British boots, or buckled shoes, or homemade clumpers. All carried shotguns and muskets, rifles, pistols, and hunting knives.

When she lifted her glance to their tanned, bearded faces and bright, merry eyes, she gasped. They had a liveliness and vitality about them like she'd never seen. It drew her toward them. She took a step closer.

A dark-headed man jumped from his horse and strode up the steps to her. Something was wonderfully familiar about his bearing, the way he walked. She cried out as she recognized John under his full whiskers.

He took her in his arms and kissed her. The men behind him whistled and whooped. They must be Marion's men. And love filled her heart for all of them.

A commanding voice quieted them. Anna watched as the obvious leader drew his horse up closer to the bottom step and called out that he wanted to speak to Ruth Garfield Edmonds.

Ruth lifted her satin skirts, threw up her chin, and stepped forward. She glared at the man through hooded lids.

"Mrs. Edmonds, I am here under the authority of General Francis Marion of the South Carolina Militia. You are ordered to return this estate to its original owners, Samuel and Georgia Vargas. Their son, Captain John Vargas will receive it."

Mammy June, standing near Anna and John, said in her bold, clear voice, "Praise the Lord."

Ruth thrust out her full lip and put her hands on her hips. "Do you think I give credence to anything a rebel might say? I am owner of this property by British command, under the authority of the Earl of Cornwallis."

A ripple of laughter came from the men behind the leader until he turned toward them. Then they straightened in their saddles and quieted.

"Mrs. Edmonds, you obviously are not aware that General Cornwallis surrendered to General George Washington at Yorktown, Virginia, on the nineteenth of October."

Anna gasped, and her head exploded with dizzying joy. She trembled from head to toe, and might have fallen in a faint except for John's strong arms around her.

Could the war really be over?

CHAPTER 19

America is another name for opportunity. Our whole history appears like a
last effort of Divine Providence in behalf of the human race.
~ Ralph Waldo Emerson, December, 1781

*A*nna rejoiced as Christmas approached—and her wedding set
for December twentieth. John's family arrived at Salt Marsh
soon after Ruth Edmonds left, and she had helped Georgia bring the
house back up to her cleanliness standards, neglected by the Tory
woman.

She came down the stairs from her old room to find John's
mother, grandmother, and the servants decorating the banisters, the
doors, and fireplaces with holly and red bows. She joined the labor of
love.

After completing the work, she pulled her future mother-in-law
aside. "I'm still not sure I understand why John had to go back to
Marion's militia until our wedding. Didn't the surrender of General
Cornwallis signal the end of the war?"

Georgia led her into the parlor to sit and rest until the servants
announced the mid-day meal. She sat beside her on a sofa.

The woman smiled. "I know how you feel. But the truth is, it takes quite a while for news from the colonies to reach England. They will not be happy to hear of Cornwallis's surrender at Yorktown, with the French fleet backing up the colonists. Then the Parliament will have to convene and formally declare an end to the hostility. John, Samuel, and Ethan think that might could happen by February next year. After that, other meetings and peace negotiations between our new nation and Britain must take place, maybe in Paris."

"But why haven't the British left Charles Town yet? I would so love to have Aunt Reba, Abigail, and Uncle Rufus at our wedding, but John said that would be impossible, because the enemy still holds the city."

Georgia patted her hand. "They may occupy our fair city until all the peace negotiations are complete. Our men folk think that could take all next year. I am sorry about your family not being able to come. Did you and John discuss perhaps putting off the marriage until they can be a part?"

Warmth rose on Anna's neck. She wanted their marriage as much as John did. A vision of the beautiful wedding dress hanging in her bedroom upstairs flashed across her mind. She wanted to wear it, not pack it away for the future. "No. We both want to go ahead, so I'm going to submerge my disappointment in faith and pray for all those peace negotiations to move forward quickly." She bit her lower lip and took a deep breath. "And I will keep praying my family and Abigail will be safe amid all the British soldiers and Tories crowded into the city. If anyone can see to Aunt Reba's needs and Abigail's and her little son, Uncle Rufus can."

A servant entered and announced the meal ready to serve.

Georgia stood. "Good mindset. I heard John say your uncle is such a savvy merchant and business owner, he could make an excellent living no matter who held the city. Do you agree?"

"I do. He is a man of many talents, who makes powerful friends and gets things done that no one else can."

She followed Georgia to the dining room, her heart lighter.

∼

*O*n the eighteenth of December, the bell at the dock sounded with such boisterous clangs, Anna dropped the cup she held. She, John's mother, and his grandmother were just finishing their mid-afternoon tea. They stood and all three rushed to the front entrance, their bouffant dresses swished against each other and the hall walls.

"Could it be John?" The question popped out of her mouth.

"Who else could it be?" Georgia clapped her hands and led the way down the steps and toward the island wharf.

As they approached the people stepping onto the dock, Anna's breath caught in her throat and moisture gathered in her eyes. John stood helping her aunt, Abigail, and Rufus onto the dock from the long boat. Her friend held a bright-eyed little Philip in her arms. William Burns was the last to exit the vessel.

"Oh, my love, how did you manage to...?" Her words ended in a sob as her aunt enfolded her in a hug.

Abigail, holding little Philip, waited her turn for a happy greeting.

Then Anna gave Uncle Rufus a warm welcome, too. A big grin creased his face. "Well, niece, you didn't think we'd miss your wedding to John did you?"

She found no words to express her joy, just swiped the wetness from her cheeks.

As servants picked up the trunks and followed the entourage to the main house, John hugged his mother and grandmother, then strode to walk beside Anna. He placed his arm around her waist and kissed the top of her head.

She sniffed and looked up at him. "This is like a miracle. How did you get them out of Charles Town?"

"It's a long story, but suffice it to say, your uncle has some powerful friends among the British officers." He tightened his grip about her and drew her closer. "Of course, they have no idea how he has aided the patriots."

Anna moved through the next day as in a dream, as her aunt and Abigail prepared her for the wedding. Aunt Reba concocted the most lovely gauze hat to match her dress, with a silver-studded head piece and a veil as soft as a summer cloud. She added red rosettes to the ivory wedding gown for the Christmas season.

The morning of the wedding, Abigail fixed Anna's hair in bouncing curls rising behind the headpiece, with thick auburn locks flowing down to her shoulders.

Her friend stood back and inspected her handiwork, then took a deep breath. "I'm so happy for you, Anna, and perhaps this is not the time to talk about it, but one day I'll have to quit living off your family. I'll need to find some kind of work and make a life for myself and Philip."

Anna's heart flipped over, and she looked into Abigail's face. She pressed her hand. "Don't you worry, dear friend. You'll always have a place with me and John. I love you like a sister."

"Well, I love you the same way, but I did want you to know my thoughts these days." Then Abigail clapped her hands. "But it's not time to discuss this. You've a wedding awaiting you downstairs." Her gentle face creased into a happy smile. She helped Anna slip into the lovely, ivory, silk wedding gown with its gossamer overskirt.

With all her attire completed, Anna Grace reached in a drawer and withdrew the ruby Vargas/Valentin brooch. She pinned it just above her right breast onto the lacy bodice. It glowed like a red cluster of berries. Would Samuel's grandmother Marisol recognize the pin?

When the time arrived to descend the stairs, she took a deep breath and grasped her full, ruffled skirt in one gloved hand and Uncle Rufus's arm with the other. Her request for him to take the place of her father had delighted him.

John waited at the bottom, his emerald eyes beaming with love. He looked more handsome than she'd ever seen him in an ivory waistcoat and breeches, with a sprig of holly on his lapel. For so many past months, his only attire was his worn militia uniform, but he was elegant in any kind of attire.

Georgia and Marisol had set up the wedding ceremony in the large parlor in front of the big windows looking out onto the winter garden. A fire crackled in the massive fireplace.

Samuel's parents and grandmother, and her aunt with baby Philip on her lap, sat in chairs, ready for the service. Mammy June, Gideon, Thomas, and several maids pressed in at the hall doorway.

Pastor Ethan stood before them to lead the ceremony. He motioned the wedding party to come forward.

Anna thought her heart would burst with joy as she glided across the room on Uncle Rufus's arm to stand before Pastor Ethan.

William Burns moved to stand beside John. Rufus moved back, and Abigail walked up beside Anna and handed her a bouquet of holly and red ribbons. Anna's eyes widened. Three red rose buds stood out in its center with frost darkened, lacy outer petals. She lifted her eyebrows at her friend. Where on earth did she find rosebuds this time of year? Abigail leaned to whisper, "John calls these patriot roses. They've survived the killer frost in a hidden place he showed me."

She turned loving eyes back to her husband-to-be, and he placed his arm around her waist and winked.

Pastor Ethan's strong voice rolled over the room, reading from the worn pages of his Common Book of Prayer. How many marriages he must have performed with the book.

"Dearly beloved, we are gathered here in the sight of God, and in the face of this Congregation, to join together this man and this woman in holy Matrimony, which is an honorable estate instituted of God signifying unto us the mystical union that is betwixt Christ and his Church." He looked up from the book and smiled at her and John, then at all those attending.

"What a wonderful time to solemnize a marriage, at Christmas, while we celebrate the birth of Christ. I've always loved this season, and I can't tell you how much joy it gives me to be able to stand here and seal marriage vows between my grandson and the beautiful Anna Grace." His voice wavered, but he cleared his throat and looked down at the Book of Prayer.

Several sniffs came from the guests. John's mother drew a handkerchief from her sleeve and dabbed at her eyes. Little Philip gave a happy holler, and then plunged three fingers into his mouth.

Anna blinked back moisture, and John took a deep breath and

tightened his arm around her waist. They confessed their marriage vows, and John placed a beautiful blue sapphire ring on her finger.

His grandfather prayed a wonderful blessing over them. "May God the Father, God the Son, God the Holy Spirit bless, preserve, and keep you, and surround you with favor and grace so you may live happy together in this life, and in the world to come, have life everlasting."

He looked into John's face. "May thy wife be a fruitful vine upon the walls of thy house, thy children like olive branches around thy table." Then he beamed at both of them. "I pronounce you man and wife."

John took her into his arms and kissed her until she was breathless.

She was still regathering her wits as his mother, father, and grandmother came to hug them, as did Abigail and her uncle.

Soon, the group entered the dining room for a joyous feast and to cut the luscious centerpiece, a wedding cake made by Aunt Reba with fruit and molasses.

⁓

*J*ohn awoke and looked into the face of his bride lying beside him. Loving every line and curve of her profile, he sniffed the soft scent of roses that exuded from her auburn hair spread out on her pillow. He kissed the tip of her nose and she awakened. Pulling her into the circle of his arms, he welcomed her warm response as she pressed into his embrace.

"Happy?" He leaned back to see her eyes.

"Completely. Thank you for a lovely wedding. Your family so amazes me. They took care of every detail."

John sat up on the edge of the bed, thankful for a little heat coming from the smoldering embers in the fireplace. He pulled the cover over her and rose.

Anna raised from her pillow to one elbow. "Do we have to get up now?"

He shrugged into his shirt and trousers, and sat on the nearby chair to pull on his socks and boots. "You are welcome to stay abed as long as you like, new wife, but I've never been able to stay down once I awake." He grinned at her. "Even with the tremendous temptation you are, my lovely one, to break that habit."

Anna stretched and then reached for her warm robe.

A gentle knock sounded at the door. John walked over and opened it an inch, then spread it wide. "Hm-m, just what we need."

Mammy June bustled in with a loaded breakfast tray. "I thought I heard folks moving about in here, or I'd never knocked or disturbed you."

The smell of eggs, bacon, fresh bread, and tea flowed over the room.

John smiled at her as she sat the food down on their small table near the fireplace. Then she reached down and pulled several logs from the stack on the hearth and dropped them onto the still glowing embers. Sparks flew and a pine scent added to the smell of breakfast.

"Thank you, Mammy." Anna slipped warm stockings and slippers on her feet and moved to sit for the meal.

John joined her as the servant left and closed the door behind her. They began the delicious repast.

He finished and pushed back his chair. "Dearest, I've something I want to discuss with you. It's been on my mind for some time."

Anna laid down her napkin and lifted her eyes to his.

"I've not forgotten how heartbroken you were about your family's plantation being burned. So much has happened since then, but I still remember. As soon as Charles Town is free again and life gets back to some kind of normal, I'd like to rebuild it and make it our home. Would that make you happy?"

～

*A*nna gasped as surprise slipped through her. She'd never imagined his thoughtfulness would extend so far. God had blessed her so much with this man. Was there no end to the happy plans he kept revealing? "Oh, John. Yes! It would be a dream come true." She pushed up from her chair and threw herself into his arms. "This is the best wedding present I could ever hope for."

He hugged her tight, pulling her onto his lap, and she snuggled into his touch. "Well, that settles it, sweet patriot rose of mine. We'll rebuild it and raise our family there."

He pulled back from her and lifted her chin to stare into her eyes. "Do you remember the verse for your birthday in Proverbs?"

She smiled into his face. "Yes, chapter thirty-one, verse twenty-five. 'Strength and honor are her clothing and she shall rejoice in time to come.'"

"Do you think that verse has worked well for you? I believe strength and honor are your clothing, or you'd never been able to rescue us from that prison ship."

Anna closed her eyes as she remembered that terrible prison ship and the cold sail to Salt Marsh with John injured but holding on to life, leaning against her. She tightened her arms around his neck and pressed her cheek to his. "Well, I can say this is a time for rejoicing, husband of mine."

"I'll see if we can't make this the first of many times."

Then John sealed his promise with a kiss that sent shivers to her toes.

Did you enjoy this book? We hope so!

Would you take a quick minute to leave a review where you purchased the book?

It doesn't have to be long. Just a sentence or two telling what you liked about the story!

Receive a FREE ebook and get updates when new Wild Heart books release: https://wildheartbooks.org/newsletter

VOCABULARY APPENDIX

1) Terminology for citizens in colonial Charles Town during the American Revolution

a) Patriots, Whigs, and rebels described citizens who wanted independence and a new nation.

b) Tories, loyalists, and king's men, defined citizens who remained loyal to the king of England.

2) Terminology for soldiers who fought in the American Revolution, both sides

a) Continentals or regulars: Trained, uniformed, full-time soldiers who fought in the American Continental Army under George Washington and his hero officers.
Major General Benjamin Lincoln was sent by Washington to defend Charles Town.

b) British counterparts were redcoats or British regulars led by General Henry Clinton, and Lt. General Charles Cornwallis and their officers. This group also included provincials or Tories who helped the British.

c) The American state militias, also known as partisans, were for the most part, amateur, unpaid soldiers who furnished their own horses, hunting rifles, and ammunition and fought successfully against the better trained and equipped British. Militia leaders General Francis Marion, nicknamed the Swamp Fox, and General Thomas Sumter, nicknamed the Gamecock, did exploits against the British in the low country and midlands. Andrew Pickens did the same in the Carolina back-country (now called upcountry). Other brave soldier leaders include Christopher Gadsden, William Moultrie, and Peter Horry. These patriot heroes have many cities, streets, counties, and even universities named after them. Marion lent his name to twenty-nine cities and towns across America, seventeen counties, a four-year university, a national forest and a small park on Capitol Hill. Horry County, (pronounced 'Orry) was named after Peter Horry and includes one of our favorite Carolina vacation spots, Myrtle Beach, South Carolina.

2) The Gadsden American flag - 1778

The Gadsden flag is an early historical American flag with a yellow field depicting a timber rattlesnake coiled and ready to strike. This snake could be found in all thirteen colonies. Beneath the rattlesnake resting on grass are the words: "DON'T TREAD ON ME." This was a warning to Britain from the thirteen colonies. It was designed by South Carolinian Christopher Gadsden.

3) Tricorn, Bicorn, and Cockade hats for colonials

The tricorn, with three corners/horns, and also the bicorn, with two corners/horns, were used during the American Revolution years. The patriots also wore a cockade.

Early American patriotic cockades were black, inherited from the British black cockades. By the end of the Revolutionary War, George

Washington felt the black cockade needed an American touch. So an eagle was added to the center and this remained the official American military cockade until cockades were completely retired in the late 1800s. Also, when the French, who wore white cockades, became our great helpers, many patriots then made their cockades of black and white to show the comradeship.

Tricorn

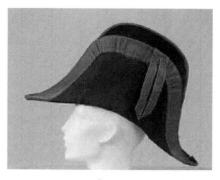

Bicorn

4) Cargo Manifest

A cargo manifest is like a passport except that is used for goods instead of persons. The manifest is evidence to the nationality of the goods, the type, size, and amount on the vessel.

5) Simmons Island, SC (now known as Seabrook Island)

Seabrook Island, formerly known as Simmons Island, is a barrier island in Charleston County, South Carolina. During the American Revolutionary years, the island was used as a staging area for Hessian and British troops during the Siege of Charleston. In 1939, the Episcopal Diocese of South Carolina rented land on Seabrook to establish a summer camp for underprivileged children. In 1951, about 1,408 acres of land were given to the church. Today there is a housing development on the island and a lovely St. Christopher Conference and Retreat Center, where I (Elva Martin) stayed once to write. Here's a link: https://stchristopher.org/

5) Tabby

A kind of masonry made of lime, sand, and crushed oyster shells popular in colonial Charles Town, and still evident in some older construction.

6) Gorget

British officers wore small breast plates called gorgets around the neck while on duty. They were a mark of rank and were made of gold or silver to match that of their regiment.

7) Reticule

A woman's small bag or purse usually in the form of a pouch with a drawstring and made of net, brocade, or beading, fashionable in the 18th and 19th centuries.

8) British Prison ships – the untold story

One story of the War of Independence that has largely eluded the popular imagination is the truth about the terrible prison ships, the "floating dungeons," Britain devised for captured patriots in most of our colonial harbors.

The British docked at least three older ships in the Charleston Harbor and packed them with patriot prisoners, like our hero in *Anna Grace*. Many, actually most, prisoners died imprisoned on these ships due to lack of medical care, food, water, vermin, and disease.

The most infamous of these prison ships was the *Jersey*, docked in

New York's East River. According to historian Robert Watson, author of *The Ghost Ship of Brooklyn,* this ship represented the single bloodiest conflict of the entire Revolutionary War. Not (the battles of) Saratoga, not Trenton, not Yorktown. The single costliest conflict took place on board this one prison ship. Most scholars estimate the death toll of its prisoners at 11,500. For many years after the war, the bleached bones of the prison-ship dead washed ashore on the Brooklyn side of the East River. Now a fraction of these bones rest atop the highest hill in Brooklyn's Fort Greene Park in the Prison Ship Martyrs Monument which overlooks the bay.

9) Breeches/Britches

The terms *breeches* or *knee-breeches* specifically designate the knee-length garments worn by men from the later 16th century to the early 19th century. The spelling *britches* is a spelling variant, not a corruption dating from the 17th century. Presently, *britches* reflects a common pronunciation often used in casual speech to mean trousers or pants in many English-speaking parts of the world.

FROM THE AUTHOR

Dear Reader,

Although Cornwallis surrendered to George Washington at York-town, Virginia, on October 19, 1781, war continued in the United States until the Treaty of Paris was signed in 1783. Our nation won our independence from Great Britain, but we lost twenty-five thousand men who battled for the freedom to speak and write what they believed, elect leaders, own land, and worship as they pleased. It's called liberty. We are the land of the free because of the brave.

The British left Charles Town on December 14, 1782, a year and two months after Cornwallis surrendered at Yorktown. Three hundred British ships sailed into Charles Town harbor to take the redcoats home and any Tories who wanted to go with them. Nine thousand men, women, and children, besides the troops, boarded these ships.

It was not a leisurely "evacuation." The liberation of Charles Town was the culmination of a well-executed military plan outlined a year earlier in a letter to Gov. Rutledge from American Army General Nathanael Greene. The American Army was encamped at Middleton Place.

From the British perspective, this event was a desperate escape.

First, the king's friends went aboard the ships, Tory families and their Negro servants, and any valuables they could squeeze aboard, including the stolen bells of St. Michael's Church. They went under the protection of the king's guns, while bad boys shouted dirty words at them from windows and trees. Next, the king's soldiers marched to the wharf and boarded.

That afternoon the American Continentals marched into the city with patriots leaning out windows shouting, "Welcome home, gentlemen! Welcome home!" Tears fell from eyes of the people and the patriot soldiers.

But Charles Town was in ruins, its neighboring plantations devastated, and its government in disarray. According to historian Robert Rosen, in the following years of 1783-1784, riots of various kinds took place, but the new municipal government of Charles Town was born in the tumult. On August 24, 1783, after a summer of civil disorder, Charles Town was incorporated and its name changed officially to Charleston as we now know it. Governmental order and restoration began with the help of leaders like John Rutledge, Thomas and Charles Pinckney, William Moultrie, and Christopher Gadsden.

During this time, Carolinian Henry Laurens, imprisoned in the tower of London, was released, and exchanged for Lord Cornwallis. Laurens then went to France and helped negotiate the Treaty of Paris with Benjamin Franklin.

Benedict Arnold, famous for betraying our country, and his Tory wife Peggy Shippen Arnold of Philadelphia, escaped to live in England after the war. He wrangled six thousand pounds from his new government for his betrayal, although he kept asking for ten thousand. Through his mismanagement, he and Peggy and their children always struggled financially. He died at age sixty on June 14, 1801, of "general dropsy and a disease in the lungs." This was one week before their lease on the house they could no longer afford expired. Peggy died three years later of cancer at the age of forty-four.

What about the beloved stolen bells of St. Michaels' Church? Luckily, a merchant later bought them and returned them to Charleston—in time for the city to celebrate the British evacuation of

Charleston in December 1782. A peal from the bells marked the occasion.

According to Ken Scarlett, President of Revolutionary Charleston, an organization that reenacts the British evacuation, December 14 is the greatest day of victory in the Revolution. Charleston was relinquished intact, the British quit the war, and independence was formally recognized. This day is celebrated annually in the city of Charleston, showcasing Charleston's great Revolutionary story to the world. Here's a site for more information: www.victory-day.org

Blessings,

Elva

Don't miss *The Captain's Governess*, book 4 in the Charleston Brides series!

Chapter One

1785

BETWEEN CHARLESTON AND JAMAICA

Abigail Welch awoke in the ship's cabin and sat up, her body stiff, her heart pounding. A cannon blast rocked the vessel again. Shouts, stomping boots, and the high-pitched grating sound of cannons rolled to gun ports on the deck above sent shivers down her back. Was the *Marigold* under attack?

She rose and gathered her robe about her, unable to control the fitful trembling within her. Plunging through the shadows toward the ray of dawn streaming from the port hole, she searched out across the white-capped sea. A low sloop, flying the skull and crossbones, pursued them across the purple waves. She gasped, and her nails dug into her clenched palms.

How could this be happening? They'd left Charles Town over a week earlier and Captain Donavan had told her last night at dinner they'd soon see evidence of Jamaica. Couldn't the British militia, now governing the island, protect it from French and Spanish pirates the captain mentioned?

Heavy, running boots in the corridor followed by a wallop on her cabin door jerked a knot in her empty stomach. She pulled her robe tight over her chemise, pushed her long tresses back on her shoulders, then called out. "Who is it?"

"I'm from the Cap'n, ma'm." His crusty voice boomed between panting breaths. "We're under attack from pirates."

She hurried forward and unbolted the door. A crewman she recognized stood there, the whites of his eyes blazing in his stiff, bearded face.

He doffed his hat and held a gun out to her. "Ma'am, the Cap'n wants you to have this to defend yo'self, in case them pirates manage to board us." He held out a Blunderbuss Pistol similar to the one her father had kept in his gun collection. It was the only one in his cabinet with a short brass barrel.

She reached for the weapon and, forgetful of its weight, almost dropped it.

The seaman steadied her grasp. "It's a wee bit heavy, but it'll sure stop anyone you want it to, ma'am."

"I am familiar with this gun, sir, and know how to use it."

He nodded. "Thank God for that 'cause I sho don't have time to show you." He pulled a bag of shot from his pocket, thrust it to her, and scrambled back up the passage.

Abigail sucked in a ragged breath, then closed and bolted the door. She loaded the Blunderbuss, laid it on her cot, then dressed as fast as she could make her fingers move over the many fasteners of her frock. Whispering a prayer, she dropped onto the side of the bed and pulled the loaded gun into her lap.

Smoke seeped into her cabin and brought on a fit of coughing. The sound of boarding picks crashed on the deck above, and then swords clashing, guns firing, and death cries filled the air. She tried to muff the formidable sounds with her hands over her ears and bit her lip to keep from fainting. Who was dying? The horrid pirates or the *Marigold* crew?

The ship began to list from side to side. Water seeped around her feet and sheer black fright swept through her. Was the ship sinking?

Father God, help me.

She stood and wrapped one arm around the bed post, then gripped the Blunderbuss in both hands and aimed it at the heavy door.

~

Captain Joshua Becket pushed his plumed hat back on his forehead and frowned as he trained his eyepiece on two ships some distance away. Cannon shots echoed across the waves, and the smell of smoke laced the morning breeze. "Lambert, I think an American ship is under attack by pirates." He handed the piece to his lieutenant and partner in adventures.

"I think you're right, sir. I see the two flags. The attacker is Spanish, the other American." The man returned the instrument.

Joshua strode to the quarterdeck railing and shouted below to his crew. "All hands on deck! Drag on every rag of canvas the sails will hold, lads. Let's help the yonder American ship under attack."

A swarthy sailor stood forward below and blew a bugle alert. Shouts and mass movement spread across the deck of the *Eagle*.

Turning the eyepiece back to the battle, Joshua muttered a curse word. Scurrying pirates fled the besieged ship. "They've spotted us, Lambert. Hope we're not too late."

The attacking sloop ripped away their boarding hooks, pulled anchor, and sailed southeast with full sails catching the morning breeze. Their curses filled the morning air.

His lieutenant turned to him. "Will we chase them, Cap'n Jay?"

Joshua gazed at the ship with *Marigold* emblazoned on its damaged side. Nothing moved on the deck. "No, let's check on the wounded." He raised his dark brows and grinned at his partner. "And let's check on the cargo, of course."

When they drew beside the vessel, he and his crew threw hooks and boarded. Bodies littered every space and blood seeped in rivets from one side of the ship to the other as the vessel tilted with the waves. His men stamped out the fires as best they could and checked corpses for any sign of life. Joshua found the captain thrust through with a sword and all his crew around him dead.

Lambert strode up. "Cap'n, this ship's been hit below the waterline, and she's taking on water. We can't tarry here."

Joshua wiped smoke from his eyes. "I know. Send the men to check the hold." He walked to mid-deck and shouted down the cabin hatchway. "We're here to help. Is anyone alive down there?" Was that a sound of coughing below or the creaking of the ship's soaked timbers?

He slid down the steps to the second deck into sloshing water and banged on doors, then kicked them open, one by one. The deathly silence of the interior ship, except for the sound of water skidding back and forth, made his skin crawl. Perhaps he imagined the coughing.

Coming to a larger door at the end of the corridor, he pounded on it and kicked, but it didn't budge.

Lambert's heavy tread sounded behind him. "Found one double bolted, huh? Here, let me help." The man slogged back a few steps, then rushed at the entrance with his full weight and bull-like strength.

The oak door split into pieces. Joshua barreled into the room beside his lieutenant.

～

Abigail's cabin door shattered from its hinges, and two burly forms charged into her cabin. *Pirates.*

She fired.

One of them collapsed into the ankle-deep water. His hat flew from his dark hair into the briny liquid collecting on the floor.

The other, of stouter body and thick red beard, cursed, strode forward, and knocked the pistol from her hands. The Blunderbuss landed on the cabin floor with a splash. Then the pirate stepped over and knelt beside the injured one. "Cap'n, you hit?" His thick voice expressed his concern and anger.

The fallen pirate sat up. "Just nicked." He pulled a handkerchief from his person and pressed it into his shirt under the red stain. He groped for his plumed hat, shook droplets away, and pushed it on his head, then stood.

He was over six feet tall, lank, and muscles rippled across his shoulders and arms. Abigail blinked and swallowed. She addressed the two of them. "You are English pirates?" Captain Donavan had expressed concern about French or Spanish rogues, not English.

The two exchanged glances and the injured one grinned. "No. We just saw your ship under attack and came to help."

Abigail stared at him and tried not to be influenced by his handsome face and bold, dark, confident eyes that tripped her heartbeat and did something to her breathing. All her senses flashed an alert. The man and his partner had secrets. "I don't believe you."

～

Joshua looked at the striking woman standing stiff and defiant before them, her lovely face pale as alabaster. Fire, however, blazed from eyes the color of the sea in bright sunlight. A beautiful, dignified woman. He suppressed a chuckle. If he had to be shot, at least it wasn't by a doxie.

He gave her a brief bow. "Please come. I'll show you." He indicated the porthole and offered his arm to assist her movement in the tilting cabin and slippery floor. "We don't have much time."

She refused his proffered arm, grasped her dripping skirts out of the bilge water, and stepped with care to the porthole.

He strode behind her and the ship tilted. She fell against him, and he breathed in her womanly lavender scent.

She turned, and for a moment, only inches separated their faces. Wide, startled green eyes lifted to his and looked into his soul, it seemed, then lowered. Pink flooded her cheeks. She reached for the cot post to steady herself and regained her footing.

He pointed out the port hole. "Now Madam or Miss, do you see my clipper ship flying the British flag? We're privateers of His Majesty, King George the Third. I am Captain Jay. Lambert, my lieutenant is with me."

She lifted her chin and moved away from him.

"We must abandon the *Marigold* before she sinks. Will you come with us?"

The woman took a deep breath and pointed. "My trunk is there in the corner. Can you please have two of Captain Donavan's crew fetch it?" She moved toward the destroyed entrance.

Joshua caught a worried look from Lambert standing in the corridor outside.

He turned to the woman. "Ma'am, you must prepare yourself. The deck is not a pretty sight. Captain Donavan and all his crew, I'm afraid, are...dead."

~

When Abigail came up on deck in front of the two men, she gasped and her hand flew to her mouth. Tears welled in her eyes, then tumbled down her cheeks. *Poor Captain Donavan and all his men.*

The man behind her, who called himself Captain Jay, took her elbow in a firm grasp. She tried to resist. Was he a British privateer or a murdering pirate like those who'd attacked the *Marigold?* She meant to remove her arm from his strong grip, but her knees trembled, then gave way.

He caught her and lifted her as if she'd been fluff. She breathed in the man's scent of sea and spice as her cheek pressed against his hard chest. One last jumbled thought flittered across her weary, shocked mind. God help her if she'd fallen into the hands of lying pirates.

GET *THE CAPTAIN'S GOVERNESS* AT YOUR FAVORITE RETAILER.

GET ALL THE BOOKS IN THE CHARLESTON BRIDES SERIES

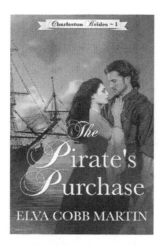

Book 1: The Pirate's Purchase

Book 2: The Sultan's Captive

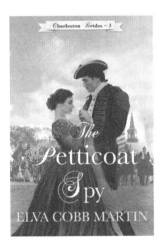

Book 3: The Petticoat Spy

Elva Cobb Martin is a wife, mother, and grandmother who lives in South Carolina with her husband and a green parakeet named Atticus. She grew up on a farm in South Carolina and spends many vacations on the Carolina coast. Her southern roots run deep.

A former school teacher and life-long student of history, her favorite city, Charleston, inspires her stories of romance and adventure. Her love of writing grew out of a desire to share exciting stories of courageous characters and communicate truths of the Christian faith to bring hope and encouragement.

Sign up for e-mail updates when future books are available, including Book 4 in this Charleston Brides Series, *The Captain's Governess*!
http://elvamartin.com.

In addition to the Charleston Brides Series, Elva Cobb Martin is author of:
In a Pirate's Debt
Summer of Deception

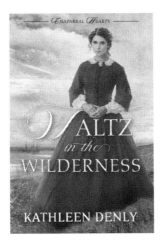

Waltz in the Wilderness by Kathleen Denly

She's desperate to find her missing father. His conscience demands he risk all to help.

Eliza Brooks is haunted by her role in her mother's death, so she'll do anything to find her missing pa—even if it means sneaking aboard a southbound ship. When those meant to protect her abandon and betray her instead, a family friend's unexpected assistance is a blessing she can't refuse.

Daniel Clarke came to California to make his fortune, and a stable job as a San Francisco carpenter has earned him more than most have scraped from the local goldfields. But it's been four years since he left Massachusetts and his fiancé is impatient for his return. Bound for home at last, Daniel Clarke finds his heart and plans challenged by a tenacious young woman with haunted eyes. Though every word he utters seems to offend her, he is determined to see her safely returned to her father. Even if that means risking his fragile engagement.

When disaster befalls them in the remote wilderness of the Southern California mountains, true feelings are revealed, and both must face heart-rending decisions. But how to decide when every choice before them leads to someone getting hurt?

Lone Star Ranger by Renae Brumbaugh Green

Elizabeth Covington will get her man.

And she has just a week to prove her brother isn't the murderer Texas Ranger Rett Smith accuses him of being. She'll show the good-looking lawman he's wrong, even if it means setting out on a risky race across Texas to catch the real killer.

Rett doesn't want to convict an innocent man. But he can't let the Boston beauty sway his senses to set a guilty man free. When Elizabeth follows him on a dangerous trek, the Ranger vows to keep her safe. But who will protect him from the woman whose conviction and courage leave him doubting everything—even his heart?

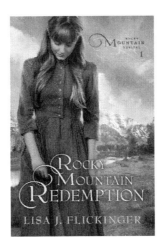

Rocky Mountain Redemption by Lisa J. Flickinger

A Rocky Mountain logging camp may be just the place to find herself.

To escape the devastation caused by the breaking of her wedding engagement, Isabelle Franklin joins her aunt in the Rocky Mountains to feed a camp of lumberjacks cutting on the slopes of Cougar Ridge. If only she could out run the lingering nightmares.

Charles Bailey, camp foreman and Stony Creek's itinerant pastor, develops a reputation to match his new nickname — Preach. However, an inner battle ensues when the details of his rough history threaten to overcome the beliefs of his young faith.

Amid the hazards of camp life, the unlikely friendship growing between the two surprises Isabelle. She's drawn to Preach's brute strength and gentle nature as he leads the ragtag crew toiling for Pollitt's Lumber. But when the ghosts from her past return to haunt her, the choices she will make change the course of her life forever—and that of the man she's come to love.

Manufactured by Amazon.ca
Bolton, ON